PASSAGE TO LAHORE

A NOVEL BY

Julian Samuel

THE MERCURY PRESS

The publisher gratefully acknowledges the financial assistance of the Canada Council and the Ontario Arts Council, as well as that of the Government of Ontario through the Ontario Publishing Centre.

Edited by Stuart Ross

Cover painting, "Four Pakistani Painters Boarding a Train for Paris," 1977, and author photo by Julian Samuel
Composition and page design by TASK

Printed and bound in Canada by Metropole Litho
Printed on acid-free paper
First Edition
1 2 3 4 5 99 98 97 96 95

Canadian Cataloguing in Publication Data

Samuel, Julian
Passage to Lahore
ISBN 1-55128-024-8
I. Title
PS8587.A716P37 1995   C813'.54   C95-932326-0
PR9199.3S37P37 1995

Represented in Canada by the Literary Press Group
Distributed by General Distribution Services

The Mercury Press
137 Birmingham Street
Stratford, Ontario
Canada   N5A 2T1

CONTENTS

1. Indonesian Restaurant: Montréal, 1985: 7

2. Plague Years in England: Surrey, 1966: 10

3. Grandfather at Noon: Lahore, 1957: 16

4. Montréal, 1985: 29

5. Frantz Fanon Conference: Algeria, 1987: 44

6. Rushdie on the Hooghly River: Calcutta, 1988: 67

7. Lipstick on Your Collar: Toronto, 1968: 78

8. Of Milk, Mice and Men: Montréal, 1983: 81

9. Progressive Sexual Intercourse: Algeria, 1987: 105

10. Indonesian Restaurant: Montréal, 1985: 110

11. Man of Empire: Toronto, 1989: 119

12. Québec and the Communal Question: Montréal, 1985: 133

13. Deep Relationships: Montréal, 1989: 145

14. The Cannibals of Maarra: Montréal, 1985: 148

15. Report of an Officer Who Was Educated in the West: 159

16. The Starry Night I Met Begum Akhtar: Lahore, 1984: 160

17. Hong Kong and the Boat People
PART ONE: Hong Kong, 1989: 185

18. Indonesian Restaurant: Montréal, 1985: 200

19. Hong Kong and the Boat People
PART TWO: Hong Kong, 1989: 207

GLOSSARY 227

ACKNOWLEDGEMENTS 229

BIBLIOGRAPHY 231

CHAPTER ONE

Indonesian Restaurant

Montréal, 1985

Monday, lunch time. I am meeting Ian and Michael in an Indonesian restaurant on Saint Denis near Sherbrooke, close to the bus terminal. We will eat outside, in a warm and pleasant Montréal summer. Late nineteen-eighties.

I wait on the sidewalk. Five minutes go by. Michael strolls along. We shake hands and descend onto the sunny patio in the front part of the restaurant. From this level we can see the bottom halves of people on roller blades trying to avoid traffic.

Michael, a tall thin man originally from British Columbia, moved to the multilingual metropolis sometime in 1982 to finish his degree in economics and development studies. He always wears hand-me-down shirts. His face is a missionary pinkish white and will never tan. His slender nose lifts up slightly on the left side. He has on tight charcoal-grey jeans and shoes with cruel metal tips, as well as a worn black dress jacket which has become shiny, a packet of Camels in the outside pocket. His brown hair parts on the left side, flopping down over his forehead.

I first met Michael on a snowy evening outside the Bar Saint Laurent, which is across the street from Schwartz's Smoked Meat. Inside Schwartz's you can, if you want, donate money for Israeli soldiers. That night, when our hands shook, he slipped me a sincerely written propaganda sheet describing the effects of nuclear war. I was moved by his commitment to the anti-nuclear struggle.

When they were in love, Michael and Ian used to kiss in a bar that a Euro-African owned. Their open sexuality made me feel good.

Back then, Michael's theory of activism was that it was a good idea to include the suburbs in consciousness-raising ventures. Besides, he was curious about the assholes of teenagers who hung around pinball arcades and needed conversion.

That was his anti-nuclear phase. Now he has risen into AIDS politics, where the search for research and support funding has become important. He's happy he became an activist and not a post-modernist, about whom he used to say, "Nothing really mattered except that this kind of thinking could produce flashy careers, loads of international travel, maybe even a noisy, safe screw at conferences in Paris, or London: hand-job sperm on a laser disc at warp speed."

Ian is shorter, sober, equally trim with a skin that tans. We see him walking up Saint Denis. He carries a shiny brown briefcase. He, too, has an AIDS-related job in Ottawa.

"Hi, guys, how are you doing?" Ian says.

"Fine," we respond.

Our waitress brings us Indonesian entrées which we start picking at.

"Nice cuff-links, Ian."

Ian smiles and places Somerset Maugham's *East of Suez: a play in seven scenes* on the table.

Our chairs squeak into position, and our elbows pull the white tablecloth tight as a drum. "I've had dinner here before," Ian remarks.

"Just leave the ordering up to him, then," Michael mutters, looking into the menu. "Everything is going to be in a peanut sauce anyway; chicken, beef, lamb, pork, all cooked with great expertise in the extract of peanuts."

Our waitress takes our order on a small pad with spiral binding. She wears large hoop earrings, maybe six inches in diameter. It is possible that they are real silver. It is possible that they are not real silver. A bead of sunlight twinkles in one earring with precarious fragility. Her mellifluously black hair gently flows back over her neck. She has on a white shirt. She whisks her peacock-flared black dress against the summer breeze and walks towards the back of the restaurant, where she is engulfed in darkness.

Michael looks at me. "Julian, don't you feel ridiculous — having thought about our waitress?"

"AZT make you a mind-reader?" I joke.

Ian, snuggling his briefcase near his chair, asks, "Isn't she the one who was at your soiré-of-many-races-and-languages? She's the woman who is doing her MA thesis on whatever from a typical ladies' studies point of view?"

"She leaves for Princeton in the fall — never judge a book by the cover," Michael says adroitly. Fire touches the end of a fresh Camel. Michael, the match, and the cigarette become one.

"It's wrong to have such an impression of her, but I agree she does dress a bit like some of all of them," Ian says flatly.

Michael adds, "And she is doing a dumb-fuck thesis like all of them, too."

We glide from subject to subject: AIDS funding strategies, the number of cases in Africa, the number of new cases in Zaire, facts, the treatments. How nationalist African-Americans visit Western African countries to bury their placentas. Placenta graveyards in Ghana, Senegal, the Ivory Coast, Gambia, Sierra Leone. "Placenta nationalism — rather different from the nationalism here," Michael snickers.

"Let's talk about tolerance," I say.

CHAPTER TWO

Plague Years in England

Surrey, 1966

The ship we crossed over on was subject to a lot of attention in the newspapers. *Circassia* had carried many Pakistanis to England. The press claimed the people had brought chicken pox with them and that they were spreading this horrible disease throughout Britain, Scotland, and even Northern Ireland. The press and those who write for it are not easy to trust, so the truth about who brought the plague over, if indeed some particular nationality or race brought it over at all, is a matter for deepest speculation. Until recently, the Canadian press was impudently and without impunity blaming the gay social structure for the AIDS issue. I remember on one occasion the CBC trying to throw up Africa as the sole starter of AIDS. Never did the media look at the situation as a product of a declining environment, which may have been a causal factor.

The plague was at work everywhere. These brown beings were spreading pox through the allotments where the suburbanites were growing vegetables. The information travelled in between shovels kicked into the ground, the consequent sods were tossed and collected into large compost heaps at the edges of the allotments, and carrot seeds were injected into the ground. Headlines generated whispers and whispers told the headline makers what everyone was to think. It was a symphony of sorts. Because of this, even the robins sang differently, their ability to change notes and scales bludgeoned forever.

The pox was flowing onto the neighbourhood holly trees in the woods, the berries were becoming acrid, orangish, overbaked, and it was no longer good to decorate Christmas fowl with any of this foliage. The risks were too great. A ritual had been destroyed. The pox had a devastating effect on the eggs of thrushes. Indeed, the ground under British society was shifting, shifting as the quality of the bird songs changed — soured, torn apart, and drowned by something like a spinning jenny introduced into the sleepy English countryside. This was the magnitude of the Pakistani Plague.

One particular day in the mid-sixties as I was sitting in the drawing room, a few light taps of rain made me turn to the window. Yes, the newspapers were right, the Pakistani chicken pox was all over England. It had moved on the vast oceans along the salty terrorist north coast of Libya, across the Algerian coast where a war was concluding, with the right side winning. It was brushing past the Rock of Gibraltar into the puffy and superficial crests of blue water in Bay of Biscay, past Brighton to Liverpool where it was pulsating and radiating out onto the living-room floors in the tranquil and innocent English suburban houses on Alexander Road, Warlingham, Surrey, via the gutter press, the official radio and, less frequently then, the television. As a child, this street and suburb of Croydon was my universe, and the pox was falling through it.

The postman shivered in fear as his hands touched packages from the Punjab, rain droplets moving down in a noisy effulgent trail from his cap rim onto the registered package. "Just sign here," he told my mother. These packages came often enough. In one case, the turmeric seeped out and yellowed the postman's hands. Silly of my grandmother to think we couldn't get all the spices for curry in England. How was she supposed to know about the history of the spice trade? In her youth she had been a Christian Girl Guide in Clarkabad near Lahore. Girl Guiding was an occupation which did not bring people into cognizance of the Pakistani plagues in the UK. Nor did it give them any sense of how Bangra and British television would have such a friendly relationship some years down the line. She could fix broken arms and knew all those other things that Guides know, but she did not know that the UK that ruled the waves for all those reasons and centuries had also travelled as far as India for rare spices. Francis Drake loved Pakistanis: there was no shortage of curry spices here. My grandmother died a few years later, after we had immigrated to Canada. It was the beginning of winter and she had had a meal at six o'clock. She felt a flicker in her heart and said that her vision had gone all historical. As my younger brother was carrying her into her bedroom for a rest, she died in his arms. I even think Marx used to go for Indian take-out from around the corner near Tottenham Court Road, somewhere near the British Museum where he wrote and did his back-breaking research. Drake and Marx were on different sides, but they both liked curry.

My grandmother even sent us garlic when we lived on Saint Mungo Street near Parliament Street in Glasgow, but we did not get any more spices when we moved to 27 Kelven Grove Park. I have a feeling that my father, in a rather diplomatic letter, had explained the nature of the spice trade to her, much to the postman's relief.

The pox was moving past the vicarage where my father took me to be disciplined by a pious preacher. Fat lot of good that did. Finally, near the preacher's house, the pox slithered into the minds of the students at school as ideology with a capital "I." It made them suddenly and slowly turn their creaking necks and vomit bile and pus in long sticky democratic lines. The slime hit walls and trees with a *tha-awap*, caught birds on the wing, and occasionally this mixture of ideology, biology, and racism stuck to immigrant bus conductors, who were made to feel the thunderhead of the pox. Thus, walking in England in that initial wave of post-war immigration cheap labour was like walking through a culture in which one removes this sticky mixture only to encounter it again and again, epoch after polite epoch.

The other students voted me out of class. Luckily the teacher was a liberal. If I had a cut on my finger – it was the pox. If I had a pimple – it was the pox. They tried to beat the *Circassia* pox out of me, but of course that could not happen without a fight; it would not happen without breaking their teeth with a T-square in drafting class. Even the objective teachers kept their distance. For fun, I projected my Secondary Modern School teachers into British India, a difficult task since I had never been there myself, being born in 1952, five years after "Liberation." I see those projected teachers as gutless Uncle Tom clerks under slowly rotating fans saying yes to everything, and not at all eager to move back to the land of steak and kidney pie. Forty desks this side of the Partition line, twenty red typewriter ribbons on the Delhi side.

Strangely, there were some English students who did not like or understand the hatred their press was spreading; they were like my professors at Trent and some comrades in Downsview, Ontario, who would help me mash jaws, blacken eyes, and kick balls. Comrades.

Without sounding homesick for the UK, I feel safe in saying that no one ever invited me for dinner while I lived there. The plague took a right turn on a road the Romans had had English slaves make and it coughed and hacked past Highgate, where it smoldered lugubriously by the grave of Karl Marx. The pox did not settle there – out of respect, I suppose; or was it out of sympathy for *The Asiatic Mode of Production* and his *Modern Theory of Colonization?* Marx spoke the para-language of why the pox came. There was no doubt that he understood the media ploy – it was the same old story to him. He knew for example that in 1871 the British press had misrepresented the Franco-Prussian War of 1870 and the Paris Communards in their fight against the French Second Empire. So, it was for all his understanding that the pox respected him; the pox did not touch him but glowed around him.

The pox respected the memory of Paris Communards who were considered a kind of plague as well. This spotted Pakistani morphology had an understanding of why cotton came to Manchester. In the late nineteen-fifties, it came to England, moving in retaliatory concert with this newly found knowledge. It took years to break the intellectual cage of history.

The swarm of press interpretation moved with grace through the Lake District, turning the water to lead. Up past the Solway Firth to Loch Ness where the monster, in a ploy against the British press, entered into a pact with the Pakistani Plague: it would take off some of the media heat by surfacing for the television cameras. One week the Pakis, next week the Blacks, mugging, and liberal opinions, another week back to the Pakis, and another the monster. It was the same year that Sandy Shaw won the Eurovision Song Contest, singing as she always did, in bare feet. It was the year that Marianne Faithfull made the hit parade with "This Little Bird." Around the same time that Diana Rigg with her sophisticated high cheekbones made it in *The Avengers*.

In its serpentine movement it spiralled up Nelson's Column and kissed him in so offending a manner (garlic tongue down his throat, oiled finger up his arsehole and rotating, and a tight unforgiving pinch to his left nipple) that his morality of silence broke through the stone, and one foggy London rush hour amid the red buses and tickering of ticker-tape in the hands of Brown and Black conductors, the stone spoke in public, spoke in an urgent headmaster Urdu to the Pakistani Plague and asked it to please stop. The rationale on Lord Nelson's behalf was that there had been too many riots. Britain was becoming too much like America. We must stop this now. It subsided: post-colonial afflatus.

Thatcher on her trapeze frozen in mid-arc; her catcher, too, a drunk, frozen in a hopeful posture, arms extended; her audience spitting out slime and cocooning her. The Empire stopped in mid-decline and hung. Something Milton Friedman, the saviour of Chile, did not predict.

The immigrants and hot political satirists got their cultural and political space on the telly and were contained: hip TV producers put on lots of Club-Mix, Black newscasters. Black thinkers would publicly take the Empire on its own terms and got tenure-track jobs for doing exactly that. Paki-Bangra disco parties for everybody to see. Fucking pluralism.

This democratizing of the public airwaves changed the interpretation of everything. Parliament even took a few tokens. During my most recent visit back to London, there were at least four articulate Blacks in the power structure. Word has it they were doing their bit, too — unlike their fellows in the South African Parliament, who were recently blown up, thank god. It was no longer totally okay to blame the immigrants. However, the intelligent right was gathering up philosophical forces to defend English culture, society, Harrods', cultural studies, history, Bounty and Mars bars, and the lack of dinner invitations.

CHAPTER THREE

Grandfather at Noon

Lahore, 1957

Il quitta sa famille
laissa pousser la barbe
et remplit sa solitude de pierres et de brume

Il arriva au désert
la tête enroulée dans un linceul
le sang versé
en terre occupée

Il n'était
ni héros ni martyr
il était
citoyen de la blessure

—Tahar Ben Jelloun, *Les amandiers sont morts de leurs blessures* (Paris: Maspero, 1976)

It was a hot day and the publishers had been talking with my grandfather about his next technical drawing book. They were in the hall of his narrow three-storey house. While Mohammed Raffi was singing love songs on the radio, my brother was having an attack of worms, amoebic dysentery, and radioitis in the backyard, sitting on the potty. He sang along loudly. My olfactory skills were acute.

Smoky worms as long as the Shalimar Express.

The walls of my grandfather's house were yellowish, cool even during the summers. The bedrooms had a slightly greenish tinge in the late afternoon, and over the centre of each bed drooped gauzy white mosquito netting. During the day, shoeless servants would twist and knot these nets high above the beds, where they hung like cloth chandeliers. In the night the netting imprisoned my grandparents' snoring bodies.

He had the house built during the summer of 1947, a summer unlike any other British India had endured. Coincidentally, on 15 August of that year, Independence Day in Pakistan, miles away in Palestine the farmhouse of the Abu Laban family was blown up by the Haganah, the Zionist military organization. Another partition and independence was about to transpire.

The Moslem publishers were discussing aspects of the trade: how many copies of which books, what schools to distribute them in, which teachers would use them. My grandfather was speaking quickly. I had the impression that these business matters had to be cleared up before the family left for a hill station — a summer resort — in Mussourie, where he would rest from the busy schedule of writing, publication, and publicity. In these hill stations he would venture out into ancient markets, selectively buying amaryllis bulbs for his roof garden. His ability to make the bulbs burst into passionate pink and red petals was renowned throughout Christian Lahore. As a drafting teacher he was very well-known throughout Pakistan, and later India. He was a sort of James Joyce of the drafting textbook world in post-Partition Pakistan. Strangely enough, although he was a Christian, he still wore his *turra* headdress, symbolically acknowledging his Sikh past.

His asthma caused him to spit a lot, especially in the morning but never in public; never near Rang Mahal Mission High School where he taught. This school was founded, my tall uncle tells me, by the famous American Presbyterian educationist and missionary The Reverend Dr. Charles W. Foreman, DD. Apparently my grandfather never spat near the Lahore Cathedral, either.

He gave private lessons to students in his office, which had greener walls than the rest of the house. Students would use thumb tacks to pin down the corners of sheets of very expensive drafting paper. They would hold T-squares along the drafting board's edge with their left hand while their right would carefully, under the supervision of their greying teacher, draw the finest lines in the world with H2 pencils. I would, when I was allowed to pass through this office, see the time-consuming drafting of square tables with elephantine legs, muscular chairs, toilets that faced in such a way as to avoid direct sunlight as well as any potential insult to anyone's religion. Once in a while I would see small English houses with sloping roofs emerging on the thin paper. English matriculation classes were, I am told, filled with poetry about dogs and wolves barking in cool valleys in Welsh villages. Who in Pakistan has a sloping roof, I wondered.

My grandfather's technical books have been published in four languages: English, Hindi, Gurmukhi, and of course Urdu. The house was divided linguistically; he spoke Punjabi with his wife, because that was the language they most shared, and Urdu with the children, because it, like English, was to become the lingua franca of Pakistan.

I would find at least five excuses to interrupt their drafting lessons. Bringing in water or tea for my grandfather to drink, I would see objects emerging on the tracing paper in oblique projection, side elevation, top plans. The students worked diligently because they had to pay for these lessons. I had the nagging suspicion that he did not charge the poorer students, or at least he charged them less. Secularism.

Many technical students still know about my grandfather's

contribution to the art of drafting plans for a house, a table, or a chair. In fact, a few years ago, when I met a Lahorie engineering student at an international party in Montréal and told him my full historical name and where I was born, a smile broke across his face. He told me he had studied my grandfather's books, although now these books are not much used. Mohammed Malikshah, the man from Lahore, was now doing research in atomic power at McGill and would soon be returning to Pakistan to contribute to the weapons program.

My grandfather wrote *A Manual of Scale Drawing* and *Technical Geometrical Drawing*, among other titles. Generations have been educated by his books and have helped, consequently, to reconstruct Pakistan from the chair up, as it were. He was also a landscape painter, but he did not become famous for his impressionistic renditions of British India. He depicted passive nature scenes: brooks flowing in and around trees with dark barks without a hint of modernist contortion; his paintings looked very English. There was a spatial ambiguity to the way he drew streams and small waterfalls: one can never really tell which way the stream moves — into or out of the picture, or if the stream is just hanging in mid-air. He was not a great draughtsman in the pictorial sense. I have inherited some of this ambiguous spatial relationship, a kind of rendition of reality that did not do much for my reputation during my phase as an undergraduate student painter.

My grandfather really had no excuse not to have been at least somewhat angsty in his landscapes, like the German expressionists who had seen some of what he had seen. The Germans saw Germany in the nineteen-thirties and -forties. My grandfather saw divisions between people and communal violence in the context of the Two Nation Theory, which was supposed to recognize a nation of Hindus and a nation of Moslems so that everything would work out. So much for the "Lahore" or "Pakistan Resolution." One has to look hard to find any conflict within his pictorial work. Not a very political man. In fact, he once did a loosely composed pen-and-water-colour drawing of flower petals. Of course, the flowers had been drafted in barely visible trace lines first, and then were built up with tiny brush strokes until they became real-looking. I suspect that he may have copied them from a *National Geographic* of the time. I have never been able to understand why he inscribed "God is Love" in old-fashioned English writing below this painted arrangement. The writing probably took as long as the execution of the flowers themselves.

His chalk drawings have a pristine luminosity, but I have the feeling they will always live outside the official art history of Pakistan. Understandable, of course; he had given up his religion to adopt another one, one from the West, or at least a religion which the West had reformulated and that grew up nearer Asia. And, as it was turning out, the promises of a secular state, as Mohammed Ali Jinnah, the leader of the Islamic state, had implied in his many pre-Partition speeches, were far from sight.

In the late fifties this religion was splintering and shattering my grandfather's family from the inside. Western ideas, such as Web-berian sociology, were laid down as career options. He thought he was just listening to the American missionaries, but there was another process he did not anticipate: religion, in conjunction with other factors such as two-piece bathing suits and Two Nation Theories, indirectly created a dissatisfaction with Pakistan and what it could not offer. This feeling of Pakistani inadequacy pulled the younger generations to London, Toronto, and Washington. It was as though this Western religion were a kind of seed planted in the older generation, to find fruition in subsequent generations abroad.

The fecund garden on the roof of my grandfather's house was L-shaped; the end of the long side overlooked the banana trees, the other side gave out to a military academy. The flowers grew behind gauze so that the savage and hungry Lahore birds would not peck off the effulgent petals. My grandfather thought the petals would bleed, he was that tender about his flowers. There might have been a problem with mice also. Missionaries picked the flowers when they came to visit: "It would be nice if your children's children could come to Sunday school." The missionaries spoke Urdu with sufficient skill to throw their victims into affectionate innocent smiles. This made their task easier.

There were large church picnics under righteous white table-cloths spread on the ground in sunny parks with fruit bats. Stern obedient servants dusted off plates before sitting many yards away to have a slightly lesser version of the same food. Pakistani men stood around with hands in their pockets, jackets done up, shoes shining. No one in full traditional garb. An occasional touch to the Sunday trimmed mustache. Wives helped by giving the servants orders: "No, over there. Bring some cutlets here and take more salad over there." Black Morrises with wooden steering wheels. This was my Lahore.

My grandfather's house was large, filled with visitors. A community of sweepers, servants, and beggars lived below us in shacks made of materials so flimsy a rainstorm would damage them irreparably. Some of the smaller buildings were made of mud. The hutty houses were brown and tidy, and I would whisk past them with my father on the back of his Triumph 175 cc motorbike.

One summer day a servant was killed because he washed an electric fan with a very wet rag. His blue and bloated body was brought out into the open and everybody wept. I only learned to fully redirect my guilt years later in Montréal, when I began to use Marxism to understand the underlying social process of self-imposed guilt.

In the blustery August of 1947 there was an attempt to burn down the house owned by Kahan Singh, which was my grandfather's original name. My short uncle was to tell me years later, "A good soul, however, came to the rescue when he revealed to the militant group that the owner of the house was in fact a Christian and not a Sikh." So really the family name is Kahan-Singh, thanks to all the kind missionaries — the ones that came to Lahore during the time of the Slave Kings of Delhi and the others who had a comparatively shorter stay. There was modernity attached to the act of becoming victims to the sweet proselytization of the pink souls from America and London.

I am not sure if my grandfather continued to paint after Partition. His house was generous, a continual train of visitors; and he had long walks after supper, often buying my grandmother a *paan*.

One memorable summer before we left Pakistan, my brother and I spent a couple of months at our grandparents'. In the hot evenings we would sleep on the open roof, exposed to the Lahore sky and the circling satellites. "Here is the Russian one," my grandmother would say. We would try ten different ways to pronounce Sputnik. It always resulted in giggling fits. My brother and I would fight with each other to get on the fan side of the grandparents. He usually won because he was younger. The electric fan reluctantly blew a more or less cool breeze across our noses. There was moonlight everywhere.

My grandmother's neck was soft. I'd place the tips of my fingers in the skin folds of her neck and count the gold balls in her necklace. If she moved in the right way during one of her boring accounts of what shapes stars would make if connected, I saw star clusters reflected in gold balls.

I countered her astrological wisdom with little stories of what I had seen during the day; for instance, how the hermaphrodite street dancers — the *Khusras* — danced. I semi-invented a story about snake charmers; stories about a fight between a cobra and a mongoose. A yellow liquid came from the mongoose's gaping mouth as the snake slowly erased the mongoose's memory by coiling around it with a steel grip. I told her about the salt taste in my mouth when I saw the thing die. I once compared her hands, pointing to the heavens, with the paws of the dead mongoose who, I claimed, was pointing to the heavens, not from a nice bed, but from the gutter three floors below us.

One of those nights the whole family, including an otherworldly religious aunt, was sleeping on the roof. We were having a riot of a time throwing things at one another while our grandparents tried to tell us mythical bullshit stories about crows and bits of cheese, foxes who would get married when it rained and shone at the same time; stories of princes and queens and aging elephants in the Lahore zoo. My grandmother claimed that an elephant was lopped up into a hundred grey pieces which were buried throughout the twelve-gated city. In the middle of her story, the sky suddenly changed colour and became a deep blue, as in one of my grandfather's more sombre paintings. The moon also deepened in tone, going from bluish to grey, then suddenly to purple. We rushed indoors. I remember saying to my grandmother that we ought to bring in my *surukhs*, my tiny pet birds. But no sooner had I spoken than I heard them behind us in the room adjoining the large roof patio. The swirling dust must have upset them. The small, burgundy-coloured birds flew in tightly arched paths in the cage. They had white spots near their eyes, sharp pointed scarlet beaks, and were tremendous fun to feed.

Some months after we had arrived in England, my mother got a letter from my grandmother saying that there had been another dust storm "just like the one when the boys were here" and the birds had been accidentally left out in all its raging twelve-gated fury. They were hurled thirty-seven feet into the banana trees.

My brother and I drove our grandparents around the bend in four days; we broke some beds by jumping on them from an eight-foot-high wall. It was a summer of homemade ice-cream, personally selected watermelons, rides in *tongas* to Chandini Chouk to see the toy sellers, green parrots in murderously claustrophobic cages, visits to people who had pet squirrels, and servants who had baths in the afternoons. We visited my grandfather's childhood schools at Kot Radha Kirshan, about three miles from Clarkabad, and Mission School in Narowal, sixty miles southwest of Lahore. Some summer afternoons I climbed a *jamun* tree to eat the berries.

There were scented rituals connected with this house on McLeod Road. There were the Moslem feasts when the moon became a sliver. We joyfully responded by taking candles to the houses of neighbours. We practised a very healthy secularism, though not really out of fear. My grandfather never ate meat when Hindus were in the house. Even then, I had developed a neutrality towards Christmas, and later on, a neutrality towards the Christian faith as well. Flowers behind gauze.

In the cool evenings when the sun was going down and the emerald parrots were returning in dusky blue spirals to their trees, we would have a reddish drink. There was chatter as the ice clinked and tinkered against the inside of the jug. Smooth dissatisfied servants wearing *shalwar kamezes* silkenly brushed the evening into blackness. The drink became pinkish when poured from the deep jug. I could see the faces of my grandparents through the glass; they looked distorted and unhappy. Multicoloured lizards with big blue-green eyes would climb high up into the night and stars. My grandparents refused to let me have a BB gun.

When my grandmother moved to Toronto after her husband

died, she told me that they used to let the hut dwellers peek inside their living room to watch their television set. Now some of those hut dwellers have jobs in Oman, Bahrain, Kuwait, and various other Gulf States. And with this injection of money into Pakistan, the Pakistani workers and prostitutes can now buy VCRs and colour TVs. All this took some fifteen years.

There were many jokes about TV; people in 1982 used to say that they had mullahs stuck in their sets who did not disappear even when the power was cut off. General Zia or his ubiquitous representatives were, it seemed, on the air every second of any Islamic day. After the 1979 revolution in Iran, Iranians used to say that their televisions had grown beards, beards oozing out onto the living room floor. Grey beards and, very unfortunately, some young raven-black ones also.

Outside, right near the front door of my grandfather's house, there was a network of open drainage that had not changed since the time Alexander the Great had paid us a visit. They were called *nalies*. The colour of the water interested me very much. At the age of eight I was able to show an occidental experimental filmmaker's sense of fascination at the changes in the colour of the bathwater, at the spirals of moving hair and soap suds in the warm water, caught by the occasional twig.

I claimed that I could tell which person had had a bath. One day after a temporary servant took a bath, the water in the *nalie* changed to burgundy, with hair oil superimposed onto the smell of Pear's soap. The spirals moved slowly and travelled down the open duct; I followed them until they changed shape and slipped under Lahore.

My grandmother had most likely given this servant the soap. Otherwise how would she have gotten it? Possession of the soap was a question of class and relative power. The servant was having her bath on the open roof near the water tank. I was not supposed to be looking at her. She was soaping her brown body unhurriedly in the sun; suds were running through her toes, which were more elongated than moon shaped.

When I look back at the event, for it was certainly an event, I feel guilty because of a highly progressive left-wing film I saw in India sometime during my first return, some twenty years later. This film depicted a landlord doing the same thing I had done as a child. I saw myself as the loathsome landlord, watching his servant taking her bath without her knowing. The landlord used to fuck her. There were no words between them. This initial sight had given me a bit of power, but I could not touch her. I suppose that feeling between guilt and access converted later in life into a phoney solidarity with the women's movement in the West.

It was a large house, but still my grandfather's children were restless to leave the country for England or America. Some even left for Frankfurt to await the ineluctable unification of the two Germanies in 1990. The first documents had already started to arrive at the offices of immigration departments. For my parents, Lahore was becoming like a train station during Partition. The grandparents were unhappy, and I see misery prevailing in their eyes in the photographs they sent over to Toronto during the following decades. Christmas 1968: long faces. Christmas 1972: longer faces. And in the mid-seventies, photographs of one prestigious funeral taken in a big church. A Christian family in a confessional Islamic state.

Soon they would all be gone. At seventy-two my grandfather died of coronary thrombosis. He lies at the cemetery on Central Road. After he died, my grandmother boarded a plane for the first time in her life. It was her first sight of Lahore from the view of the parrots. She joined us in Toronto. The other grandmother is buried in Glasgow.

Sunset. October, some year in the late nineteen-fifties. We have pushed up through the Suez Canal. The sea pulls us down, the sea pushes us up. Salt spray all around. Flying fish dead on the deck, snagged on rigging in the night. Wings of flesh. Elvis in Karachi. Elvis becoming the sea, the air. I remind my mother that if she had paid a particular radio station in Karachi more money, perhaps they would have played Paul Anka's "Oh, Diana" on my birthday. On my birthday we waited, but no Paul Anka. Instead, they aired a bit of semi-classical music by Ravi Shankar accompanied by that famous fiddler from the West — Yehudi Menuhin.

There is a man talking to my mother. He is British and she is beautiful. My father is already in England, living in a small flat with a newly bought gramophone. We are moving up through the Red Sea. The Englishman has on a blue blazer and holds a tall flared sweating glass of cool beer in his stubby English hand. His shirt is open and the collar is folded out over the blazer. Still, he does not look good. My sister is sitting on a deck chair, reading *Jane Eyre*. We are on the promenade deck. The man's fingers are nicotine-stained. A plume of smoke floats towards Pakistan. He inches nearer my mother. Her scarf flutters like Isadora Duncan's when she dies at the end of a black-and-white film.

The white captain with a megaphone tells us, in Urdu, which surprises us, to move away from the deck's edge. Stormy weather. Human cotton moving into Britain.

It was late afternoon when we boarded a large passenger ship with an oily black hull. I sat, waiting for the vessel to pull out of Karachi harbour so I could see Pakistan fade into the Arabian Sea. When I awoke it was night, nothing but the rising and falling of sea and the hissing darkness. Lunar sounds of the inky water. We had departed. Liverpool was to come much later, two or three weeks later, in a northern sunset. We stopped in Aden, and then slowly moved up through Gamel Abdel Nasser's well-organized Suez Canal. Out on the sandy distance I could see people picking dates. Groups of camels stooped in twos and threes out on the watery desert.

Port Said. Dolphins in the smelly Mediterranean. The Rock of Gibraltar and the Bay of Biscay. A strike by dock workers at Liverpool — a vision of the great West.

The Lahore house was empty. In Agincourt, a plaza-ridden suburb of Toronto, there was talk that we ought to sell the old house to a Christian family. When I went back to Lahore in 1982, a carpet dealer had a *soosth* shop there. The carpet dealers were discussing General Zia in very negative terms, which made me feel good despite the initial shock of seeing my family history turned into the fine, redundant weaves of moderately priced carpets from Kabul.

The grandparents had failed to hold things together. A persistent cool breeze, like the one that deepened the colour of the moon and killed my pet birds, had blown their kids into the distance; my mother, father, and brothers and sister had made the dusty train journey to Karachi, then by ship to the port of Liverpool. They rode an old smoky coal-driven train to Middlesex and Wimbledon with its sunny gardens and the smashed shell of a pet tortoise. The English neighbours were disgusted by the Pakistani kids who had used tennis rackets to open its shell.

CHAPTER FOUR

Montréal, 1985

If Needham's account of Chinese technological competence
and superiority over the West until the latter's sudden surge
forward is correct, then it is even more striking that
Chinese and Portuguese overseas exploration began
virtually simultaneously, but that after a mere 28 years the
Chinese pulled back into a continental shell and ceased all
further attempts. Not for lack of success, either. The seven
voyages of the eunuch-admiral Cheng Ho between 1405
and 1433 were a great success. He travelled the breadth of
the Indian Ocean from Java to Ceylon to East Africa in his
seven voyages, bringing back tribute and exotica to the
Chinese court, which was highly appreciative. The voyages
ceased when Cheng Ho died in 1434. Furthermore, when,
in 1479, Wang Chin, also a eunuch, interested in
launching a military expedition to Annam, applied to the
archives to consult Cheng Ho's papers on Annam, he was
refused access. The papers were suppressed, as if to blot out
the very memory of Cheng Ho.

—Immanuel Wallerstein, *The Modern World System, Vol. 1*
(New York: Academic Press, 1974-80)

My quarter is nationalist Francophone, unlike boulevard Saint
Laurent, a few blocks away. Saint Laurent, sometimes called "the
Main" by the older Anglos, is a street running from the Old Port

to the treeless northern suburbs. Saint Laurent is a mix of every nationality except people from Ulan Bator. Just off this street, which divides Montréal into east and west, one is able to see the economic centres of the so-called cultural communities; on either side and on Saint Laurent itself, the major immigrant group is Portuguese. As one moves east of boulevard Saint Laurent, the neighbourhoods become exclusively Francophone.

A walk through the McGill student ghetto in the other direction puts one in Waspish lawn-laden neighbourhoods with optimistic robins who come in May, red-stone public libraries, concerned kindergartens and churches. Churches are ubiquitous in this city and many of the streets are named after dead priests. In the humid summers, men in side-street cafés off Saint Laurent listen to soccer games on crackly short-wave radios. Some bars that have made it big show off their profits by mounting dish antennae as large as those used by astronomy departments to gaze at supernovas light years away. Football matches from Uranus.

Soccer season fills the bars to capacity. Inside, through the smokehaze, large screens remain a noisy videostatic green until September. To hoots and cheers, mechanical football players in knee socks run from one end of the beer vapours to the other. The rippling video green comes from Brazil, Italy, Germany, and the hooligan-filled United Kingdom. After the soccer games end, American football lights up the screens. Announcers with southern accents. And now the salsa bars are filled with students from the Anglo universities, many offering their virginity to the swaying exiles from Central America who now have to pay a $975 head tax on top of a $500 processing fee before entering Canada.

This general area, once a more Portuguese neighbourhood, has been transformed into a neighbourhood of artists, humourless ecologists, and women who publish illustrated theories on female ejaculation. One is also likely to meet left-wing politicians in their late thirties who claim they will do their best to prevent the licensing of any more bars.

In the early part of the twentieth century, Jews gathered here from Europe. Most of them have left the area now. Many famous Canadian writers, such as Mordecai Richler and Irving Layton, spent their childhoods here. Leonard Cohen with his black suits, white shirts, and chicken-skin neck can be seen on occasion, if one is lucky.

Some of the Portuguese immigrants, one could say, are actually African. They came from or were born in Angola, where, in the mid-seventies, another Black revolution was unleashing a power that would establish an independent nation-state. Consequently, some Portuguese settlers immigrated to Montréal. But these Angolan revolutions were mere irritations — interruptions in the history of European settlers in Africa. Portugal, in conjunction with South Africa, was always able to contain the uprisings, more or less.

Mozambique's leader, Samora Machel, addressing an audience in Zimbabwe, said approximately: "Those of you who were colonized by the British feel you have inherited brilliant parliamentary struc- tures; those among you who were touched by the French flame of civilization know that you have remarkable intellectual traditions to lean on. But I — I was colonized by Portugal, the most backward country of Europe." The Zimbabwean audience burst into laughter. Rumour has it that some of the Portuguese factory owners and workers who came to Montréal blew up their factories before leaving Africa. Some have now become very successful in the restaurant business. Peasants in fur coats.

Saint Laurent has many Hungarian sandwich shops, at least four new Lebanese restaurants, a Cairean fast-food shop, a few Rumanian shops, and a Vietnamese cloth shop which has not gone under yet, but I am sure it can't take recessionary pressures for long.

I enjoy going to the German shops to ask for curry powder. I usually do this with one of my darker Asian friends — one in particular who is capable of speaking perfect high German.

The Main hasn't any Indian or Pakistani shops north of Sherbrooke. South of Sherbrooke, the many Indo-Pak stores sell *halal* meat and spices, and some even have bitter cucumber. Heavy smells of spices blending with *ghee* in hot pans waft from a small restaurant below Sherbrooke. The Pakistani shops do their trade in electronics; they have the best deals in town if the *Salam* is appropriately Karachiesque. Lots of *Salams* on Saint Laurent; Iranian political refugees, Bangladeshi political refugees, Tamil political refugees, and the occasional Pakistani political refugee. On the right day, with the appropriate amount of sunshine, one can *Salam* oneself to high heaven.

I often walk in this area of Montréal with Nabil, who had to leave Pakistan because of his keen ability to organize labour and direct trade-union activity. He is a tall jolly man with a protruding round gut. He has been in prisons. Chilies up his arse, skull fractures, days without food, and two slightly distorted fingers, but he still has a sense of humour. Years of exile in the fractured *dunnia Arabia*, the Gulf States. Punjabi soldiers collectively spitting in his face. In this neighbourhood Nabil has the ultimate in street cred because he has been in the prisons of both the phoney Maoist Bhutto regime and the subsequent CIA-imposed Zia and Benazir regimes. Actually, he says, all were CIA.

Nabil trashes the Karachi ghetto of electronics merchants. "*Yaar*, I not wanting to humiliate the situation here in this area but all I see is devoted pray on Friday — the North Africans in one mosque, the *bhenchood* Pakis on the other side."

I say, "Why resent these people trying to conduct an honest

business in electronics, *somosas*, *paan*, and video cassettes? Why are you after these poor souls?"

"Well, this is all *chouth-key-chutney* if pardon to me, I like to telling you that indeed you romanticize these reactionary types — these bastard are just roaming the street — cigarettes and *paan* — these bastard are victim of Two Nation *bhenchood* Theory. I want to say fuck off you."

We pass an electronics store. "Look," I say, "these guys are making a killing — and they do international transfers from sub-continental PAL-SECAM to North American NTSC. Don't you think they're providing the community with a good service?"

I call Nabil Captain Choodie because he has taken to having two or more lovers these days. He has a weakness for very voluminous southern Italian or Euro-Canadian women; they remind him of his childhood in Multan.

"Yes, great service — *ma-ka-laura* transfer this to that, that to this — these *bhenchoods* don't even look at title of video-shideos they rent and then smoke in front of TV screen."

He does imitations of political refugees gushing smoke out in front of video screens. "You're not seeing the objective reality, *jinnab* — they're victim of Two Nation Theory. Some say political refugees — but I'm sorry to say I don't believe they sincere refugees. No, I don't believe, I don't believe. One hundred times I say I don't believe. You believe because you went to private school in Karachi and wore tie and shorts, proper *bhenchood* British imitation. You just enjoy life — even if sometime you go on welfare — *array yaar* — welfare Canada Council artist you — just fuck *yaar* and listen to my objective interpretation — not emotional.

"Where you think they go after Friday meetings in splendid mosque which they rent from European Jewish — some of them, I mean — not all of them, just some of them — of course there're sincere august types here. And what you think this room that they rent from...you think this is splendid? No, not majestic architecture like Alhambra in Spain."

He looks directly at me to see if I've noticed his use of the word *august*.

"Tell me," I insist. "Who are these august types?"

Nabil stops in mid-stride, turns to me with the confidence of a cop, and takes off his sunglasses. "You make fun because I use word *august*? Well after prayers — well you think — you tell me."

"Captain *jee*, I give up. You're the one that's wanted for treason, Captain *jee*, you tell me."

He smiles at my repeated use of the word *Captain*. "What is logic with false political charge on me and where they go after prayers — please tell to me, but think you study political science — you just make fun and enjoy at me?" He pauses, then smiles widely. "Pinballs arcades, *yaar* — you not able to guess? You have gone to private school, Saint Patrick's with imitation English grey shorts on and tie, you not able to tell me — they go to *mather chood* arcade, *yaar*, run by Chinese who eat frog. *Bhenchood* arcade sharcade."

His fingers spiral upwards. "And you know — please don't to be shock: one green-grocer tell to me that about Rushdie — he should to have his hands paralysed — *gandoos*, you distart and ramantize issue, with simplistic official multicultural anti-racist analysis."

We round the corner at Ontario and head towards rue Saint Denis. "Nabil, how was I supposed to guess pinball arcades — they are mostly video games now, aren't they?"

"Okay. Videos-shideo games. Okay, video. Same point. Same point I make. Guess what happens after? They discuss with prostitutes — please to believe me, I'm not lying. They discuss with prostitutes — they not asking how many times All India Radio playing Schubert music like when you visit homeland, *jinnab* – they discuss with prostituted women."

"What? For a fuck, Nabil?"

"Yes, you see relation I pointing or not? Sometime even they make them to receive blow job — they ask to prostitute, 'You can make to me a blow job?' — what is this? Correct religious teaching, what you think?"

"Captain, I see relation."

"Why you enjoy at my English — why you enjoy so much my English? I'm telling you *bhenchood* truth — I can give it you in writing."

We enter a grocery store. He is trying to get the owner to place an advertisement in a local, sometimes progressive, cultural magazine Nabil works for. I, however, have a lunch date with two AIDS activists.

If one continues on boulevard Saint Laurent below de Maisonneuve, below boulevard René Lévesque, which was formerly named after Lord Dorchester, one passes through a small bustling Chinatown. No recession here. No Chinese shops have gone under. This Chinatown is hemmed in by large ugly concrete French-Canadian institutions. Yellow Peril.

I often think of the past in England and Scotland. This thinking about one's past can be a lucrative process if one can publish books or make films based on memories which can be made cultural or multicultural and framed in what is now called post-colonial discourse.

England has no shortage of such entrepreneurial ex-immigrants. In Kelven Grove Park in Glasgow, a big bully is making me kneel down in front of roses and is kicking the shit out of me. A white straw-haired Canadian friend, who is doing a soft, descriptive, and empirical work on the media at an impressive Montréal university, and who did not like using condoms in the late seventies, tells me when he lived in France the same thing happened to him, *even though* he was white. However, when I write about or discuss my memories I can, if I want to, call it racism; he can't. I can try to make a profit out of it, even get a grant; he can't.

Recently this man and I had a falling out because we applied for the same job. When I told him that I had sent off my CV to the same place, at his suggestion, he immediately turned cold and bitter like the winters here. He demanded back the two hundred bucks he had lent me. "You told them you're a Paki, didn't you?"

Another day there was a fight with John Macgrottie. I smashed his Glaswegian face repeatedly with my brown fists. A tight circle of his Scotty friends stood around. Another kick to his little stomach, buckles in pain, a boot to the balls. Another full-force fist to his face. He got up again. I opened the little fucker's face with another full punch. Teeth on the kerb. Scottish blood: Pakistani fist. He came to school the next day with two black eyes and a torn lip. A very small anti-colonial victory, another possible world relation. Brown first with a condom. He never called me darkie or nigger again, but his friends ganged up on me, so I busted his head yet again. Ah! the cycle of sweet Fanonian violence.

My parents, in a transitional religious phase, were planning for me to be an altar boy. I used to go to church at lunch time, and sometimes on the way home: "Bless me, Father, for I have sinned; I have committed the following sins. I have been fighting with Scottish boys. That is a sin, isn't it? Father, I have stolen money from my sister."

"Your sins are forgiven, my son; five Hail Marys, stations of the cross once, the rosary once; your sins are forgiven, my son."

Saint Patrick's School was on Saint Mungo Street, in a working-class district of Glasgow with coal fires. Saint Mungo is the patron saint of alcoholics. But a little out of this area one could see nice things in the toyshop windows: large model ships drifting on styrofoam seas like at the Glasgow Museum.

The way they broke my smaller brother's nose at playtime is an image that I still treasure today. He is now a member of a Canadian police force in a city that's locked in snow six months of the year. This history of violence sets me apart from my white friends. Their ideas are not much to beat down anyway: neo-Althusserians at best, mixed in with the borrowed language of people from the earth-shattering Frankfurt School. Poor Walter Benjamin. Some of these intellectuals have kissed the French thinkers goodbye. The very best of them employ Edward Said's mechanical critiques of Orientalism, safely launched from Columbia University, where the Jewish Defense League makes things difficult for him by wrecking his office.

Occasionally, tough feminists invite me to their classes to show my work — cultural studies types; they give me grants, to show that they are racegenderprogressive. I go into their galleries to give talks, show my videotapes: on the Algerian War, the Orient in the Occidental imagination; the fall of the Caliphate of Granada, etc.; to discuss things like the depiction of Third World armed struggles in the CBC state media. Afterwards we sing happy birthday to Nelson Mandela in whose honour the municipal government has named a park.

In a grey Glasgow schoolyard at breaktime, white knees in my brother's face. Outdoor toilets with freezing urine and white caustic soda to keep the plague off the kilts. Broken English absorbed from the teach-yourself textbook in Lahore. No one wore kilts in Glasgow, of course. Stories told in the hickory-dickory *tongas* of Clarkabad. Brown, undernourished, overbeaten horses: rib cages in the Orient. Why did we leave? The Moslems were not that intolerant, were they? More like the Chevrolet Dream. Cheap visas? Follow the gold to London. No. Not for my class of immigrant. Middle class; Jains on one side, more or less educated Sikhs on the other. Pounds Shillings and Pence...Pounds Shillings and Pence...*Allah-O-Akbar*...Simple Simon Simple Simon was a pieman...on McLeod Road in downtown Lahore. Paris of Asia. A land of silk, sun, spices, and full-colour posters of General Zia. My little brother's face, bleeding, nose smashed. The only little Paki in the schoolyard. Simple Simon. Boots in the balls.

In Glasgow some of the preachers who taught us were addicted to giving the belt. In their offices, Joycean coal fires in green-tiled fireplaces, shiny pokers. "You're nothing but a playboy, Samuel." Now why did he say that, I would wonder. *Playboy of the Western World*, I think now. No. Surely he could not have meant that. Hard to say. The black strap for incorrectly calculating vulgar fractions; Father Seenin, the man with the strap which has three long fingers. Grey eyes grey hair grey suit sallow skin.

There were petitions signed in school in Warlingham, Surrey, to get me out of class. "Because your father has come to take our jobs — wog." Very reminiscent of my Canadian friend, some twenty-five years later in Montréal, with the same sentiment — the one I owed the two hundred bucks. "Give back the money by the middle of the month." Back in England my feelings used to get hurt, but not without breaking someone's nose or smashing a T-square across someone's teeth.

I did have a few loyal friends, like my professors at Trent, which is a little British mimesis in grey concrete beside a polluted grey river. The teachers were from Oxford, Cambridge, and Canterbury, Empire-educated clones, ideas frozen on the Bayeux tapestry of higher learning. Some were progressive homosexuals and died in the late eighties.

One thinks about all this later in life, after the heat of the moment, after the fists have stopped smashing the Scottish face, after the ship has pulled in to Liverpool.

Though I was trained to see in neo-Marxist terms, I was never really political during my undergraduate years at university, but I always had a bloodthirsty attraction to the Palestine Liberation Organization. My interest in world politics must have evolved because of the intricate influence of thought and action that my liberal professors exposed me to in the mid-seventies via Georg Lukács, Jurgen Habermas, and Roland Barthes, the French dandy. There were no women social critics or Blacks on the courses back then – unless of course it has been recently proven that Lukács or Habermas had mothers or fathers from Senegal or thereabouts.

One of my professor friends writes political plays involving postal workers in Peterborough. He slips them Brecht and beer on the side and gives them Mao caps. I'll always admire him for this. He drives a blue Porsche. He put $2,300 Canadian into my first book of angry poems against Canadian support of dictators in zones of military conflict. He often visits me here in Montréal and takes me out for dim sum. He went to school at Oxford, subsequently carrying an Oxford version of F. R. Leavis's revaluation of English literature to the University of Hong Kong. He was a personal friend of Chou En-Lai, saw Mao from ten metres on a sunny day, shed tears over the Suez crisis on the lawns of Oxford, had a son in Hunan province in China, sucked off a man from Samarkand somewhere on the Silk Road en route to a teaching post in the cultural studies department in Ontario. He loves condoms – even, I think, likes to jerk off in them in front of his video camera.

The professors minimized Joseph Conrad's questionable anti-imperialism. In *Nostromo*, Conrad refers to Natives as "a torrent of rubbish." I found this out much later of course, in the epoch of political correctitude and cultural policing.

Constant fights in high schools in Toronto and in Warlingham. A girlfriend I had at the time in England was called "wog-lover" by her friends. I think this used to hurt her — she promised me that she would not feel sorry for me.

Then, after twenty years of never having touched British soil (except for a plane transfer at Heathrow en route to Kuwait and Delhi), I went back to England. I was researching a film on the Algerian War. I sent my childhood sweetheart a postcard from Hackney, where I was staying with a union activist friend.

My postcard worked. She called just eighteen hours after I had dropped the thing in the nineteenth-century mailbox. Such is the power of the British postal system. She remembered everything: the walks in the woods, the holly trees, the Christmas carols, the chilly winters, the walks to and from school, the chips in newspapers, and very reluctantly, the racism I suffered as a child. She moved past the question when I brought it up. She must have felt the sting also. It was obvious that she did not know how to assimilate the bicultural ideology of *Sammy and Rosie Get Laid* in yet another term of Thatcherite Britain. When I lived in England, Enoch Powell was all the rage. The words "Paki-nigger-darkie" in my face.

Perhaps she had never seen such cinematic gems as *My Beautiful Launderette*. This gem has a Pakistani sucking off a progressive white ex-fascist, or was it the other way round? This kind of cinema calls for people to treat us nicely and accept us. The harder, more violent cinema, which is constantly being produced, is not polite enough to make it to big public screens, so we have to be contented with brown on white on brown blow jobs in renovated laundromats. It must be hard for her to consider trendy race issues. After all, she's only known the track-and-field Paki. The fishing-pond Paki. The tree-house Paki. She has been in the same white neighbourhood since birth. It is an international fact that suburbs make you silent.

Before I zapped off that postcard to my old girlfriend, I locked myself into England by catching the tube from the Druidly titled Seven

Sisters metro stop to London Bridge to East Croydon, and then that bus ride, a Green Line bus, to Chelsham Road, followed by a walk to 58 Lime-green Road.

I walked past the house where we used to live, past the hedges where white boys with plumbers for fathers and toast-and-jam mothers chased me on their bikes.

The cornfields flowed smoothly into Farley Common, where an old black horse used to stand in the rain, the blanket on his back dripping ruefully into the stupid British countryside. Walking past our old house, I thought I saw another ex-girlfriend, asked if she or her family still lived there and yes, they did. The blonde stranger with a tartan skirt and white knee socks said her parents still lived in the same house, but she had moved to a house with her husband and kids.

When I got back to multiracial Hackney, she phoned.

"Are you married yet? What do you do?"

It felt sweet and nervous at the same time to talk with her. "I make films and write a little, but mostly I make films about history, films that do not get shown."

"Oh, why don't they get shown — are they ever on TV?" The bad connection crackles her voice. "Can I come and see them?"

"Well, actually I'm not sure if they are ever going to be shown in England."

In fact they were being shown at the London Filmmakers Cooperative, but I thought it was safer to retract into my avant-gardist role than to invite her to London to see my mixture of post-colonial hybridity and resentment against the Western press.

A little back and forth through the green years. I did not see her: too close a skirmish with something beyond me, just way too empirical. She tells me she now raises finches and ducks, and the ducks swim in a small pond in her garden. Their house is in Warlingham. Croydon is near Warlingham. Swan and Sugar Loaf.

Warlingham is in England. England is a little island with a great mail system. I wonder if they have central heating. We are reconnected now. She writes letters to me in cold Montréal.

Green Line bus. The yellowing corn fields pull out into the distance as I move back to London Bridge, back to the safety of Hackney. The trees I used to play under remain unchanged. I remember the touch of the tree bark in 1986. Dogs barking in the cool damp distance, iron nails rusting in the tree, the same nails I put there when I knew England through a tongue that could not quite pronounce V as in *vice*. Boys at school thought it was funny. Wind in the grass in the sand dunes on Munora Beach, Karachi. My ear close to the hissing.

On my third trip back to London, my Pakistani friend Jamal and I drove back to Warlingham. We had met that preceding winter in a New Delhi art gallery in front of a painting called "Night in Benaries." He had round glasses and I could tell that he was returning to see his past. I found my ex-girlfriend's address in my computer-printed directory and Jamal and I headed out to visit her. An old woman came to the door. My ex-girlfriend's children and husband were away and this old woman was house-sitting. "She has not been at all well. Last Christmas the doctors let her come home, but she is not well. Yes, she has mentioned you," said the frail woman. "All she could say were a few words." Our memory had become one-directional. She had suffered a stroke.

We drove back to an expensive Camden café and tried out English attempts at coffee. Jamal was born in Lahore some years after I was; weird that I should meet another Lahorie in Delhi and we should walk in the Warlingham woods together a year later.

Independence Day, Lahore, 1958. Martial law, jeeps, martial law, a coup, more martial law. It would be dishonest to try to connect our departure from Pakistan with this coup. It would make us as virtuous as some snobbish Chilean refugees, but we did leave shortly afterwards.

CHAPTER FIVE

Frantz Fanon Conference

Algeria, 1987

In perhaps the most eloquent epitaph on the Communards ever uttered by a non-Marxist, Auguste Renoir (who so narrowly escaped with his life in those days) said of them: 'They were madmen; but they had in them that little flame that never dies.' The memory of Louis-Napoleon's glittering masked balls at the vanished Tuileries had been swallowed up by the mists of the past; little enough is still recalled about Trochu's spiritless defense of Paris; and in France even the humiliation at Bismarck's hands is largely forgotten. But the 'little flame' of the Communards continues to be kept alight. The link between the brave balloonists of Paris and the spacemen of ninety-five years later may seen a tenuous one. But the course of history often flows down strange and unexpected channels. In 1964, when the first three-man team of Soviet cosmonauts went up in the Voskhod, they took with them into space three sacred relics; a picture of Marx, a picture of Lenin — and a ribbon off a Communard flag.

— Alistair Horne, *The Fall of Paris* (Middlesex, England: Penguin Books, 1965)

Algeria keeps coming in and out of my head, because it was one revolution that I studied less superficially than other revolutions.

And, of course, the memory of that Black medical student I met at Houari Boumedienne Airport on the afternoon of my departure returns every once in a while.

The crossing from Paris to Algeria was fast — epochs connected by eighty minutes' air time. Air Algérie served us *El Moujhadid*, a state newspaper, along with Algerian beer ("*Mais oui, c'est alcoolisé*"), concrete proof that Algeria is hundreds of years ahead of other Arab regimes. Or perhaps it is not proof of anything at all. In a year or so Algeria would see that its own *intifada* made it resemble the Jewish state. We also had some pastries trapped somewhere between the ancient Arab world and industrial French baking.

I turned to the centre pages of *El Moujhadid*, which had details about the Frantz Fanon conference that I was to participate in, and a large obituary on James Baldwin. Baldwin was Black, so was Fanon. Although I had not been introduced to any of these intellectuals, I could feel their presence in the humming body of the plane — earth-shattering talk about publishing this and that. Deadlines for the next conference on technological revolution, and whether Jean Baudrillard was going to accept an invitation to their precious conference.

They turned and looked at me. I noticed them; they noticed me. I noticed them. The revolutionary class. An African man who had become my conference friend told me later, "*Ah, les intellectuels, penses-tu qu'ils occupent un certain espace?* Politics is all about noticing other people, *n'est-ce pas?*" He told me this as we boyishly pissed outside the British Embassy later that evening, after a supper paid for by the Algerian people.

We stayed at the swankiest hotel in Algeria, the old Saint George, now the El-djazair. Large, chandelier-filled dining room, foyers as big as football fields. A bit like the old Batista-era hotels in Havana, except that here in Alger, the orchestra was still playing, at least for the duration of the conference. Every morning we were driven to a large shopping mall-like building, where the conference took place. There were several lecture halls connected to broad spacious corridors.

I was standing in a city in which an old colonial power had been defeated, sent home, and the contemporary power even succeeded in retaining a few French intellectuals who had made Algeria their home, forever turning their backs on France. These people would loudly claim during the conference that this was home. After '62, "We stayed because we could not go back. We had become Algerian."

Their presentations at this conference were graceful, and I could feel one culture overlap another through the black skin of Fanon, who died at Bethesda Hospital in the United States at the ripe age of thirty-six in 1961. He is buried on the Algerian-Tunisian border at Aïn-Soltane.

I became friends with a Burkinabé man during the six-day conference. After a late evening supper of lamb and couscous in the palatial dining hall, British-Canadian-Québécois-Pakistani and Burkinabé urine once again mixed on the pavement in front of the British Embassy.

These days the FLN — Front du libération nationale — is in a lot of trouble because the FIS — Le Front islamique de salut — is picking up steam, and it is not as easy to contain as the modernist FLN, which is not really racist.

More or less the reverse is true in Québec, where the official structure is not healthy for non-white immigrants and Natives. Québec consists of a dominant white tribe, a historical residue of pre-revolutionary Jansenist France.

The Québécois can just barely hold their heads above the ideological swamp of Parti Québécois manipulations like the French-language-threat-illusion and a half-baked desire for a Québec outside the federal fold; earnest desire, all this talk of "independence" — but it will be no better than the partition of British India. There, Partition produced three states where the sleepy upper and middle classes got to replace the Raj and send their kids to England for schooling. India turned out to be the Largest Democracy in the World. Great achievement. Québec will not do much better — it will become the second-largest French-speaking democracy in the world. It has fewer internationalist intellectuals than India, for one thing, and there isn't even an equivalent to the bourgeois-Indian-nationalist-Fabian-socialist Jawaharlal Nehru. Is there even a pseudo-secular-separatist like Pakistan's Mohammed Ali Jinnah in Québec? Jinnah's secularism-in-theory makes the PQ leaders look proto-Nazi, as the leaders of the Anglophone parties tell us. Québec will just produce a ruling technocracy moving in concert with self-satisfied Québécois, and sooner or later it will fall into the hands of the Americans.

There is a massive difference between the nationalist vision in Algeria pre- and post-revolution and the québécois non-counterparts. The québécois regime in the summer of 1990 called in the army to "solve" the Natives' attempt at stopping the construction of a golf course on their ancestral lands at Oka, near Montréal.

In 1988 there was massive repression in Algeria — as bad as the repression in the occupied terrorities in Israel. The American-Palestinian member of the Palestinian National Council, Edward Said, called this uprising Algeria's *intifada* — an injurious comparison for Algeria. There were very intelligent riots in the streets in Alger. Militarism comes hand-in-hand with the nation-state's drive towards modernity.

An Algerian novelist, Rachid Mimouni, who smoked at least as much as René Lévesque, told me Algeria was actively not racist. "It is not so easy to say that — there is right here in Alger a synagogue in the heart of the Arab world. Pluralism. And moreover there is a Jewish writer who lives here and he is loved and well-known throughout the country."

Just as I thought Mimouni was going to conclude his statement, he ironically added, "You know, Samuel — *pardonne-moi*, Julien — Islam has always been tolerant of Jewish religious practice." In fact, the rule in Spain since 711 was keep to yourself, pay taxes, don't proselytize. His cigarette moves to the side of his trousers. "I'll try to find your book when I get back to Montréal."

Years later, in June 1990, to be exact, I saw an extract from *Le jardin*, another of Mimouni's works, published in *Le Monde Diplomatique*.

He mentioned the other minorities who live and work in Alger — the Kabyles, who have had more than a little difficulty with the Arabization movement, for example. Algerian academics, writers, and intellectuals are extremely used to international guests. Their answers roll off Sorbonne-educated tongues in two or more languages.

The morning session of presentations is over and we are all having coffee. I overhear a conversation between an Asian Kampalan-Marxist victim of Idi Amin and an Egyptian woman who is not presenting a paper at the conference but is part of the international audience. She is the only veiled women here and is holding a coffee cup in her hand. The Kampalan man beside her is trying to involve her in conversation, but before she can give her shyness full rein he places his question: "I really would like to know why you wear the veil."

She continues to look directly at the table. The question does not derail her; of course, it is not supposed to. There is a confidence in the way she stands. Her fine veil of embroidered black lace is a little more eye-catching than it might have been had anyone else been wearing one. The relative blanking out of the rest of her facial features gives her eyes added power. I am pulled in from a distance. I am trying hard not to stare. Her eyes are fine: irises hazelly green, with tiny black slits and constantly expanding and contracting pupils.

As she leans to place her cup on a nearby table, an elegant line forms around her hips down to her sandalled high-arched feet. Politically incorrect observations? Who cares? Fanon wasn't orthodox either. We are here to reflect on his works, and his works embraced sexuality, French propaganda, white skin, Black women, Black men, white masks, religion, French propaganda, and modernity. And the configurations under her garb are beautiful. I can't be sure, but I am sure.

Her veil fluffs a little when she speaks. His directness does not make her shy away. However, before she can formulate a response — I can tell she is about to begin something — he adds his next question: "Is the Islamic movement on the rise in Algeria, as it is all over North Africa, affecting you directly? Is the *Ikhwan* in your own country affecting you?"

"Well, this is a complex question. I can only answer it in a direct way," she replies. "The veil is become an economic question inside a religious one — there are many other reason as well."

The nerd Asian Kampalan sociologist tries to look reflective, pensive, concerned, all evidence of an upper-class colonial upbringing.

She asks, "Are you with the university here?"

"No, I am from the School of Oriental and African Studies, but if I can ask you, why is the veil an economic question?"

"Well, for the lower-middle-class woman it has become a way to get out of the competition of the glamour, and I am not saying that glamour is a Western phenomenon."

The Kampalan is showing educated surprise — a thin trace of a smile. His mannerisms have taken literally years of training.

"You see, it is not for the religious reasons alone that we are wearing the veil. If one has not the money to buy all the expensive creams, the cosmetics and lipsticks, you see, it is a bit easier this way."

His face moves to express satisfaction and even surprise at her answers. There is, I am convinced, a generous sophistication to him. It all but sets the Egyptian woman at ease, but he is suspicious of her answer.

He senses the presence of an Algerian woman who has moved into the orbit of conversation. She is standing beside them, on the verge of making a contribution to the subject. Her hair is black, leather dress cut unIslamically above the knee, though not quite a mini. Tanned legs. Flat black shoes from the northern coast of the Mediterranean, tissue-thin pyramidic silver earrings. The requisite cigarette, international symbol of liberation, moves down past her forehead, past her high cheek-bones and into her mouth, a mouth sexier than Jeanne Moreau's. A few strands of jet-black hair are placed back in line.

The Kampalan has to negotiate the Algerian's very acute frontal sexuality as well as the veiled woman's understatements, which are sexual though in different terms. In fact, the Algerian's projection is a beautifully embroidered mix of the left-unsaid.

The impatient Kampalan asks the Algerian woman, "Do you think the FLN can contain the drive of the fundamentalists here in Algeria?"

The Algerian woman answers in English. There is a *sympa* tone of internationalism for the Kampalan brother in her voice. Her accent is somewhere between Green Park, Southall, or Brixton. No. I'm wrong. I track their conversation with CIA closeness; this woman is a product of summer school at Oxford, a crash course in English. Later I discover my observation is right. She is to present one of the most challenging papers at the conference, "The Limits of Fanon's Resistance: The Impermanence and Collapse of Imitative Modernity."

"This is a complicated question: you see, I cannot answer it with the confidence of my Egyptian friend. However, I can tell you how Algerian women face the Islamic front."

"And how is that?"

"We are very scared and annoyed by it. The Islamic movement could put us in a very inferior position. It could undo many advances that even the FLN, with all its limitations, has made. This is not merely a class question. This FIS is using every means to try to bring poorer women into its fold."

The Algerian woman continues, but her English loses composure: "*Le FIS* makes life a little less complicated rather yes for some women than having to put up with sexual competition. It makes things easier and besides the FLN do not understand *la dynamique* of this group which *le FIS exploite...* It has a charm these days, and underestimates their ability to listen, act, and reform, *et tout ça. Et le FIS* — they are animals: *ce sont des animaux* — there have been talks even of them burning women dressed in short sleeves and dresses with acid — *imagine-toi? — effrayant* — also they have been telling *merde* about women taking jobs from men which is not true."

The Kampalan, who shows no signs of being overcome by either of these women, reminds her of his original question. There is a smile across her red lips. Another conference session is about to begin in the lecture hall. The Egyptian and Algerian leave. A grey robe flutters away from me in the modern building.

The Kampalan, alone, faces the universal question of whether to refill his cup or follow the women to the next panel. The remaining crowd of twenty people scatters, then gravitates towards the door of the hall. A chilly breeze off the sea blows through the building. Other members of the audience congregate at the hall doorway. Cigarettes are brutalized on the marble floor. The next panel session has started when we walk in: ten students from the university are reading small sections from Fanon's work.

The first student, a woman, reads from *Towards the African Revolution*:

> For nearly three years I have been trying to bring the misty idea of African Unity out of the subjectivist bogs of the majority of its supporters. African Unity is a principle on the basis of which it is proposed to achieve the United States of Africa without passing through the middle-class chauvinistic national phase with its procession of wars and death tolls.

The young student looks to her left and passes the *parole* to the woman sitting beside her. Something about this collection of readers catches me in an unexpected way. It is some twenty years after Fanon's death; he was not a great political philosopher, not even a great tactician, nor even a great shrink. He brought different fields of human resistance together. Here, for example, are people who might not have gotten together: an Iranian about whom we will hear later, the FLNKS fighters from New Caledonia, a Pakistan-Quebecker-Brit, many Black Americans, one Ethiopian psychiatrist from California.

The young Algerian starts to read:

> And off we were, across the one hundred kilometres of dirt road. This part of the Sahara is not monotonous. Even the sky up there is constantly changing. Some days ago we saw a sunset that turned the robe of heaven violet. Today it is a very hard red that the eye encounters. Aguerhoc, Tessalit, Bouressa. At Tessalit we cross the French military camp. A

French soldier, bared to the waist, gives us a friendly wave.
His arms would drop off him if he could guess whom these
Arab outfits conceal.

Then a German student studying in Algers reads from *A Dying
Colonialism:*

> For the tourist and the foreigner, the veil demarcates both
> Algerian society and its feminine component....
>   We shall see that this veil, one of the elements of the
> traditional Algerian garb, was to become the bone of
> contention in a grandiose battle, on account of which the
> occupation forces were to mobilize their most powerful and
> most varied resources, and in the course of which the
> colonized were to display a surprising force of inertia.

Other students read sections from Fanon's work on the role of
the French radio and his analysis of the role of Algerian women in
the struggle.
    I cannot imagine this reading occurring at a Canadian univer-
sity.

In talking with Algerian women I found that they had rather direct
answers when asked: "Do you think Algerian women are well-repre-
sented in positions of importance?"
    With an air that suggested they were confiding in you, letting
out a state secret, they would say, "Yes, but it was, I would think, a
political revolution, not a total change. I mean, some of us still have
our differences with how it all went."
    Women did have a range of positions on the revolution: some
were dissatisfied; some were, in light of the imminent revival of
Islam, a little too cautious to slam it outright. Veils, European

dresses; dynamic contiguity. On many of the main streets one could survey the dress codes, from the tribal feudalism of the hidden woman to hip-hoppy skirts on women with a sharpness that would make Simone de Beauvoir look like a philosophy major in a small-town Canadian university. They did their bit as commandos, as armed liberators, and now they must enjoy their little bit of post-revolutionary freedom, their little bit of forgetting. In recent elections, the FIS won 853 out of 1,541 communes – enough to terrify even uncritical liberal women.

After the conference, an army official, who I think doubled as minister of culture (and who, it was rumoured, ordered the troops to fire live ammunition on demonstrating children in October of 1988), invited us all for a special parting supper of first-rate vegetables and a huge fish in the centre of the table. The army official was very cultured and had given a memorable speech at the conference.

The waiter served us with two large spoons held poised in one hand. I had several helpings, and drank lots of wine. Some of the conference participants had been to Algiers before and had seen bread lines in the city during the day – something, no doubt, the regime would like to have hidden totally. The most refined Fanonists, a breed of political animal trapped somewhere between Trotsky and Iqbal, renamed the FLN the DISCOFLN. Nasty irony, given the generous invitation to dinner. In the huge basement of the huge hotel where the regime installed us was a gymnasium-sized vibrating disco filled with lots of men dressed in shiny black suits and women in leather minis.

"Just like a virgin." My conference buddy was telling me that he was going to fuck someone that night. "I think the one with the Paris education. *Moi! je vais draguer ce soir.*"

"Why her?" I asked, because it was a system within which he could communicate, a system produced by colonial history and factored into a frame of French enlightenment. A tailor-made discourse that French colonialism had prepared exclusively for him, a hand-job on the rails of intellectual practice.

His country had had the pleasure of being a French colony. This process of *draguer* was a kind of process snagged between the army official, Cuvée du Président (an excellent wine, if you like wine that is really full-bodied and rather *corsé*), the revolution, and the just-so-correctly-fried vegetables and the charming translator who played with us.

The translator was also dressed in the latest styles from Paris, though not avant-garde: she had pink nails and said she was frequently flown in by the Libyan head of state to translate his words into the patient ear of the Western press. I have written to her but she has not written back, nor has she sent the tapes of Algerian music I asked her for. Her English was good, but when I tested her with phrases like "Pissed me off" and "Take the rap for it," she failed. But hers was nevertheless better than the English spoken in Québec. I learned more new French words in Algeria than in my eleven-year stay in Montréal.

The Black thinkers from Zaire, Senegal, Martinique, New Caledonia, and America said that the Algerians were sort of forced into holding this conference because Martinique and Brazzaville had previously hosted Fanon events. Fanon had seen no borders in the world. He was Black, from Martinique, and Algeria was racist. There was an underlying tension between the Black Africans and the Arabs. There always will be.

The Kanak leader from New Caledonia gave a talk that explained everything, including the history of French atomic-bomb testing near his country. He explained the make-up of the French mercenary constituency there. Algeria understood this man from New Caledonia — they heard him in reverent silence. He said they would use the FLN example to free themselves from colonial rule.

Standing ovation. But what really tore the roof off the place was:

"Algerians and the people of New Caledonia have met before in history — this is not the first time. And, my friends, when have we met before?" He pauses. "We have been in a French prison...we were in a French prison in the 1870s when France exiled many of the Paris Communards to our homeland — New Caledonia. My friends, Algerians fought alongside the Communards in 1871."

My Burkinabé buddy from Africa cannot control his excitement; he bolts up from his chair. His notes — in colonial French penmanship — trickle to the floor. Everyone else is clapping. His eyes are watery. I feel part of something. I think about what the socialist François Mitterrand said on November 12, 1954: "Algeria is France. And who among you, mesdames, messieurs, would hesitate to employ every means to preserve France?" He was at that time minister of the interior.

Later I discovered that indeed Algerian "immigrants" had fought alongside the Paris Communards. Many were exiled to New Caledonia, among them Louise Michelle, a leading Communard, called the Red Virgin. Indeed, "History flows down strange and unexpected channels." France faces ineluctable defeat in New Caledonia as it did in "Indochina" and Algeria. But one is never sure about liberation struggles in the New World Order. There were no Pakistanis at the conference, despite the fact that Fanon's writings do exist in Urdu. The translation of Wretched of the Earth is Uftad Gannie Khakk – "Those that have been thrown on the ground like ashes."

A Palestinian named Abouali, whom I had befriended, was bored in Algiers, though he did not wear it on his face. He always smiled, and when I spoke of Canada he listened with a strange closeness, as though he had been somehow starved for news. Occasionally his bitterness leaked through, but it only took a whiff of Palestine to bring out something not visible initially. "I was born a refugee," he said in the only bitter tone he ever used to express himself. "I want to leave Algeria; they will not let me teach journalism or film studies. The Algerians don't want my skills."

"The Quebeckers don't want mine," I say.

I called the Canadian Embassy on Abouali's behalf, and got a québécois accent on the other end of the line. "Hi there, comrade from Québec. My friend Abouali wants to move to Canada – can you help him? He's been to school for years, very educated, a West Banker. He is a great journalist – a non-smoker – he's everything we need in Canada."

Abouali hears me repeat the embassy lines. "And it would take a year or so and – what! You want him to apply from Rabat – what? – he can't apply from Algiers?"

Canada has recently sent back hundreds of Turkish refugee claimants. Canada and Québec are not as open as Abouali thought. In fact, some of Québec's politicians are Catholic when it comes to race, class, and accepting the blame for the effects of the massive arms industry here and the subsequent production of political refugees from El Salvador, Guatemala, and elsewhere. "Of course, Abouali, you know that Canada sells arms to El Salvador, Guatemala, all those places where we Canadians get refugees from. You know this about Canada, don't you?" The positive images of Canada, Québec, and pine trees vanish from his face.

Some Québec unions have discussed the idea of quotas on the number of immigrants in high schools. Abouali found out that Montréal has one of the world's largest arms industries. Montréal is in the Canadian province of Québec. Québec has tried to shed its catholicity, but what it got in 1976 was a micro-nationalism, singularly the worst sort of sickness, though not as bad as a communal riot during the Partition of British India. Algeria's nationalism has concretely helped some liberation movements.

Québec has done nothing to help a single international liberation movement, except for a few Toronto-style bake sales and solidarity dance parties.

Abouali brushes back his black hair, twists his ruby-headed ring off the knuckle of his finger. I see the tight impression the ring has made in the Palestinian's skin. He replaces it, then reaches for his wallet: "I'll pay for the tea this time." I will not be allowed to pay: I am in his world, in his injured and fractured *dunnia Arabia*.

A few tinny dinars tinkle on the table. We leave the café.

He is not saying much. He softly holds my elbow as we re-enter the conference hall to listen to a paper on the Iranian thinker Dr. Ali Shari'ati. It has been rumoured that Shari'ati was killed by British forces in 1977. Shari'ati's tyrannicidal interpretations of the Koran helped to fuel the 1979 Iranian revolution. The talk is prefaced with something that was written by Dr. Ali Shari'ati but could have been written by Fanon:

> Come, friends, let us abandon Europe; let us cease this
> nauseating apish imitation of Europe. Let us leave behind
> this Europe that always speaks of humanity, but destroys
> human beings wherever it finds them.

The talk is about Shari'ati's translations of the works of Fanon. Dr. Ali Shari'ati is the first to have translated Fanon's work into Farsi. Many of my Iranian friends say Shari'ati was a confused religious modernist and a fundamentalist all at once. The paper was given by an Iranian woman who, later, in a coffee-break conversation, said she visited Iran often.

"I change dress codes in the washroom of the 747 somewhere over Bulgaria," she playfully explained.

Abouali and I are impressed with her talk. "Canada is a nice safe place which can be racist. I live from welfare cheque to arts grant. Abouali, I know about a small town, Um-el-Famnn, in your part of the woods," I say. His face lights up. I tell him about *Palestinians Under Israeli Rule*, a film I once saw in Montréal.

As we become familiar with each other he builds up the courage to scold me: "Your film on the war that you showed is useless: the editing was bad, the acting was a damn joke, and you exploited footage of West Bank riots only to dilute this analysis of the Algerian War — what an utter shame you wasted all that money! I can't even understand why they gave money to someone like you to make such an inconsequential work — it's a wonder they don't send you back to Pakistan — and they should make you apply for re-entry from Rabat."

We got to be conference buddies. "Abouali, all your years at that underfunded West Bank university have not done you any good at all — all that suffering under Zionism has undercut your education in film studies. Besides, what do you Palestinians know about Brecht?"

He leans back in laughter. We have found another café. The beautiful glottal hiss of Arabic surrounds us. "We know everything there is to know about Brecht, my Pakistani-Canadian conference friend."

Defensively I add, "If you lived in Canada, you would fast become intolerant of documentaries that use boring methods to explore boring themes."

He was being watched by the Algerian state. We exchanged addresses, phone numbers, handshakes, a few loving ironies. "It's a shame that even the powerful Edward Said could not get you a scholarship to powerful Columbia University." Our goodbyes became actions.

Then just as we are set to leave each other forever: "Hey, Julian, maybe your film was so bad because you have been wasting your time at all those underfunded Canadian universities."

"Abouali," I said, "it was not a film but a videotape — not everything with moving pictures is a film."

I watch a chugging Russian-made taxi take him up one of the European-engineered roads.

I look out my hotel window at ships slowly pulling out of this city thrown into a hillside. White pillar-like houses shooting up into the cool mornings. I want to stay on in Algeria. I send out scores of postcards. I call Sophie in Paris: "Can I stop in for a few days?" The conference organizers are not willing to pay for a three-day extension. I move to the Hôtel Regina on boulevard Ben Boulaid Mostéfa. Not a five-star hotel. Breakfast is included in the price of the room.

One descends five flights in the cage elevator to a small yellowish lobby with one large light bulb. One morning, I pushed the button and, while I waited, poked my head over the metal fence to look down the elevator shaft, not realizing that the heavy cage was above me, slowly descending. I heard a squeak, looked up, and barely missed having my head crushed between the fence and this greasy mass of steel. I was almost decapitated. A cleaning woman who caught the end of this event sucked back a sympathetic gulp of air, thanking Allah.

The breakfast consisted of two not-so-stale rolls with jam and coffee, served in a small room adjoining the yellow lobby. A proud and morbidly silent man worked at the desk. Foreigners did not impress him. I could not invite a woman I had met up to my room. In the five-star hotels where the FLN hosted its guests, however, this international practice was not questioned.

Riadh El Feth, the arts centre which hosted our Fanon conference, had Madonna blasting out of large TV screens elegantly bolted into concrete pillars every twenty feet. This is the evolved historic *souk*, a marketplace. No sand on the floor. Occasionally one would see people from the far south, wearing huge midnight-blue Afghan-like turbans rising augustly skywards, and long flowing *djellabas*, ordering hambooorgers with fries at fast-food joints.

Algeria has one of the youngest populations in the world. Seventy percent of the twenty-four million Algerians are under twenty-five years old, almost sixty percent are under twenty, and fifty percent are under fifteen years of age. Maybe Fanon's prediction will pan out: Algeria, a second revolution? This second change of air, however, will not resemble what Fanon had in mind; it won't be something that he could have easily predicted. The Islamic response to Western imperialism has not been a weak one. People no longer invest much hope in "*la gauche sourde*," the FLN.

I had met and become friends with a woman. We would disappear for whole chunks of time during the afternoon sessions. Walks mostly. We would see scenes of about twenty or thirty youths dressed in skin-tight blue gathered around the TV monitors. I made some claims to Yasmin about the effect the tube was having on Algerian youth.

"Yes, but that view is so outdated. How are you going to prevent the outside world from coming in? Everyone has a TV and an '*antenne parabolique*' – *notre société... tout à fait parabolisée* – you know the leader of the FIS has two *antennes paraboliques* – everyone says he looks at more porn from Sweden than all the rest of Algeria put together. *Et quand même*, so what's wrong with Madonna on the screen – *vous-êtes khomeniste ou quoi?*"

I say, "Yeah, I suppose you're right, but there could be more debate instead of all this time devoted to *Les Clips*."

She does not believe in what I am saying. "We often get lots of French intellectual broadcasts like Pivot on *Apostrophe* – do you think the Algerian TV *intellos* would put on programming that good?

Imagine-toi. I mean, how do you think we would find out about Umberto Eco? about the Channel Tunnel? about, *oui, Madonna? Alors pourquoi pas Madonna?"*

I back down. I retreat into my well-rehearsed barrage of negative commentary on Canadian TV, Canadian immigration, Canadian institutions of higher learning. "Television in Québec actually educates, refines. Such is the power of the traditional Canadian educational system." For contrast I compare the lack of pluralistic political spectrum on Canadian TV with what I have seen on British television. "Canadian CBC and Radio-Canada is devastating — utterly boring."

I bring up what Noam Chomsky repeatedly exposes in all of his books.

"I have never heard of this man, Noam Chomsky. *C'est un Juif américain?*" Yasmin asks as we walk around another glass-windowed boutique.

"Yes, *un Juif anti-sioniste, très critique de l'État sioniste* — he exposes its connection to the Pentagon." The Yankee media does not have Chomsky on the airwaves at home. He is popular in Europe.

Yet the presence of foreign TV in Algeria was as powerful as it was in Cuba, where, during a winter vacation, I saw Madonna as well. Not all Algerian youth were glazed by the tube. In Cuba, one minute it was the bearded Castro and the next minute a young Cuban would be slipping in a video cassette of Madonna doing her nickel-and-dime choreography. Here in Algeria, state TV piped in Frankie Goes to Hollywood, Marianne Faithful, and Sting.

Towards the end of the conference, I was interviewed by an intellectual in his mid-twenties. We went off to a side of the building which overlooked the city. He questioned me in French while writing out my remarks in Arabic. Some of the younger *intellos* in

Algeria knew all about Western power configurations to the smallest liberation struggles everywhere, including the strike at Université d'Alger, and why the Algerian press did not cover it. By comparison, Canadian youth must have the lowest level of international awareness in the world. Algerians knew where Maputo is. Québécois youths don't know or care where Luanda is or when Maputo was a Portuguese colonial centre.

After the conference, on the way back to Paris for a few days, I meet a medical student near the Air Algérie check-in counter. People don't line up there, they just form a circular critical mass around the ticket agent who, despite even rude attempts to get his attention, remains cool, polite. "*Oui, mon frère, oui, attendez une seconde, je vais le faire pour vous.... Attendez, s'il vous plaît.... Vos billets pour Paris vol 1871. Attendez, s'il vous plaît.*"

The medical student and I connect souls during a twenty-minute meeting before his flight out of Algiers. He is from Burundi and tells me that Algeria is not all that racist any more, or not as racist as my African conference friend has told me it was while he was a student there in the seventies. I don't really remember how we started talking about race. Perhaps because it is one of those subjects that transplants such as myself talk about when they are transplanted. Very much like two hockey fans talking hockey when they meet each other for the first time.

Our conversation dissolves with the fluttering of the flight announcement board:

AF 407 Brazza embarquement immédiat.

I walk my friend to security clearance. He goes on to Brazzaville, where he will change for a flight to Bujumbura, then by road to somewhere nearby. A few minutes later I leave for Paris, Lahore of the West.

I cleared Algerian customs. After some nonsensical questioning by the inflated ego at security about why I didn't have any bank exchange receipts, I walked through the checkpoint, hand on my boarding pass, and slipped into the sunset.

As we left the tarmac I thought how I had betrayed the revolution by exchanging French francs on the black market. The exchange rate on the popular market was many times better than what the socialist state was offering, just like in Cuba.

I was invited to the Fanon conference because I had produced a documentary on the representation of liberation struggles in the Western press. Also my videotape is the only one in the history of the Western world to have dramatized the work of Frantz Fanon. It is not a major work; Channel Four in London did not want to buy it and a French film festival of ethnographic work was not interested in including it in their program. I made General de Gaulle look like a dysfunctional prick.

My tape is a compilation of archival footage with dramatic scenes culled from the work of Fanon. In London, I did manage to do some research on the Western media's depiction of the Algerian War and on liberation struggles in general. But it was not until I had returned to North America — Washington, DC, to be exact — that I did any serious archival research for my documentary on Algeria's struggle for independence. Officially, this surge for liberation was launched by the Front du libération national in 1954 and ended in 1962 when the Algerians won a political victory. Of course, Algeria did not fare so well in its post-revolutionary-post-colonial phase. Few Third World countries do.

Archival footage is in the public domain in the United States. All rights are protected here in Canada, even if we have paid for some progressive CBC journalist to provide us with unbiased objective reporting. Frequently, Canadian journalists use the *inter-*

view-the-police-commissioner-for-the-real-version method. In Canada and the UK, the state holds on to archival footage in self-protective ways. The CBC charges hundreds of dollars for the use of a few seconds of "their" footage. The Library of Congress in Washington, DC, knows it does not really matter who gets a chance to see and use the past in whatever context; democratic pluralism will rule.

It is twilight. The undercarriage slides out from beneath the fuselage with a rheumatic creak and thud. The lights of Paris flicker underneath me. Paris: built on the graves of the Arabs. We are on the other side, the northern side of *mare nostrum*. The driver of the airport bus is a *frère* from Algeria. The métro takes me to Place de Clichy; I walk in a wintery drizzle along boulevard de Clichy up rue Forrest to Sophie's house. From her kitchen window one can see the Cimetière du Montmartre and almost, though not quite, Émile Zola's grave. I say hello and go to the kitchen tap to get a glass of water. She and I laugh at the French over-concern for history.

I once sailed past Alger — in 1958 to be exact, in the city's most violent anti-colonial phase; there were thirty to sixty political killings a day. Jean-Paul Sartre played the concerned French moralist along with his *Sammy and Rosie Get Laid* wife. Crafty French folk.

JP introduced Fanon to Europe, then to America, then to the world. Sartre got tons of credibility by making hefty supportive statements about the suffering Algerian people.

What was I doing then, when we hordes of Pakistani immigrants sailed past Alger? I was seven or eight years of age, on the deck of the *Circassia*, looking at comic books; bang, splat, bash: reading the classics of liberation theology: the story of Abraham Lincoln and how he saved the slaves.

I was watching English ladies and men drink draft beer for the first time in my life and perfecting my English: "May-I-please-have-a-pound-of-butter"...pounds shillings and pence... pounds shillings and pence. Sigh for me, nightwind, in the noisy leaves of the Red Sea. "*Ici c'est la France.*"

My first sight of Liverpool. Twilight. A middle-class slave, of sorts. Others have made the crossing before, only without walks on those decks or Biblical allegorizing of the breeze in the Red Sea. No English ladies drinking teetering drafts on the high seas, no kind orders in Urdu. It wasn't until recently that I discovered that sixteenth-century Liverpool had a Black population. This knowledge locks me into a particular history, although I am not totally a part of it.

CHAPTER SIX

Rushdie on the Hooghly River

Calcutta, 1988

The dockside had a massive pool of quicksand next to where the boardwalk merged into the river. Partially submerged in this quicksand was an old boat with sections of its hull ripped out, like missing teeth. The grayish soil had a hint of blue because there was a large moon. The moonlight made the ground look like the back of a black wave or a whale. No motion, just the hint of it. Deep striations on its back, as though a giant claw had mauled it.

The old half-submerged boat appeared to be riding on the back of this sandy, moonlit slush. The boat had a large still eye painted on its side. The party crowd gathered by the dock to board the midnight cruise up and down Calcutta's Hooghly River. There was a rustling of saris; perfume mixed with the night air. Our boat bobbed up and down as this class of tea-plantation administrators boarded. Tasteful saris mostly, but a few overly bright ones. Midnight blues with grey shiny borders. Highly educated wives. There were no freelance artists on board; professionals mainly. A class on the deck, rotating to Madonna; another class belowdecks, less drunk, heating the food.

My brother and I had just arrived from Canada. It was December of 1988. The month before we had seen our media give extended coverage to two whales trapped in the Arctic. People were making efforts of all kinds to free the whales. Heads of state were making statements on the issue.

In West Bengal we sort of confused people; we looked like we were from somewhere right there, perhaps the northern part of a nearby country. Yet our accent in English set us apart as returnees or foreigners. The flight to India was awfully long and I remember puking on the 747 between Amman and Calcutta. It felt like the plane itself was trying to vomit me out. I have the feeling that I was getting ready for culture shock, but this time back there was no shock — Calcutta might just as well have been another stop on the London tube. There was a tight security check at Amman.

Our friend, Dr. Mukherjee, had picked us up from Dum Dum Airport and the chauffeur had given us a drive through some of the worst slums in imperial history. Kalamudeen, our driver, was fluent in Hindi and I practised my Urdu with him. I once saw him mixing a white powder with some green leaves; he would get a bit alert-looking after he had put this under his lip.

Right after our arrival we had a breakfast of eggs and went out on the balcony to see the city. From the fourth-floor apartment we were able to see palm trees and a few street vendors and beggars. Large buildings surrounded the apartment block this tea company owned. I had been told that the company had very good and fair relations with its workers; some tea pickers would get as much as fourteen rupees a day which, given the scale of things in India, was just enough to contain revolution.

I had the feeling these large houses below us were from an epoch when history was more British than Indian. Large patches of green algae grew down some of the walls. Later, in the moonlight, some of the algae became shapes that reminded me of images of Lady Mountbatten, Jawaharlal Nehru, and of course George V who fades and is replaced by a portrait of a white-suited, dashing, fully decorated Lord Louis Francis Albert Victor Nicholas Rear-Admiral Mountbatten, Viscount of Burma, soon to be the first Sea Lord.

Kalamudeen's driving skills were very modern. He was never in his life going to hit anyone or anything. He was able to miss a cow by two centimetres at sixty k.p.h., with four people on bikes in front of him. And our executive guest, whom I had known when he was doing his doctorate in experimental organic chemistry at McGill, told us that the driver was well aware of the consequences of slamming into cows. We were not to pity him if anything did happen. Even in secular West Bengal the immediate repercussions would be odious. I shudder to think of a street mob, a bleeding, injured cow, the Moslem driver at fault. Even as passengers, we could not expect great treatment at the hands of such a crowd, however accidentally the cow was hit. I always got the feeling that Kalamudeen was from East Pakistan but did not want to talk about it. He drove so close to people that we could hear bits of their conversations. Pedestrians scratched their noses as they dodged the Indian-made Ambassador. Pakistan does not have the infrastructure to make cars.

It was terrifying driving with him, but not as terrifying as reading Gunter Grass's articles on Calcutta. Grass was staying in "Cal." An Indian magazine called *Sunday*, somewhat less politically uncompromising than it is now, featured his dull writings on poverty and dirt. His work read like that of one of those short-sighted Western thinkers, a little like VS Naipaul, who did not do much to educate themselves on the real reasons for the ravage of this city and this part of the world. Did Grass expect Cal to be like Hamburg or Frankfurt? But he had enough Western literary clout to get published and was talked about on the boat ride on the same inky river that has made French orientalists and filmmakers go all misty.

Kalamudeen drove Allan and me to see the Victoria Memorial about three times because Dr. Mukherjee gave us a lift downtown every day. His office was on Bishop Lefroy Road and from there it was easy to start our wanderings. The memorial is a series of dusty rooms layered with paintings of the various rulers that have passed through Calcutta.

New Year's Eve was spent on a rented boat on the Hooghly River, which cuts Calcutta in two. The Christmas decorations on the boat caught the light breeze. The tape deck motivated dancing and touching. As the evening moved on, it became obvious that the sound was suffering from dying batteries. Tracy Chapman was sounding more and more like Ray Charles.

The driver of Dr. Mukherjee's bulbous white company car came along with us and was sort of a stowaway in the hold of the boat as it trudged towards the Howrah Bridge where people were sleeping. This is how Calcutta's Departments of Transportation and Housing merge into one mutually concerned civic body.

My mind kept being pulled to the quicksand in the harbour. There was a little chill in the air. A middle-aged single woman made a beeline for my younger brother, Allan. We both wanted to have sexual experiences with her, but I felt she had an adverse reaction to the greying hair at my temples. She kept talking about discos in London, and how cruel Indian society was to a divorced woman with children. We told her how different and advanced things were in North America, where women can do what they want.

The river was silent and flowed against the boat's movement. There was a tipsy-teetering large Bengali man who would get hugged frequently by one particular woman. His movements countered the decorations in the breeze. Allan and I had the feeling it was her way of publicly demonstrating her friendliness. Liberal West Bengal. The hugged man almost fell in the quicksand when we docked.

Some very hot chips were passed around and they actually hurt the mouth. The driver of our host's car was down in the engine room, where it was warmer and where there was a soap opera trapped in the black-and-white TV. The boat crew watched it while heating up the feast for us. The driver and I became friends. He told me that he had seen a dead body floating down the river. Allan thought he was serious. There was nothing in Kalamudeen's face to tell us otherwise; there was mischievous honesty to him. Some of the dancing guests said there was indeed a possibility of a body.

"So what to do?"

"Call the police," someone said in alarm, "for the benefit of the Canadians. We can't have the Canadians thinking we don't care — look, it could have been a murder mishap. Yes, definitely a police investigation is in order. It's after all a body floating down the river."

Someone else juts in with, "Maybe it was water poisoning from the river — maybe the person just fell in and that's what happens."

My brother chuckles, "I didn't see no body."

The slightly tilting man, parting some of the decorations, says, "You people from Canada. I just don't get it. A friend of mine from Glasgow wanted to save a dog hit by a car. She was a red-blooded Marxist too."

As the woman with whom Allan was talking moved to refill her glass, we looked into the dark and turbulent waters. Two brothers looking into the river. He thought about sleeping with this travel agent. Post-colonials who live in Canada never get a chance to get together with women from "back home," as it were. And if we do, they are never post-modern enough, and no matter how many free tickets a glamorous travel agent gets to London or NYC, there is a modernity of incongruity which puts distance between such encounters and, of course, the possibility of a good lay. She is back with her glass of something looking like a curried version of a Bloody Mary. "Yes, I do get to London often." Their modernity is neo-feudal, far enough from the Indian male power structure but never independent of it. Our modernity is based on two or three hundred years of economic rape.

The boat burred noisily as we chugged under the Howrah Bridge, the busiest bridge in the world; a river of humans and metal — cars, bikes, cows, human flesh, all knotted together. But at night, the great loop of British-masterminded steel and concrete becomes hushed as winter fog engulfs the city, shifting over the water and enveloping the bridge. We are under it now. Our boat's engine echoes under the bridge. I see the whites of my brother's eyes as he looks up. "Holy smokes, will you look at that?"

Dr. Mukherjee comes over to where we are standing and sees the astonishment on our faces. "Just a few minutes and we are into another year of Rajiv Gandu's reign. *Gandu* means arsehole: Gandhi is his real name — ha ha."

Allan says, "I know what *gandu* means."

During my first trip back to this part of my past I saw a film in Delhi in which there was a circular pan shot of loads of people sleeping on this bridge. The film was about a single Christian woman school-teacher, so it was only right that we heard Christmas carols on the soundtrack. "Silent Night" was sung by what sounded like an Indian boy's chorus from the famous upper-class Indian private school in Dehra Dun. This particular scene was supposed to externalize the central character's feeling of loneliness; the bridge as a metaphor for the outstretched hand; her Christianity in a land of Hindus and Moslems. Touching and intercultural.

At night, people populate this large cement bedroom in blanketed huddles; as the city faces daylight the warp and woof of human life removes the sleeping jetsam from the bridge and the flow surges and scatters like bits from a shipwreck. Many lefty intellectuals say that things would have been a lot worse in West Bengal if the communist government had *not* come to power. It is hard to doubt Indian intellectuals. Even harder to dismiss what they are saying as foolishness. Foreigners like myself see the observations of "the Native" as well-developed cynicism — enlightened realism.

They laughed at Salman Rushdie's *The Satanic Verses*.

"All pre-orchestrated cheque-book fiction. The Moslems have

fallen for it. All the dates and milk in Paradise can't save the bugger now."

"Ha ha." More Christmas decorations fall onto the deck. Fading blaster batteries.

An eloquent woman interrupts: "And the government of Rajiv Gandu must do its bit to save them from the cruel barbs of *The Satanic Verses.*"

"Smart man, that Rushdie." And in a hushed whisper at my shoulder from a man who wants to let me know he is smart enough to use bad words: "Smart brown cocksucker that Rushdie. I hate the bastard."

Yet another voice emerging from the inky blackness: "He is popular in the West because he shits on us and our walues."

The teetering man: "What values? You see how we treat the bodies on this river, full of piss it is. He died of water poison — no doubt of it. You know I went to school at Cambridge. I find it hard to adjust my university-educated politics to India. Very difficult."

His red tie slips out of his pants belt like a masala- covered tongue. His glasses are thick as Coke bottles. My brother notices me looking at his specs. We laugh together. The drunk looks at me directly. I push my brother into his vector of conversation and try to escape along the outside gangway of the boat, but it's too late, the teetering man has engaged us.

"You in the West are on about the freedom of expression *gandu* bullcrap, but when push comes to shove you liberals always go back to your Judeo-Christian-Marxist roots and support this freedom of expression — horse balls."

"Yes," I admit.

But the passive approach does not stop him: "Look at all those poor Pakistanis that got killed because of his experiments in avant-garde writing. He's not a heretical thinker either, though he is magnificent on the question of royalties, you'd agree?" he asks, showing all his teeth.

"But it would be a real loss to the world of literature if he were killed," I offer, sipping my drink.

"Yes, real loss." He smiles to his nodding wife.

His monologue is like the endless plume of smoke from the boat's chimney: "This issue of freedom of expression is one that cannot be separated from the cultural practices that come into existence because of the political systems that depend on imperial expansion: the continuation of this system, your system in Canada and this Bengali piss in this pissing river which passes itself as water, depends totally on the relative denial of rights of other world citizens while a wide variety of rights, and riches, get naturally acquired, as it were. Canadian rights, like 'freedom of expression,' are not naturally acquired but are politically produced and enter the ethical mainstream — your ethical mainstream, I might add — through the checks and balances that are required for the stable problem-free exponential growth of your fascist 'democracies' in the West.

"One reason why the acquired rights of one culture dominate the ethical, cultural, and political scene over the acquired rights of another is because imperial Europe and North America, the super-dominating powers in the world today, have the means to project the problem into the world for their own economic good through the high modern media.

"So rights in the occidental expression of the term appear to be the ethical by-product of imperialism. They are acquired rights which become naturalized in Western culture, and are inextricably glued to imperial expansion which continually overturns the rights of others to produce new rights, ethics, and freedoms. Farmers in India who had the right to grow a wide variety of food in the seventeen-hundreds were forced to grow just cotton — cotton which was used to fuel the Industrial Revolution. 'Freedom of expression' is one of the rights that follows from the industrial epoch.

"Canadians, friends, here is a question for you: is it possible to say that nineteenth-century women became feminists because industrialization inadvertently organized urban labour? Perhaps this is one example of where rights were produced in the West by direct exploitation at the 'periphery' — India — the overturning of the 'rights' of Indian women in India at the time."

"Yes, I see your point," I say.

He rolls on: "Unconsciously, what the damn Rushdie affair did was to jab at one site where rights and subsequent authority are produced and reproduced. And I thank him for this."

His wife says, "Thanks, Mr. Rushdie." They both laugh. "Oh, thanks, Mr. Rushdie, thanks ever so much for the rights."

"Tax-paying Moslem population in the UK should have the same protections as other religions."

His wife chimes in with: "Like the Jews."

The teetering man rolls on and on: "The only expression the whole affair got was the superiority of one culture's level of tolerance over another — which by the way is hard to argue against — except if one accepts, without doubt, that rights fall from the sky and are not manufactured at staggering rates of exploitation or water pollution. Ha ha."

I pretend to look around for another drink. "Yes, I can see the hypocrisy. Had we not engaged in imperial expansion then we might not have been able to produce these rights which look natural, humane, god-given, feminist."

"Fast thinking on your part," he says. His wife takes him to the makeshift bar for replenishments. We feel humbled.

I remember crossing the bridge during the day; people carrying pots telescoped into one another like long heavy oil drums. About fifty different kinds of bleating car horns; horses, donkeys, men, women, a history of transportation since the beginning of time within a noise system that sounds like an avant-garde orchestra in New York.

Silently, the boat turns its nose towards where we came from. We pass under the concrete bedroom again. Rushdie is swallowed by the waters along with all the grammatically perfect Indian English. A few months after our boat trip, Khomeini orders Rushdie's death for having twisted the Holy Koran. The *Fatwa*. Just another temporal issue for secular West Bengal. The water in the river passes, the issues pass.

Calcutta in this darkness looks like any other city, the architectural differences taken prisoner by the night. Only small lights give us a hint of the shape of the buildings. The vague sea-rivery smell is also not enough to separate this place from another city. It could be Karachi. It could be Montréal.

There was more dancing on board; fat, middle-class bumpy people bumping together; not involved with any oppositional movements, and definitely not guilt-ridden because of it. Surprisingly, the music was totally current. From the Pet Shop Boys to Tracy Chapman. A visiting Englishwoman told me how bad the telephones were in Calcutta. I replied with, "Every time I tried to call my trade union friend from the British Museum at his office on Great Suffolk Road I got ten different kinds of oil companies, in Bahrain no less." So piss off, you English, I thought as the gin began to make me feel like Lawrence of Camden or Islington or Hampstead Heath. Swirling desert sand. The Gulf of Aqaba in sight.

I am not from here and so what if the dog had a crushed rib cage? Oughtn't we to save it? My brother took a photograph of a flattened dog on the road to Fullipur.

The boat wriggled and tilted starboard. A scattering bunch of smoke furiously bubbled out of the water. The plastic glass fell from my hand into a memory of Montréal. So fuck you, English. She moved away, not fielding any further questions.

At about one-thirty in the morning we pulled dock-side. Safe and sound. No tragic happenings for the *Calcutta Telegraph*, the *Times of India*, or *The Hindu*. The remaining food was distributed to the boat workers, and Kalamudeen took some for his family. The quicksand was shining but from a different angle. The moon had scarred the sky. The gouges in its back were somehow more painful looking. The sunken boat's still eye was almost blanked out by the darkness. I threw two Indian beer bottles into it to see what would happen. One bottle hit with a thud and sank. My doctor friend encouraged me to try walking on the muddy surface.

I watched the other bottle for a while to see if the whale would swallow it, but it did not. The servants carried all the cleaned pots and pans and plates, loaded them into the trunks of various waiting cars with their respective drivers. The travel agent did not give my brother a goodbye look. Her reputation. The national papers. *Quickie in the Quicksand: Calcutta travel agent seen with Christian Pakistani Canadian returnee in harbour quicksand. Several photos, see SANDY and MUDDY, page 3.*

We drove through the yellow morning fog past the effulgent Victoria Memorial, still brightly lit by the taxpayers, past BBD Bagh; the tires grumble over the tram tracks. The deserted shopping district, the central square of the city. People slumbering in the streets. Over more bumpy tram tracks. Thud thud. Past the place where I had my rubber stamp made: name and address, thirteen rupees. We turned onto a street which had a hundred-foot-long graffito along a wall: CALCUTTA CITY OF WORLD PEACE. Past Ballygunge Place and into flower-filled upper middle class Bright Street where the night porters were waiting for the party.

CHAPTER SEVEN

Lipstick on Your Collar

Toronto, 1968

She was making curtains, spent the whole day measuring, cutting, and stitching the ugly patterns. Already some of the smaller windows had orange figure eights, pink cows, black dogs, orange Harley Davidsons drifting in the Italo-Torontonian July wind. The very off-the-boat colours could do nothing but brighten the otherwise gloomy place. Taste had nothing to do with it; anything would have worked; the place was that sallow. It was their first house in Toronto, in one of the many Italian areas. Italians had built Toronto. There were lots of greaseballs on the street corners. *Chapattis* and pasta. They had arrived from England. After a short stay on Keele Street, they had moved to their home on Grand Trunk Road. She worked painstakingly, finger-picking the needle through the cloth which was half of something and half of another.

When the father came home he broke a broomstick across her back and face. Her face started to bleed and this shocked him. However he did not stop; the beating continued. Silent neighbours. It all became a poetic memory for the sons: a new house – a new country – a bleeding mother dizzily turning round the kitchen getting a slap, a kick; her hair leaving her skull in slow-motion pulls. He loves me He loves me not He loves me He loves me not. Airborne chairs. Connie Francis singing. At Anglo-Indian parties in Karachi they used to fox-trot or tango to "Lipstick on Your Collar." Infesting locusts and the rainy season doing their own sort of dance. All the steps came from those do-it-yourself dance books and of course from the inescapable influence of Elvis movies like *King Creole*. Beat-your-wife books. Schematic trajectory diagrams dash-dash-dashing out the route that, say, a chair may take to the wife's forehead or cheek. Klonk. Thud. Seat cushions spilling out of the flying chair. A quick glance at the instruction book.

His day at work had not been so good. He worked at a local clinic. A new Canadian professional. She refused to press charges — they all do, I am told. She said she had wandered around a park all night for fear that he would hit her again. She had returned in the afternoon. He slapped her several times in England also. He hit her in three different countries. They both used to slowly walk on the paths in Lawrence or in Shalamar gardens in the cool dark green evenings in Lahore, hand in hand; commitment, smiles. They had met some time in the late nineteen-forties and worked out the outer dimensions for a romance, which broke up, and she left with another man who lived in Quetta, the capital of Baluchistan. In the blustery Partition riots of August 1947 they had fallen in love.

They met at a Bible meeting — she was very knowledgeable in the New Testament. Their eyes had connected somewhere between Noah's Ark and the part when someone turns into a slab of salt marble or where lambs drink from the stilled Red Sea. They did not read the Song of Solomon. Church meetings were different then. Television had not been introduced into the public mind. A bishop of Pakistan, who was their family friend, had no idea what television would produce later on in the New World or even in Pakistan where, during the Zia period, it was to surpass the turgid sexual power of any preacher in the American Bible Belt of the nineteen-eighties.

There are many photographs of her in various stages of pregnancy, and judging by the way she dressed, she looks like someone who had adjusted intelligently between two cultures. Here she is in a dark-green sari on a chair with a sloping back. Prize of Lahore. Here she is in a white dress with a V-neck. There she is in a badly composed photograph, in a row-boat on the River Ravi, smiling and pretending to be scared of alligators. His arm is around her. Here she is beside the first budding rose of their love on a clear thrilling inexorable winter morning, on the roof. Quite pregnant.

He had adopted Western dress traditions before her. She had a certain ability to mix traditional patterns of both dress codes. The curtain material was not exactly proof of that. Photographs of both of them are filled with post-Partition sunlight and there is little remorse in their faces. There are orbiting birds in cages, and a static parrot so committed to movement one would think he were sculpted from wax and painted. There are freshly born kids on towels in the garden. Pre-literate servants hanging in the background, fuzzy, as yet still out of focus; the revolutionary future of Pakistan. It is Sunday; both of them have resolved the incident. He likes the curtains. She loses, always. There is the smell of cucumber mixed with yogurt, sharp biting chillies taking the tongue. The memory of blood in her mouth and a husband who tells her he is sorry, ever so sorry. As his hand moves across the table for more chicken curry, she pulls away, pulls away into the riot-filled Lahore of 1947. Blooming flowers. Pregnancies not graced with slaps. In the years to come the apologies become just neo-colonial lies, until the sons grow and require the father to consider plastic surgery for his bottom lip.

CHAPTER EIGHT

Of Milk, Mice, and Men

Montréal, 1983

We are starting with the fundamental principle that we are
all citizens and equal citizens of one State....Now I think
that we should keep that in front of us as our ideal, and you
will find that in the due course of time Hindus would cease
to be Hindus and Muslims would cease to be Muslims, not
in the religious sense, because that is the personal faith of
each individual, but in the political sense, as citizens of the
State. You may belong to any religion, caste, or creed – that
has nothing to do with the business of the State.

—Mohammed Ali Jinnah, Founder of Pakistan, August 1947

As for the injustices which the Québécois have been, and
remain, victim to, they in no way compare with those borne
by the Palestinians, the Bengalis, the Rhodesian and South
African Blacks, the North American Indians, and countless
other Third World cultures. However colonized it may be,
Québec is still nouveau riche in the eyes of the
poverty-stricken colonials of Africa, Asia and Latin America.
It is the suburb of *Joual* in that vast, imperialist metropolis
called the 'West,' otherwise known as 'the Free World.'
    It is a suburb as rich as certain European countries,

such as Belgium, and it belongs to the White race to boot —
that race which is presumed destined to reign on earth
evermore.

—Pierre Vallières, *The Impossible Québec* (Montréal: Black
Rose, 1980)

From 1980 to 1984 I lived on rue Saint Dominique, near
Schwartz's Smoked Meat on boulevard Saint Laurent. Across from
Schwartz's is a local international hang-out, the Bar Saint Laurent
and the Cabane. On winter nights when the wind blew eastward
across the mountain, David and I would smell the various meats
being smoked or cured. Late at night we'd meet in our kitchen: we'd
make coffee or maybe have a midnight sandwich. After a quick chat
he would return to his essay on Jean-Paul Sartre and I would return
to my essay called "Denis Diderotian commentary on Jacques Louis
David: The beholder and Belisarius receiving alms in relation to
Greuze's 'La jeune fille qui pleure la mort de son oiseau.'" Or
something like that.

I'd go to the Hebrew delicatessen with a skinny québécoise
art-school friend, who wore black miniskirts so short that the hem
line was a few inches from her crotch. She had developed an
irremovable Parisian accent after a six-month stay in Paris. She was
appalled at this eating place, repeatedly saying, "*Quel carnage!*" She
would never eat anything here. Featherless dead smoked ducks,
smoked and spiced chickens, enormous sides of smoked meat hung
from the walls of the restaurant. At the back, thigh-sized slabs of
liver and steaks were being charcoal grilled. The all-male staff
consisted of happy-go-lucky-curt-for-the-sake-of-it rotund Greek wait-
ers.

I had moved from rue Durocher, the noisy McGill student ghetto, under cover of a starry January night, illegally breaking the lease. My new apartment was on the top floor of a small block of five apartments with a dangerously shaky balcony overlooking a Turkish steam bath. Our rent was initially $100, but as time went on the landlord pushed it to $135.

David, my house-mate, was a small-framed, blue-eyed, white liberal from Ottawa whose father taught journalism at a university in Montréal. The father had a BA from Oxford and the requisite accent. The British media activist, Tariq Ali, in his *Street Fighting Years, an autobiography of the sixties*, wrote: "The *Guardian* correspondent – " my house-mate's father " – was notorious for his hostility to the Congolese leader. His report on the Independence Day celebrations criticized Lumumba's indictment of colonial rule as 'offensive' and the newspaper had shamelessly headlined the dispatch as 'Congo Festivities Marred.'"

There is no doubt about it, I was instrumental in turning David from a Zionist sympathizer to someone who looked at the Palestinian question in a deeper way than *The Gazette* | – it labels all liberation struggles as terrorist movements. Back then, remarks critical of Israel made him cringe. He is now a fan of Noam Chomsky, whose endlessly repetitive exposés of the American press don't bore him. And it is all my fault.

For someone whose experience was altogether anchored in Canada, David has moved through a smug conservatism endemic to the Ottawa Valley to a highly race-sensitive Ontarian NDPism fashionable in the nineteen-nineties. We sometimes have long conversations on the phone about such issues as management-worker disputes across the country. He is a union activist for Bell Canada workers, loves Natives, and is doing a doctorate in labour history, "The Retraining of Steel Workers," at an Ontario university.

He has tried to find his father's nineteen-sixties *Guardian* article in the Robarts Library, to no avail. I would not have understood liberalism had it not been for our life together.

The walls of this small apartment were cracked, the white paint peeling off to reveal a darker grey followed by yet another layer of navy blue. I imagined how close this small apartment must have been in a dark navy-blue. The landlord refused to do any repairs or even get our dingy walls painted. In some of the cooler winters, regiments of mice would migrate inwards towards the warmer walls of all the houses in our neighbourhood. Neighbours would often talk about the invasion of rustling creatures.

There was an old woman who lived below us on the street level whose house stank of cat piss. Between David and me on the top floor, and the lonely old woman with a son who rarely visited her, were two high-cheek-boned undergraduate women; they studied foreign languages at McGill and had rich parents in Westmount. They always fucked Hispanic or "other language" guys. They wouldn't fuck me because I was a Paki, not entirely appropriate for those early eighties. Recent British films starring Pakistanis changed all that.

In this apartment Montréal winters were bitterly cold. Every fall of every year, I was terrorized by the thought of how cold it might get. I used to worry that I might get chilblains like we did in England. On the coldest nights, at forty below zero — maybe even a little colder with the wind-chill factor — I could almost feel the mouse population's collective body rustling next to mine for heat, with only a few inches of plaster and peeling paint separating us. Whiskers, expressionless full-stop beady eyes against rough post-World War II plaster. I had a small space heater but it didn't help. It was like a candle in a frozen-food warehouse.

One night I set traps to kill mice. At three in the morning I heard a click. Was I lighting a cigarette for a friend? I awoke to the squeaking of a mouse caught by its tail in the trap under the oven. I was scared to touch the mouse. I was troubled by the pain it could be in. So I brought out the vacuum cleaner, took off the sweep-head, zeroed in on the mouse and then, *woosh*. The screeching mouse zipped past my eardrum into the post-colonial world of dust and asphyxiation.

I found it hard to contain the hate I felt towards the landlord who made money from these cool walls. I fantasized about murdering him in the manner that the South Africans murder police informants, with long dull knives. Slashes to the kidneys, the neck. Knives with masking-tape handles, bricks to the side of the head, and, finally, a burning tire around his fucking neck; flesh and tires stinking to high heaven.

At night, through my dusty window, I could see continuous nebulous clouds of steam pouring out a vent at the side of his Turkish baths. The clients went in at all hours of the day and night, the steam waggling into the winter.

Back then, I used to borrow money from a friend who, in the late eighties, grew a trendy retro "phoney-tail." He lent me forty or so bucks in the last weeks of a few welfare months. Time was defined by this cheque; rather a different conception of its philosophical dimension than I had learned from Saussure's analysis of currency in defining differential linguistics at Trent University. My generation of graduates has difficulty getting jobs.

My poverty had made me angry, misguidedly so. One winter I composed a letter to the welfare office; of course, I did not have the courage to send it, let alone carry out any of the malicious and naive acts suggested in it. Some eight years later, back on welfare, I still harbour these feelings.

"It has come to our attention that you welfare agents may soon be forced to carry out policies and practices that could possibly have a negative effect on us. Collectively we realize that this is NOT your fault.

"BE WARNED: THERE IS GOING TO BE LEGAL AND ILLEGAL OPPOSITION TO THE POLICIES THAT YOU MAY HAVE THE CHOICE TO PRACTICE. WE SAY CHOICE BECAUSE YOU DO HAVE THE MORAL CHOICE TO REFUSE TO HASSLE US. IF YOUR SILENCE MAKES US GO WITHOUT FOOD AND SHELTER THEN WE WILL ACT AGAINST YOU.

"On the legal level we may put this undercutting of human life on the public agenda by trying to use the press. But we have no illusions about the press.

"If that does not work we will be forced to use methods that may cause harm to you personally and your children. We are already beginning to find out where some of them go to school.

"Our feeling is that if you treat us with respect, dignity and kindness, we in return will respect you as people who have to do a job. But we need a cheque as well. We understand that delegating public money to us is your source of income: eliminate us and you will eliminate yourself.

"YOU HASSLE US AND WE WILL GET YOU.

"We have no choice: take that little bit away, or reduce the amount we get, and YOU personally will start something that will be violent.

"WE ON WELFARE WILL NOT BE KICKED IN THE FACE WITHOUT RETALIATION. WE ARE NOT IDIOTS; PLEASE UNDERSTAND THIS."

During one application for social assistance I was asked to prove that I was a Canadian citizen. I showed the welfare people my Canadian passport and my citizenship card, which was dated 1973, as proof of my nationality. But the québécois welfare supervisor asked me to provide him with an IMM 1000 form (which takes two to three months to get) from Canadian immigration. I came to Canada in 1966. I was being asked to prove that I was a Canadian after twenty-seven years and after holding a Canadian passport for over two decades. *Québec tsé.*

My landlord was part of the first wave of post World War II European immigrants. He wore opulent fur coats and ate large amounts of smoked meat, and once or twice made pejorative remarks about my mother. He had a pink clean-shaven face. A thick gold chain on his wrist. His shoes were shiny.

The landlord had dark, smoke-coloured windows on his large American cars with spotless white-walled tires. He had a few other houses up on rue Laval and wore two walnut-sized gold rings on one hand. When the landlord was not in his office, his son would take rent cheques from us. He was cool towards me and would have nothing to do with my suggestions about a little home improvement. He shared the father's money-minded cruelty. I'd open his face one day.

In this apartment I began the style of life that effectively meant I was dependent on arts grants from the Canada Council. When those did not come through, I would read histories of the Third World and British and French imperialism, waiting for the welfare cheques guaranteed by liberal democracy. It was in this apartment that I left my Christian-Pakistan background and became interested not just in talking about international politics in a way that defined my public persona, made me attractive, a little jagged, "interesting," but also in organizing pro-Palestinian demonstrations. This kind of political organization made me feel warm inside, as when I saw *The Color Purple.*

It was in this apartment that I began to improve my Urdu, a language that had evaporated off my tongue since my days in England. I had become more or less fluent in French, but that did me little good. Life is impossible in Québec, which has its own history of struggle for self-determination. But in the early nineteen-nineties, I found myself saying more and more often that I did not want plural acceptance from Quebeckers. All I wanted was the multicultural cheque to make films and write scripts for the mass media. The tax base in Montréal is seventeen percent non-white; so what the cultural ministers do is take our money and give it away to white artists. Robbery pure and simple. Québec is the best case for a quota system that I have ever experienced.

After years and years of rejection by Québec I just wanted the money that was being snatched from me in the form of taxes – the taxes I pay on food, for example. At long last I was beginning to understand what Pierre Vallières meant when he titled one of his books *Un Québec impossible.*

David stayed with me for about two and a half years.

He used to come home for lunch from school, buy Portuguese potato bread and cut it off with his Opinel knife. Often we'd buy a roasted Portuguese chicken and pick at it together on those long cold nights. We became very close, but not trendy university homosexuals.

I have the nagging suspicion that our bonding was based on some kind of historical compensation for his father's newspaper imperialism: the Man Friday syndrome. Or was it my Othelloism? Our friendship grew deeper than that of brothers. We read and re-read Frantz Fanon's books together, poring over sections, dissecting them piece by piece like the barbecued chicken. Some years later, the liberal, by coincidence, met a Christian Pakistani Stalinist woman and left for the Northwest Territories with her. There he helped Natives run a progressive newspaper which in the late eighties was utterly destroyed by the conservative government's funding cuts.

I lived on my own for some years after David left. This routine was broken for a few months by a Pakistani student, Saleem, from Karachi. He was feudal in terms of housework; he could not wash pots, but he was a star student in cancer research at McGill, a womanizer, and excellent at finding liver infections in mice. Rumour in Pakistan had it that he had been arrested for subversive activities against the state. He told me that he had been puzzled, for some months, by a liver problem in a series of mice he was working on. Saleem could not figure out why the mice were dying.

On a wall in his bedroom just above his pillow he had tacked up ten technical photographs of mice cleanly cut down the abdomen with all the internal organs splayed out under a numbered grid. Screwing his friend one night, he began to stare at the photos. As his gaze wandered away from her committed eyes, her committed breasts, he discovered an inflamed liver in one of his patients. He got extremely excited; blood retracted from his erection. In mid-thrust his hands went up to his head. "Here it is, here it is — this is why all those fuckers have been dying." Finally, he could explain all those dead mice. A sort of thrombosis of the liver; a key solution to many problems that had been holding back his experiments. She got dressed, and left, never to return. He got gobs of research money from his department. And soon he left Montréal for Boston where he started a post-doctorate research program. My mother said I ought never to have bacon in the house because my Moslem flat-mate could be offended by it. He had little trouble eating BLTs.

Then another Pakistani student moved in. Zulfikar was quite a bit older with a well-developed sense of humour, and was devoted to an analysis of bourgeois nationalist discoursing as well as being a part of it. He was short and had an impeccably well-groomed moustache, ironed his jeans, wore repulsive aftershave and smoked his cigarettes Punjabi-style. He had a photograph of a group of Pakistani intellectuals surrounding a past head of state of Pakistan. Zulfikar appeared to be about two metres away from this brilliant politician in the picture. He only showed it to me once, because we disagreed on Bhutto.

It was in this apartment that I, along with Zulfikar, started to translate a few short stories by Sa'adat Hassan Manto, the Pakistani writer whose stories were set during Partition. I would sit at the typewriter while Zul would read one of Manto's stories of rain and innocent girls playing in it. I would tap out my version on the typewriter, which, after a quick discussion, would be corrected. Zulfikar's idiomatic English was very good and he was always too shy to translate dirty words. The giggling girls of Manto's stories wore *kamezes* which became transparent in the endless rainy season. The male protagonist would end up meeting one of the girls and would drive her to work; he would discover much to his shock that she worked in the oldest profession. The semiotic feminists I knew at the time would emotionally label this the "male-observer-narrator discourse."

Zulfikar stayed with me during one of those cruel bone-cracking winters. He politely wondered about the sound in the walls. He had a roundish Ismaili girlfriend with a beautiful hooked nose and a shock of long black hair. She would waltz into the apartment: "I am dedicated to the concept of God, but you see, I can easily slip into the most comical tirades against fundamentalists of any religion. You just name it, any fucking religion." She would jiggle her head in a West-Bengali-Dakkaesque way and burst out laughing.

Zulfikar would add, "Don't let this Moslem shock you. She is very much a true believer."

She told us a story about when the Prophet (Peace Be Upon Him) was besieged and very short of food, and he asked his colleagues if the *ulama* could *halal* crows — bless them so they could be eaten.

At the tail end of that winter, Zulfikar finished his doctorate on how and why Henry Kissinger had compromised the independent development of Pakistan. Zulfikar was a bourgeois Marxist.

He had some anthropological interests as well. He told me about a tribe of Black African-Pakistanis on the Makaran coast near Sind. Some people might never have admitted that they were Black Pakistanis. "Little work has been done on them," he used to say, turning away from his IBM typewriter to defrost his butt against the gas heater in that cool March.

The kitchen served both as a kitchen and as a United Nations conference hall, with representatives from Haiti, Afghanistan, Chile, Bolivia, and Québec. My Iranian friends, who would put mint in melted butter on rice, introduced me to the revolutionary Islamic work of Dr. Ali Shari'ati. Zulfikar, with his bifocals dropping over his nose, would say, "You see this area," pointing to the large map of Pakistan, "some centuries ago, this was Arab Sind." And he would proceed to punctuate his tracing hand with one of his theoretical questions: "Why does Pakistan have to go through every possible stage towards a social state? Why can't it just go from a nice dictatorial client of the Americans to an Islamic Cuba?"

One day in one of his fits of noisy Punjabi theatricality he took a wide-nibbed marker, drew dotted lines all over my large full-colour map, and wrote "Disputed" in large letters.

Zulfikar and I would sip cardamom *cha* with cinnamon during breaks from our studies. He showed me how to curry lamb and how to use coriander. "You just put it on top at the very last moment, before you put on the *garam masala*, and let it just settle for a few minutes with the heat off."

His Punjabi manner of cooking was different from the way his girlfriend from Dakka did things. For me her meat curries were strangely made. She would do everything in more or less the same way as Zulfikar did: brown the onions, add the ginger, garlic, the five or so spices, and then a slight browning of the meat at the end of things. But just when we thought the curry was cooked and ready to eat, she would add the pre-soaked *basmati* rice to the reddish-orange meat dish. She was not making a curry but a *pallu* which was slow simmered in *alu bukhra* — dried plums which were added in the beginning just before the onions became transparent. It tasted great but the process was really foreign to us.

In the winter of 1983, under the guidance of Zulfikar, I read about Sind, what used to be called "Arab Sind." "A lot of archae-ologists like the area. Some, I am told, like it even more than Mohen-jo Daro," he pontificated, moving his arse in direct contact with the new gas heater. Karachi, once the capital, is the main city in this province. The article was about Sindhi resistance to the British; Feroz Ahmed described how the people in this province became a people dispossessed in the same way as the Palestinians in Palestine and of course the Natives here.

That winter I felt an affinity with the Sindhis in Pakistan. I am from the Punjab, from where eighty percent of the military is recruited. The army is used to put down opposition in Sind.

When we lived in Karachi, when I was eight or so, my parents were planning to send me to military college, but we emigrated to England, and my father became a professional after having worked on roads using a pneumatic drill. If we had not moved to England, I could have been a foot soldier of some influence in this army. There was some talk that I would have become one of the few

Christian generals in the Pakistani army. Sometimes I regret that we ever left. We went from slightly upper-middle-class people in Pakistan to poor immigrants in the UK, until we returned to our class origins in Canada. My father's colleagues in the places where he worked would ask with well-practised ambiguity: "How was the research trip to Edinburgh? Err...Mister, do you like England? When are you planning to go back?" Of course the "back" was nothing to do with Scotland.

Punjabi generals have snatched land in Sind; their disco-dance parties last deep into the night. The Sindhi language is suppressed; it was illegal to publish journals in Sindhi without the approval of the Islamic government of General Zia. Some of the streets in Karachi are named after Urdu poets, not Sindhi ones. Linguistic identity and determination, political symbolism, and street names are taken seriously in Pakistan. But of course when street names are changed it doesn't really mean anything at all. The same people stay in power even if a hundred Marxist playwrights write a hundred plays about how one hundred percent corrupt nationalist leaders are. Shortly after the death of the premier of Québec, Dorchester was renamed boulevard René Lévesque. All that is on the horizon in nineties Québec is a separate nation-state, a "liberated" Québec. Impressive.

Not long ago in Sind, graffiti were continually appearing on walls in the morning: SINDHU-DESH. The "Desh" at the end of Sind echoed the process of Bangladesh, which grew away from the East/West Pakistan equation in 1971 in a more or less revolutionary way. The Karachi Dawn ran stories about dogs and donkeys with "ZIA" painted on their backs. Even intelligent nationalist movements such as the ones in Sind show little concern for animal rights; the Punjabi army moved with unction against these dogs and donkeys.

There were problems with Zulfikar's Sindhi nationalist friends who dropped by. They would show us tracts they had written: *A Declaration for Peace and Amity in Sindh*, Committee for Amity and Peace in Sindh (CAPS).

"Aliens residing in Sindh illegally should be apprehended and deported," one of the tracts read. "They are not only a strain on the scarce provincial resources but are also a serious threat to the security of the country."

One particular Sindhi even advocated the expulsion of a small Burmese community in Karachi because "They come to Pakistan to take our jobs and the sister-fucking Iranians and Bangladeshi so-called political refugees should be sent back also."

I asked one of them, "How goes your application for refugee status?"

"Oh yes, very fine, thank you. Canada is nice country."

A few Gulf Arabs staying at fancy Karachi hotels were shocked by the way the army was killing graffitied dogs and donkeys which were carted away by the truckload. But who were they to be shocked by this violation of animal rights? Some Gulf States have hired Palestinian historians to excavate their history because their educational institutions are unable to produce historians. This is the view of a British travel writer, Jonathan Rabin, whose *Arabia Through the Looking Glass* offers some proof.

Here in Québec, the same sort of graffiti were appearing: "Loi 101 ou 401." Bill 101 is the law that made French the official language of our province. It is illegal to have store signs in any language other than French. The 401 is the highway that many miffed Anglophones used in order to leave this province in the late seventies.

My Québec provincialist friends would compare the struggle in Palestine with their own "fight for liberation." They would say, "If you agree with the struggle for Palestine, then why can't you see that it is the same thing here?"

Invariably I would rebut with, "I think the PLO has an international awareness which this place and its fight for cultural identity does not foster. Here we see a nationalist attempt on the part of a moneyed Francophone class, not exactly a liberation struggle.

"A liberation struggle is something different," I would angrily say.

The Palestinians I had met in Montréal were aware of liberation struggles in many parts of the world. Some of my Palestinian friends had even come to terms with their anti-Black feelings. The Québec provincialists were hermetically sealed within the PQ's array of pre-orchestrated disputes on language and shop signs. I find it very difficult to identify with nationalism of the shop-sign kind. Dime-store nationalism not worth a fucking shit.

My disagreements with the revolutionary class always produce bitter hostility. "If you don't like it here, then leave," was always what they said.

The PLO was internationalist in its outlook: Czechoslovakian handguns, Bengali freedom fighters, Russian AK-47s, rocket-propelled grenades from Moscow, Bulgarian jam, Danish bandages and medicines, and condom-wearing Canadian surgeons. Comparatively speaking, the PQ's vision is provincial.

Roland Ducharme, whom I met at a café called *Le Funambule*, had become my friend. Our friendship came to its apogee during and after the 1980 referendum on sovereignty association: "*Toi, tu t'identifies pas avec notre culture, parce qu'on a une histoire qui a commencé en 1600 ou quelque chose comme ça — et puis —* so what — it is not good enough *pour toi? Alors, qu'est-ce que tu veux? Une maudite pyramide sur le Saint-Laurent?* Can you please tell me what you yourself know about your ancient history, *s'il te plaît?*"

I had not yet begun the process of historical excavation. I was silent. I didn't know where to begin with Roland. I could only mouth the typical things I had heard Third World radicals flippantly saying when trashing Québec: "Well, there is Mohen-jo Daro – three thousand years of civilization or maybe even more, who knows, thirty-five-hundred years old. Just a little bit better and older than the Plains of Abraham. And who gives a shit about the few arsehole playwrights who have elevated your popular language to a court language? A so-so novelist who has lecture halls dedicated to him in universities which look like churches? And there is more debate in the Indian press than there is here."

"*Tu dis Hubert Aquin? Mais oui* – he is better than your Rushdie. *Mais notre lutte pour l'indépendance, notre lutte, cher Julian, n'a jamais exclu les immigrants comme toi – pourquoi tu te sens en dehors de nos projets?*"

"Roland, yes it fucking well excludes me. I just want the fucking money. Fuck pluralism. *A ce moment je voudrais que la société provincialiste me donne du fric pour tourner des films, point final. Et elle ne me donne que de la merde c'est tout. Une porte fermée. Fermée toujours et pour l'éternité. Et, en plus tu sais, mon cher Roland, que c'est la vérité. Il faut pas 'découilloner' la réalité.*"

Roland buckles up, ready to defend himself: "*Pas de problème. Je suis d'accord avec toi sur cette question de fermeture, Julian. On l'a dans le à cause des médias et tout ça...mais, il faut que tu comprennes...tsé, Julian, mais qu'est-ce que tu connais de cette époque de l'histoire de Mohen-jo Daro? Toi, tsé, tu as passé toute ta vie dans l'Occident mais qu'est-ce que tu sais du Pakistan – sauf les jokes cute sur les politiciens. Fuck ça. Ne fais pas de prétentions de grand intello* – because you're not one, anyway. What can you fuckin' tell me about *tout ça – relire Marx* – for Christ's sake?"

My snobbery is being dashed to bits. True, I correctly pronounce a few names like Taimur, Babar, Humayun, Akbar, Jahangir, and Shah Jahan, Taj Mahal, *Times of India, The Calcutta Telegraph, The Karachi Dawn.*

"I am not a historian of British India nor of Pakistan — why expect so much of me — does every immigrant have to be an expert historian — *réponds à ça? Alors, si tu dis oui, tu es malade.*"

"*Parce que tu es un snob total. Tu viens ici pour chier sur ma culture et me fourrer et aussi*...and you know fuck all about your own political circumstances and history. *C'est ce que je voulais dire.* Even if you come from an older culture than mine you should not shit on mine *tsé* — after all, we were damaged by the same force *les colons anglais* — *eille, tsé* — don't forget that."

Roland stopped coming to visit as often as he used to.

He was like having a Michel Tremblay play in our kitchen.

I saw him ten years later. He had his long hair cut and was working for the Canadian International Development Agency in Ottawa.

The Québec nationalists are Machiavellian in the way they distract and manipulate people by the many fogs of defending the precious québécois language while, when they first surged to power in the late seventies, butchering the labour movement and social programs. Amnesty International even published a report exposing the cruel treatment of prisoners at Archambault Prison. In the late twentieth century, immigrant-threatened québécois nation planners were thinking up ways to move new immigrants into small villages in the countryside surrounding Montréal where they would not upset the "real" people of this city.

When I lived in Ontario in the late seventies, I was impressed with the Québécois' sense of national self-determination. However, when I actually came to Montréal to do my Masters in fine arts, I discovered that this nationalism's sense of *fermature* towards immigrants and non-whites was absolute, and only a violent race riot would make them open-minded.

No one who was not a white Francophone, or was not open to

becoming a Francophone, was allowed expression. One could not be critical of Québec intellectuals without losing them as friends. Not a squeak of daylight. Even Toronto — a suburb of London, as a Greek writer friend of mine likes to call this model Canadian city — is more open. In Toronto, race and multiculturalism are flamboyantly displayed like decorations on the Christmas tree of democracy. Many post-colonial-post-modernist Chinese homosexuals and reggae stereotypes fall for the multi-game — hook, line, and sinker — except my Greek friend who came to visit me on 17 November of a certain year in Montréal. It had barely begun to snow.

Ares Velhoukiotis came to watch the *Bill Cosby Show*.

I flip on the TV and his commentary flows: "These fuckin' white cacksuckers are always so happy go fuckin' lucky in this oreo show, eh Jules, you rust-painted half-nigger? These A-holes make me sick."

"Hey, Ares," I ask, "do you think the Canadian TV producers can do any better? And as far as I know, Bill Cosby does not degrade Afro-Americans."

"Afro-Americans?" Ares repeats. "Very correct, Jules. But that's only correct if you are livin' in Jimmy Carter's America. The term is African-American-or-he-she-person-Canadian-African — get it fuckin' straight."

I can tell by the look in my Greek friend's eyes that he is not going to really respond to my statement. Ares reaches forward and turns down the volume, puffs methodically on his cigarette like one of the characters in his recently published book. A thin funnel of smoke issues from this character's mouth as he drives a longish emerald Greek car made in Detroit. Ares is about to say something big: "When these middle-class Canadian fucks at CBC do somethin'...like with *Urban Angel*...I mean, all first-generation Canadian-born greaseballs don't necessarily 'tawk like dis all da time,' especially if they're allegedly detectives, editors of scholastic Hellenic journals, pizza-wops, cops, or high-class gynaecologists."

I understood this nationalism as a process similar to the one which consumed British India during "The Jewel and the Crown" era, when a sense of nationalism, of national identity, consisted of a struggle against a British India dominated by the Hindu ruling class.

This process of Moslem and Hindu identity also produced a sense of total exclusion of the many minorities that live in Pakistan. The Hindus, the Christians, the Ahmadis, Parsis, the Buddhists, the Sikhs, and others have a problematic relationship to the dominant group, to say the least. And, of course, nationalism, as it evolved in the pre-Pakistani British India context, was used as a sneaky ploy, on the part of the ruling Moslem and Hindu *salariat*, not to share power with each other; rightly, the Moslem minority was worried about being overcome by Hindus. Québécois nationalists are roughly the same labour-union- and Native-bashing group of arseholes that exploited the divisions among the peoples of British India. Of course one could write tons of books on narrow-minded nationalisms, but they do not deserve the exposure.

Québec's move towards "independence" is locked into the language and the non-actions of nationalism; not *liberation* in any imaginative sense.

By now even those seventies romantics have come to terms with the fact that Québec's is not an international liberation that wants to foster lively debate, practices, and pluralism.

In the eighties the pious provincialists otherwise known as nationalists would say, "After independence we will have our chance to talk, but now we have to settle the constitutional question and we must establish ourselves as a country, as a state independent of Canada. Then, and only then, *cher ami*, you will have your ANC and PLO offices on Sherbrooke, and, anyway, we will call it avenue Charles de Gaulle."

At once I asked, "Can we please have the ANC and the PLO offices on either side of the Israeli Embassy?"

Back then on cold nights, in front of the new gas heater, I would muse over the human phenomenon of nationalism with my Muslim Pakistani comrades. They taught me the pejorative for Christian in Urdu: *Krranta* – those who like to use electrical appliances. How would it be possible to create a movement for national independence that would not suppress the minorities? Why are non-Anglo-Saxon minorities here seen as a group antagonistic to nationalism or, rather, antagonistic to liberation? Why can't a critique of nationalism be offered within a phase of nationalism? Was it all biological? Why can't a critique of it all be offered on the public airwaves? Was nationalism a product of an irrelevant political structure imported from nineteenth-century Europe? Why was it not relevant to immigrants in Québec?

These questions preoccupied us until we were all talked out, till all that was left was the hissing of the gas heater. In this late-night silence we would walk over to the door overlooking the fragile balcony to pay homage to the permanent plume of steam across the street which marked off the nights until spring.

I told Zulfikar that it reminded me of the smoke stack on the ship. On many evenings he would listen to my simplistic stories of racism in Toronto and England, express shock and bid me good night, slipper off to his small bedroom, fall asleep, and dream about returning to sunny Lahore, star-filled Lahore; returning to his comfortable tenured job at the University of Punjab. But one evening, out of the blue, Zulfikar told me about a television program he had seen on a London TV channel in which a group of white working-class lads smashed up a few Bengalis because the Bengalis scabbed at a factory undergoing one of those vicious English strikes. "That's awful — did the program take sides with the racist bastards?" I asked.

Zulfikar looked at me, drew on his cigarette, then looked back at me, saying, "This was nothing to do with racism. This was class politics — racism is just a bourgeois Christmas-tree decoration."

I was an outsider, the vacuum-killer of mice.

Zulfikar often recited bits of Faiz's poems. In particular he loved to hear me repeat, after him, the following lines of a poem on Partition:

Ye daagh daagh ujala, ye shab gazeeda sahar
Woh intezaar tha jiska, ye woh sahar nahin hai

This stained dawn is not the one we waited for.

"*Arrah yaar*, your accent is just like those missionaries who came and went." Then he would ask me to repeat it all until I got it right. And I did. I did.

After having turned off all the lights I would have one last look at the cross on the mountain. I would return to my cold bedroom, occasionally slip in a cassette for a few late-night tunes to ease me into sleep. This particular night I listened to "Silver Dagger" by Joan Baez, followed by "I'm a British Subject Not Proud of It" by UB40. Occasionally, I listened to *gazals* sung by Begum Akhtar, whose elegant voice I had learned to love in my thirties. I had never heard her in my youth.

"Taste for this kind of music never fades — even with generations that have not really heard this music. You see, it is like a seed planted in you. That trip back to Pakistan was the water, but how

can you understand what the songs are about?" Zulfikar brooded
with condescending wisdom. The tap in the bathroom trickled into
a sleepless February night.

Richard Stevens came for tea on 15 August 1983. National Independence Day celebrations in Pakistan. He was working for a horrid
little gutter-snipe of a paper called the *Sunday* something-or-other. His
contribution to radical popular journalism was to delete the word
terrorist in stories that came off the wire. He wanted to deflate the
consensus-generating capacity of that particular word with new-world
word objects like *freedom fighters*.

He resented cultural-studies types who were able to make a living
out of useless academic exercises. He was once the editor of the
McGill Daily, and proudly remembered it.

I was broke. Richard bought the milk for the tea.

He deeply understood the world system of international corrup-
tion and knew how to organize resistance at every turn. He now
works for a union on Great Suffolk Road back in London, "a world
centre of the trade union movement." He claims that workers in the
newly liberated Eastern European states are lining up to join the
union he works for.

I remember once walking into his apartment — at the corner of
Saint Laurent and Fairmount. The door was open. I heard him
speaking dead-fluent Russian. As I closed the door, he hung up right
away. He knew I'd heard. I said nothing about it. "How's it going,
Jules?" was all he asked.

He found feminist theorists (both women and men) stupid and
apolitical because: "They are unable, in fact cannot, because they're
so stupid — they can't — don't integrate or problematize the historical formation of the nation-state."

He hated the pink in maps, but never disfigured my maps. He

was cagey, tactful, an instant expert in almost everything to do with Sufi mystics, off-shore radio stations, negative income tax in Scandinavian countries, why Arab liberation movements don't like Czech handguns. But he was a lover of Québec nationalism.

Lots of my friends left Montréal. Some friends and I – Colin and an ex-hippy – took Richard to Burlington, Vermont, one gusty summer day, where he caught a flight to New York, then another across the pond to London. During the last ten years, all my friends went back to where they came from: Lahore, Paris, Cairo, Karachi, Washington, Delhi, Cape Town, and, of course, Toronto. Montréal in 1990 is what Lahore must have been like for my parents in that epoch when George Cukor's *Bhowani Junction* was shot in that city. No room for the niggers in Québec.

Richard thought nothing of paying for the milk; it was an act of international solidarity. He walked down the brownish steps through the dank green hall. From the balcony, I saw him cross the street to the Greek pastry shop. He was walking his funny walk back to my door. I heard the main door close behind him, *thud*, heard his knock. He poured in the milk, followed by the tea, very English. From the small kitchen window which overlooked the mountain with its lightbulb crucifix, we discussed Afghanistan via Delhi, Moscow, and Washington, DC. Agreements were hard to come by in those days.

He was born in London and continually reminded me that he was of working-class origin, despite the fact that his father had become a professor at a major university. His father, unlike the liberal David's father, was an expert on the decolonization process in Anglophone Africa. I'm sure Richard was working class, but only for a few minutes after he was born. His father wrote the definitive book on Cecil Rhodes, the nationalist. His father is sympathetic to Québec nationalists.

In 1987, I went to see Richard in Hackney, where he drank milk non-stop. Sometimes after work he opened the fridge door and poured a carton down his throat without even putting it in a glass or offering any to his international guests. British milk is so much better than Canadian milk. Even Chernobyl did not scare him off the white stuff. In Hackney, it ran down his cheeks. Once when we were on our way to see the Algerian singer Cheb Khalid, he downed a pint of milk at the Elephant and Castle underground station. I broke out in sentimental laughter at this trade-union activist drinking milk in a station called Elephant and Castle. At least once a day he flew down the steps to Safeway to get more. His fridge was always stocked.

When I lived in England in the sixties, I was so ashamed to be brown-skinned that I drank milk during recess with the hope that I would turn white and my smelly garlic breath would go away. I am still brown. The prime minister, a Labour racist, or someone like that, let the school kids have milk. Thatcher took it away but I drank lots back then.

CHAPTER NINE

Progressive Sexual Intercourse

Algeria, 1987

Descending to the level of the visible world, the relation between Adam and Eve is seen by Ibn 'Arabi as one that is governed by a mutual and perpetual attraction to unite, culminating in the physical act, and the continuation of Divine manifestations. The ontological Adam (male and female) is conceived in the image of the Absolute in its Singleness, but when the Absolute desired to see Itself in concrete form, the female element, Eve, was extracted from Adam to make Divine manifestation possible. The love of the male toward the female then, is due to his love for himself, as she is his inward part, whereas her love for him is due to her love for her place of origin. Similarly the Absolute's love for Adam (male and female) is Its love for itself, and Adam's love for the Absolute is a yearning to go back to one's essence.

— Huda Lutfi, "The Feminine Element in Ibn 'Arabi's Mystical Philosophy," *Apif, Journal of Comparative Poetics*, no. 5, Spring 1985 (The American University in Cairo)

The day was sunny, and we had just been told that a Canadian had designed the conference centre in Alger. This was easy for me to see, because I am sort of a Canadian, and Complexe Desjardins, the tackiest piece of architecture in the Western world, is a few blocks from my Montréal apartment. Its mistakes in human scale calculation have the same grey blunderous tone and echo to them here in Algiers.

The building was hard to read. A waste of time. Montréal in the early nineties was turning into a vast parking lot with more than just a few inane buildings.

The points of attraction were the usual: one culture being played out against another. There was little time to go through all the arguments: at what stage in a developing country was it necessary to increase the absorption of Walkmans; at what stage was it okay to introduce computers in primary school and car assembly plants. At what stage in a developing country's move towards emulation of the West was it right to introduce safe sex via television; and without doubt, what would be the role of unions in a new African state? Not everything was possible. All these ideas faded as the real issue became obvious.

Foreplay in Algiers was a little different. Their pubic hairs snagged right away. She was part of the larger culture. The male was part of an immigrant configuration, steeped in politics, dipped in all the interesting aspects of the haze and fuzziness of theoretical post-colonial violence with a painterly – even a Frankfurt School – sense of social change. She had offered to take him for a tour of the city in a cab. She had dominant-culture scent, but he liked that. Minority scent really bored him. He licked her tits for 6.5 minutes, at least as long as it took for the Algerian television news to expire into the next memory of a living revolution. Her legs were higher in the air now. Their breathing changed, he saw something new in her. Not the woman he had met in the building the Canadian arsehole had designed. Another historical, architectonic power had taken over. However, her ideas remained – powerful, contentious, radical, much beyond his thinking; tinkering echoes of the heady days of the FLN.

Her movements, initially coming from what he thought were the under-theorized sections of women's studies, were short, and at first he thought them to be reluctant, but given the orchestration they couldn't have been more perfect. As the session progressed he expected she felt as though she were in the company of a man who had tried hard to understand the oppression of women both in the West and here in a country where nasty orientalist French anthropologists wrote in newly learned Arabic. Algebra, Algeria, Mars bars, pirates off the Barbary Coast, more wars of liberation, boycotts of Olympic Games.

The Western women he had fucked changed from someone just having coffee in front of him to one who was integrating an oppositional sense of it all with stiff nipples ready to be male-sucked. His dick was mean stiff and he was not willing to make apologies for what his forefathers had done. If push came to shove he compromised his ideas to fit the necessary ironies, but only to demonstrate and convince women into the sack. That was politically suspect. He did not give a shit.

Patriarchy was perhaps their problem. He really tried hard to apology-screw her, but couldn't. He thought about balcony-bonking her but the very important buildings, some symbolically important, were altogether too, too visible, or not visible enough, depending on the positions and references one needed to make. Resolved political discussions at the hotel, Cuban ships in the harbour, other ships from the Eastern bloc countries leaving vaporous trails as they slid away to the civilizing shores of Europe and beyond. After the long tit job, he hoped she was feeling that she could integrate a really good post-colonial stick-suck job. But she did not go down on him. He wanted his cock sucked badly. Perhaps her sense of historical compensation, he ruefully thought. He sensed the imbalance, accepted it. In fact, it became a sort of silly male victory for him. She felt his immigrant post-Partition brown stick move slowly in and out of the first millimetres of her vagina. Then he stopped fucking her, just like that, looked into her eyes and sucked her pussy again. Her vaginal lips became like the slight waves in the Algerian harbour and every time he returned them to their original position he thought of them as cresting, drifting out to sea. Touching. Very touching. She was doing really nicely. He grabbed her hair a little too urgently and licked her face and yelled into her mouth. He thought this put her in a spin, and she was happily losing it. Another victory for her. Another presumption on his part. Again from behind her neck he pulled her hair, perhaps with too much vigour. "Sorry, sorry, I said I am sorry."

"*Ça va, ça va, lentement, continue, continue.*" He touched her arsehole in a brotherly way. They were sort of standing and with grind sensibility she pulled at his hips and troubled down into him, her other hand on his nuts. No sounds. Just a cooing Christian inside a different mode, a different history. A thorn in the side of the French.

They were in the embassy quarter of Algiers and they had forgotten about the conference din for a few moments. Chattering intellectuals. He was operating through the myth that Muslim men did not suck cunt. He thought that this limited and essentially racist view of a social code could be demolished by any reasonable progressive interpreter. He moved on her, and she was taken out of a certain colonial construction of the Other. He thought hatefully of Camus in the garden of Imperial French Gethsemane; in 1962 French privilege was forced to collapse. Only a million deaths. He had always found it hard to turn Camus into shit with his North American friends. Everybody loves Camus; he did not have a very deep understanding of the Algerian war. Three thousand liberation-related deaths in Paris. At times he took his dick out altogether. Was it a code that instructed, Don't lick it, don't lick the organ where piss comes from? He wondered if Christians in his own country, Pakistan, sucked. He did not push the idea too far. He knew the answer was mostly negative: if Benazir Bhutto could not just now develop a substantive distance between Zia's clerical residue and the more or less progressive constitution of 1973, then he was surely in no position to wonder too deeply. The fucking continued, and it was sincere. Really sincere — he was going to be in Alger for three more days.

They turned out all the lights in the hotel room and his back was to the television which threw out a socialist cathode hue. The TV, an import from the home of the revolution, the USSR, flashed different colours. Her face went red, went blue, green, until they turned on the stark overhead light again. He told her a few stories about television preachers in America.

The TV program was a history of Hungarian music, in French and Arabic, if I remember correctly.

CHAPTER TEN

Indonesian Restaurant

Montréal, 1985

Michael's response is quick; he passes me the chicken-in-cashews. The conversation continues: "Who gives an altar-boy fuck about this. My obsession is with the church these days because Ian's brother heads a parish and I've always wanted to give liquid holy communion to the head of a parish — a kind of student-paying-back-the-teacher kinda thing. Bit idealist, I admit, but I'm an idealist.

"These days churches have come under an inordinate amount of moralistic criticism," Michael goes on, reaching for more wine, "don't you think?" His T4 cell count is low, though the final waves of sicknesses have not yet struck. He keeps us abreast of all the new cures. "Yeah, the Church. Forget your tolerance bullshit. Besides, I know what you're up to — you're going to connect it with homosexuals. Why don't we talk about the media's marauding of the Church? God only knows *what* goes on in the Church these days. One must try to look at the acceptance of gay culture as one of the nice things about liberal theocracy."

I refill the glasses with Montréal's version of Algerian red wine. "How do you know what I am up to, Michael? I haven't even begun to make my case."

Michael eats his salad, looking at me all the while. "Your argument going to be better than this wine? *Très corsé.* Rubbish this wine, but thanks anyway — cheap civil servant — saving for a house in the burbs?"

We were all close enough friends for a good argument. Things would never get too heated. It would stay a nice formal cool and, if things did get huffy, then I was willing, I had made up my mind, to let the Indonesian chicken guide us.

Michael pushes his brown hair across his forehead.

I offer, "So it is not really the right time to expose how the super-production of condoms is putting a strain on Third World labour. Therefore we ought not to criticize Rushdie, because if we did, the fundamentalists would use what we say to further their cause, *n'est-ce pas*, is that the nature of the beast?"

"Rushdie got an $800,000 US advance from his publishers — Health and Welfare Canada gives us fuck-all," Michael retorts. "Some say Rushdie got £800,000 sterling — maybe AIDS groups should start a campaign against the Prophet."

"Here is a little about the Third World," Ian says, reading from a book he has brought along for the lunch. "'By 1991, the United States Public Health Service expects to have a total of two-hundred-and-seventy-nine thousand cases of AIDS. If present trends continue, at least one-hundred-and-eight thousand of these will be among New York Blacks and Latinos, most of them living in low-income inner-city areas.'"

Ian sighs, leaning forward into the wineglass, and the white tablecloth buckles into a small wave. Elbows. A few drops of wine sink into this cotton crest, red islands in an Indonesian sea.

Ian's hand reaches across the table, bringing the warm wine to his lips.

"Tell us again where you were born," Michael asks me.

This was becoming a ritual: "Temple Road, May the 7th, 1952, the anniversary of Dien Bien Phu, in the kitchen, Taurus, Temple Road, in downtown Lahore, the twelve-gated city, Temple Road, May the 7th, anniversary of—"

Ian interrupts. "One of those well-known facts, being shamelessly repeated. Not going to tell us anything more? The charming story about watching that woman servant bathing? The homosexual servants who were homosexual because of the unavailability of female donkeys? All those nights on your grandfather's rooftop in Lahore? The hermaphrodites? Charming childhood you had."

Ian asks, "How gated is Lahore?"

In one unhesitant flowing sentence, I deliver: "Bhati, Mori, Lahori, Shah Alami, Mochi, Akbari, Delhi, Yakki, Sheranwala, Kashmiri, Masti, and Texali gates."

"Wow," Ian says.

Michael looks outside for a moment, rubs his eyes. "Julian, you've told us all this before, you repeat things. But you know I'm sort of grateful." He smiles. "Let's take this discussion to the confessional boxes of social change."

"Shouldn't you stop making fun of Ian's brother?" I ask. "Hey, Ian, got any condom samples for us?" I ask.

A lone puffy cloud passes overhead in a deep blue sky. Ian puts on his $300 sunglasses. Some more unserious stillness; Ian examines his fork. The condoms, all bright colours, are being passed around. "Red one for Julian, blue for Michael, orange for Michael, purple for Julian."

For no apparent reason there is a generous smile across Michael's thin lips. He moves all his condoms across to me. "All for you, big Julie."

Michael pauses thoughtfully. "Yes, so what if rubber production is more labour intensive now than it used to be 'cause of AIDS? It's not my fault I have to use condoms; I got to use more condoms these days 'cause I can't stuff anyone nor get fucked without them. Anyway, are we having lunch or a fucking history lesson? And from whom are we getting this history lesson? From one of the most ill-informed historians in Plateau. Besides, fuck all this serious shit talk — I need to start some sort of religious life."

Ian's brothers butt in on the agenda for the next few minutes.

I sanctify our meal: "dóminus vobíscum" and a sign of the cross. Some peanuty chicken oscillates down Ian's Ottawa-funded throat, followed by a quick gulp of wine, a drop of which follows the glass's stem to the tablecloth.

Ian's glinting, slow-motion fork catches sunlight, touches a bit of hot green sauce which has slivers of red chili mixed in with it, and glides over towards Michael's mouth. His lips close down on the morsel. They become lovers in a John Donne poem:

Our two soules therefore, which are one,
Though I must goe, endure not yet
A breach, but an expansion,
Like gold to ayery thinnesse beate.

I am excluded from this embrace of homosexual memory. The conversation spins out of the lovers' embrace and warps back into real time: I am the straight breeder in front of them.

Ian was a bright productive student who got his assignments in on time. He met Michael at one of his classes on Chinese history. And then it became a love-hate-but-more-love-than-hate relationship. "Julian, remember that summer — was it two summers ago that we went to visit Ian's brother at the monastery where they make cheese — you were expecting to see him in an easy-to-reach gown?"

Ian is in government-sponsored seminar mode: "Here is what the British paper *The Sunday Telegraph* of 21 September 1986 published: 'Stringent health checks, including blood tests, for all visitors to Britain from three Black African states must be introduced to prevent the spread of the deadly AIDS virus, the Foreign Office has been told.'"

Michael points his long nose at the waitress.

Ian asks, "What would I prefer? The Indonesian chicken or a

session with her faeces — sorry, thesis?"

"But one has got to come to terms with tolerance. Because if we understand the limits of liberalism, then we can go further. Even sexually," I say.

Gentle Ian swallows his food. "Aha, you've been reading again," he says.

I continue, "Even further than mere handcuffs, and double dildos, dogs, pigs, snakes, hamsters, and gerbils, or in the reverse order: gerbils and hamsters. Hamsters are usually bigger than gerbils — even diesel-dyke orthodox lesbian-approved bondage. Bondage so nice that it has the Germaine Greer pap smear of approval. Double dildos in Mecca?"

"The tolerance that one connects with liberal democracy is something which has cost someone, in Malaysia, for example, a fuck of a lot — rubber workers who, if they strike, will face harsher repression than the miners in Newcastle," I say.

Ian smugly asks, "Does the IRA allow the use of condoms?"

"And this repression," Michael ponders, "is all our fault for wanting to bumbang, extract cream, and include small animals in those Fire Island sixties, seventies, and perhaps not so much the eighties — all those guys in uniforms."

I say, "Yeah, why couldn't you all stick it into a vagina — keep the white tribal population of Québec intact, stop the non-Judeo-Christian immigrants from taking over Québec? That way society wouldn't have fags-in-the-army-navy-airforce problems — things would be normal, just like in tenth-century Cordoba."

Michael fiddles with the condoms. "We're playing condoms and repression, are we? All civilizations have had plagues which have wiped them out or reduced their power — this is going to be *the* solution to the Pentagon. We're sitting around beatin' our meat on a non-issue. Let's get on with the priest-brother who makes foreskin cheese."

Ian is not amused. "Some of us here are dying of AIDS," he breathes out. "The our-tolerance-their-superexploitation bit bores me. Why make us feel guilty? There's a Third World here also, you know. The rates are the highest among Blacks, Hispanics and, of course, we can't forget the poor whites, all those poor working-class whites."

Michael rolls his eyes, exhales smoke upwards. "Yeah! All those tolerant assembly plants."

"The health bureaucrats in Ottawa gave HIV sufferers six million dollars," I say. "The wing section of one F18 fighter plane costs twelve million. The Humour Museum got ten million Canadian dollars."

Michael giggles. "Ian, think about it, we need the F18s to defend our source of oil and its by-products in the Gulf. Oil products, honey, think: lube jelly. We need the surplus-value-leisure-time so we can slide our boners inside selected or unselected bums. We need the time to write and think about solutions to AIDS while rubber workers and oil workers bust their oily little nuts off among the green trees and grey elephants."

I look at Ian. The red wine has outlined Java, and a thin brown dribble of peanut sauce has traced Marco Polo's voyage.

I puff up. "The English working classes unify, because of the possible and actual degree of industrialization largely as a consequence of the extorted cotton from India. The Indian peasant goes hungry; the cotton-spinning Gandhi represents them in vaguely the same way that recent Moslem fiction tries to improve Islam by scripting Mohammed's (Peace Be Upon Him) wives to be all leather slaves of Satan. Rushdie got what he deserved."

Michael tries to stop my flow. "The family order is being replaced by the anarchy of another order — serfs hitchhiking off the land and into the factories. The need for an industrial work force is the most important thing. The money capital shifts from Amsterdam to London, for the first time in history. Women leave the kitchen for the factory, for a relationship with another man or another woman, for a braless midnight basketball game on July the 4th... for whatever. A role in a Spike Lee film on all fours."

After a pause, Michael adds, "I am not sure what kind of homosexual training people get in the Church, either. They have produced a bunch of squealers-to-the-media — not guardians of the trade."

"I bumfucked five guys yesterday," Ian boasts. "One exotic dark man, oh I don't know from where, somewhere east of Istanbul, north of East London, I suppose. Where? you're going to ask. Well, in the park at midnight, dog-style. Oh! weee, crescent moon. One in an alley and there was teamwork — I got it in the same park again, Lahore-style. There was this class-struggle peroxide sperm commando, holy fuck, little leather jacket, I loved it when his arsehole was tight in the beginning and then I was in there with my dick, stroking in and out — taking my heat-seeking missile out all together and bursting in again whenever I felt like it. I was fucking him deep. More jelly. Then another queer had his mouth, irremovably, on my ball-bag in the most meaningful way possible, and you know it was the closest thing to pre-nineteen-sixties cream-piss exchange — shucks! Techniques have changed so much — ask any faggot over forty. Know what I said before I came?"

"Shoot cum, not Arabs," Michael answers.

"Is that a comment on gay ethnicity?" the sociologist in me asks.

Michael, again fiddling with the condoms, looks at Ian.

"Adulterous bitch, that's give or take five condoms."

"What about the Church? We can't neglect Michael's interests," I ask.

Michael swells with erudition. "It is the last bastion for early training. I, in fact, am rather grateful to my preacher. He taught me everything — including confessional-box sixty-niners. Why are you asking about the brother — I had my eyes on him first. Oh-oh, Julian wants to fuck Ian's head-of-the-parish brother also?"

Ian's brother's sex organs hang mythically over the table.

"Oh, sure it's true that some boys got abused," Michael rolls on, "and if they did, the preachers ought to pay the price for having forced them into unnatural acts. But as for my own personal experience, it was a window on another world — blood down my thighs. Busted new A-hole. A new world order."

"And it changed your life?" I ask.

I was wondering why there were no buses on this north-south street. Saint Denis — no buses. A shitty thumping Celine Dion tune blasts out of a new red BMW and evaporates like a plume of exhaust. The new Front de Libération du Québec. Smoke from Michael's mouth issues like early industrial England.

Michael contemplates death: "Maybe I'll come back as a curried condom in Agra?"

"Maybe. But you'll have trouble getting an Indian visa because of your condition," I say.

I think of Marco Polo's ugly search for spices and good dark-native mouths and cunts before he returned to oily Lisboa or wherever he came from.

Michael affectionately draws towards Ian. There is a lull in the conversation. Traffic noises. A few people in effulgent late-eighties neon colours drift by. Tight black bicycle shorts with glowing green designer labels, twenty-five-speed bikes made of the same material as the space shuttle. A skinny mime artist slow-motion jogger with a very long gait dreams by, Walkman hissing. Bunch of shit.

I think about one particular day when my sister was sailing from England to Canada. She told us how the Rolling Stones used a sitar in "Paint It Black." This song had not crossed the Atlantic yet. I remember listening to CHUM 1050 for hours on end, waiting for the hit from the heart of the Empire. Finally one day I heard it. Mick Jagger made the South Asians feel wanted by using one of their instruments.

It felt good to have lunch with these homos, though I was not sure about Michael's ultimate polarity. I had the feeling that if one took his positive pole and pointed it to a negative cock or vagina or arsehole, it would show all the normal properties of magnetism. But that might have happened before the HIV stuff started. In their company, I could say things without the dull sting of orthodoxy. I could even say mean things about a Stalinist dyke we knew and learned to love. She always wore nun black.

The rise of capitalism in Eastern Europe was having a good effect on her. One by one, as the East European governments fell, she too was replacing the old with the new. She was now screwing men and had become, rumour had it, a blow-job specialist. A traitor, some of her ex-colleagues thought, but her colleagues were all crashing bores. Elizabeth Arden products were accumulating in her bathroom, and she smelled nicer and ate more vegetables.

CHAPTER ELEVEN

Man of Empire

Toronto, 1989

My uncle is coming to pick me up so we can join relatives and my parents at an aunt's house. It's mid-February, and a few wispy clouds are hidden behind a defeated sun.

Snowflakes hang in the air before settling on the road. A small snow storm is forecast. Inside, it is warm; bright red carpets from Lahore, green wallpaper with embossed gold leaves from Canadian Tire. A collection of old rupee notes behind glass; one note has a picture of Mohammed Ali Jinnah, the founder of Pakistan. Inside the hallway is a framed picture of my grandfather beside a portrait of Trudeau. My parents' house in Toronto is a celebration of our almost-upper-middle status on a tranquil treeless road.

It is getting harder and harder to distinguish this neighbourhood from the others where we have lived — for years I've been living in Montréal and have somehow lost touch with my suburban roots. Some cars pass the main intersection a hundred yards away. I am alone in the house. A black Mark 10 Jaguar with a yellow indicator light blinking slowly through the snow husses up our driveway. I put on my coat and give the rupees and pictures a nod before joining my uncle.

I slide into the Jag. He slowly backs out of my parents' driveway. More snow gathering on the freshly salted roads. Windshield wipers sweep across our vision. His hand comes to his mouth; he is about to say something but he hesitates, giving the impression of having recalculated his words — a phoney attempt at precision.

"This Jag has an FM radio," he says. A snow-covered sign for Warden Avenue glides by. Large dynamic Canadian fluorescent lights.

My uncle has a brown hookish nose that he frequently traces back to the Slave Kings of Delhi. Aristocracy. He believes in British quality products; one summer he bought a Mini Morris with hydro-elastic suspension. He ran out of gas several times because the "petrol gauge did not work; otherwise the car was fine." Our best discussions always transpired in one of his many English cars.

We drive for a while, then abruptly the front left side of the car whimpers down as he speeds up. A flat tire in a medium-scale snow storm. He wrestles with the steering wheel. "I was just about to tell you about my days when I was a pilot back in Pakistan and now this has happened." Someone honks from behind. Passing car tires rip up the grey slushy snow. The sun has almost set and the suburban landscape looks hostile. We are like the first Pakistani astronauts landing on the moon.

In the snow with his brown tweed jacket and a tie made of knotted silk, he is telling me that he was a pilot in the West Pakistani Air Force doing airlifts in one of those epochs when a coup-like affair looks like a surge for independence or when a surge for independence looks like a coup.

We are stopping on the Macdonald-Cartier Freeway to change a flat tire, not radioing in to the control tower, nor telexing the embassy to confirm facts about an airlift. "The wheels on the plane we used to fly were twice the size of these damn wheels and rarely would they go *phutt* like this one."

"Yeah, Murry—" I'm on a first-name basis with him " — these tires are really bald." He has a bad heart and the slightest accident could kill him.

My Uncle Murry was responsible for the airlift of refugees from East Pakistan. He fought to expose the Rawalpindi conspiracy of

1953: the government of a general or civil politician leader with green eyes decided that the communist forces in Pakistan were getting too large for comfort. "Oh yes, the powers were scared that Moscow's domes would come floating down to Jail Road in Lahore via Switzerland, or perhaps even through Kabul."

My uncle was the chairman of a poetry club which met regularly at Faiz Ahmed Faiz's house. Faiz, the editor-in-chief of the *Pakistan Times*, was the most famous poet that Pakistan has produced, and my uncle was there right beside him in Beirut when he got the Lenin Prize for writing. The Soviets had flown my uncle there so he could help out with the ceremony.

My uncle was a saviour pilot and a close friend of Claude Lévi-Strauss, the world-famous anthropologist. The airlifts took place in a war that a leading political exile Pakistani predicted would follow after Mother India had been divided. Even the most refined plastic surgeons' hands could not put her back together again. In goes the needle to sew the nation together, out gushes the blood and pus between the stitches.

This maiming of the sub-continent all caught up with Lord Mountbatten, the last viceroy of India who, on a blustery day in 1979, was killed by an IRA bomb while yachting in the Irish sea. I tell my uncle the joke about the last viceroy: "How do we know that Lord Mountbatten had dandruff? They found his head and shoulders on the beach."

He tells me bits of his regular Partition stories:

In 1947 blood becomes a kind of Hindu-Moslem treacle clogging up train wheels: trains to Pakistan ambushed by rival religious groups. Bogies crammed with dead bodies. Lord Mountbatten has been appointed by Churchill to offer solutions, terribly English solutions. The Quit India Movement has taken shape and is being led by Mohandas Karamchand Gandhi and a few other Western-educated nationalist leaders. He puts forth his theory on the war on the British home front: decolonization is the least embarrassing route for the Empire to take — "Look, they pulled out of Africa, didn't they? And the whole decolonization hubbub was London thinking, wasn't it? They were the first ones to leave."

A version of parliamentary modernism is somehow being imposed on India by its own leaders. Smoke in Amritsar. Gangs of Hindus toss buckets of circumcised heads of cocks into Moslem restaurants. Sikhs, Moslems and Hindus go on a rampage and start killing. The Quit India generates a movement all of it own.

My uncle is a storyteller of the highest quality and his stories deepen my knowledge of my own past. I'm not sure what his stories do for him, but they push me into the library to extract the truth and to undermine his bullshit.

When I try to verify his stories with my relatives, they say, "Your uncle is the best inventor in the world. Believe him if you want — the bugger once told me that he had an affair with George Eliot."

"Pass me the jack, Uncle." I sometimes call Murry Uncle. He walks around to the back of his favourite car and brings out the jack. Then he opens the car door and reaches in for his cap made from the skin of the fetus of a sheep. In Pakistan they do this by cutting open the stomach of the pregnant animal, ripping out the premature fetus and curing it, followed by a month-long tanning by smoke with the cinders of Rushdie's book. Hats by "choice," as it were. Murry stands, gloved hands behind his back, watching me inch up his black snowy car into the twilight.

The wheel squeaks off. My hands freeze cranking on the spare. We put things back in the trunk. He throws an old blanket over the jack and the flat tire.

"Afraid that flat tire will get cold, Murry?"

"It'll make much less noise," he says, slipping the key into the ignition. "Thank God I found the keys — thought they had fallen somewhere." He chuckles.

The engine does not start. His nose moves closer to the cold steering wheel. Then, as the engine chugs to life, he makes a cartoon face expressing relief.

"Oh by the way, I did like that joke about Lord Mountbatten, but you're so bloodthirsty." His cheeks puff up into a smile. "*Wrooom*, look, immigrating into the westbound traffic," he says.

The airlift starts. I am with him on this one, I don't argue, I don't try to refute dates and names. I'll confirm it all later with the aunts and uncles in another treeless, sunless, silkless, spiceless Toronto suburb.

Murry is not in bad shape, though I've the feeling that the final heart attack is around the corner.

"How's the health — still taking those dynamite pills?"

"No, I'm only supposed to take them if I'm near the pearly gates. Modern medicine. I hope what's-his-name, on the radio — you know, the one who puts in all those stutters just for show — dies before I do," Murry replies. He pauses.

I break the pause. "Imagine, just imagine, Murry, having your cock sucked by someone who stut-stutter-sucks like he talks."

The remark does not affect him. After a few more exits, Lawrence Avenue or Eglinton Avenue, he compensates for my attempt to shock with his opium story. I let his pre-Partition drugs-in-Lahore narrative roll without interruption. Nothing has been added nor subtracted from last year's version.

I was hot off the fall-winter term during my third year at university. My head was full with Aldous Huxley's *Eyeless in Gaza* and *The Devils of Loudun*. Also Walter Benjamin had been a hit that term; his beautiful analysis of photographs and how mass reproduction took the romance out of everything had become important, and my relative fluency with some of his theories helped get me laid several times.

"Do you think that your friend's — Claude Lévi-Strauss's —

structuralism..." I say "structuralism" with a bitterness that Murry acknowledges by turning to look at me. "Do you think that his structuralism was a project that was socially relevant? Or was it more to do with visual anthropological history without knowing the world in Marxian terms — you know, leaving out all that class-struggle stuff and showing all those magical masques. Shouldn't he have shown it all, how structures relate to international capital?"

Leaning back, Murry clutches the steering wheel and braces to give his response.

"You see," he says, indicating left and immigrating into the right lane again, "I don't look at structures of history in those terms. It is a kind of intellectual investigation that is important — your problem is that you get too far too huffy, you're so dogmatic about the science of observation — you're not very controlled anyway."

I'm getting him upset. His heart is racing a little too quickly. But the drag is I have to annoy him slightly if I want the story to be a good one. I use Claude Lévi-Strauss to get him going. That's my past experience. Use something else to drive the story you want to hear. But as he grows older a hazard comes into play: perhaps if I annoy him sufficiently, or make him defensive enough, I'll kill him. Murder via heart attack: Slave King nose frozen to the Canadian steering wheel of opportunity like a dead green parrot. A few last pre-rigor-mortis pecks at diagetic seeds. His nostrils are expanding. I ease up. "Okay, so what else did you talk to him about?"

My mother would blame me. She would not forgive me for getting his heart to stop in the middle of the Don Valley Parkway. So I ease up, though not totally.

"But if he was a close friend of yours, then why don't you know what he might have thought and what he might have suspected about Western observation systems and concepts of history within so-called primitive peoples? Why didn't you question him about the politics of it all?"

Murry turns on the radio. I dream him into Lahore in the fifties with a brown Morris Minor. He's a geography teacher. I immigrate him to London, throw him in a London suburb after having him masturbate a few English ladies — Gandhi-style — enema tubes, fasts, Saran Wrap or the post-colonial equivalent of the period — after gin and tonic. I settle him in a liberal suburb where some crude white niggers throw a petrol bomb through his mailbox. I dream his son into a performance artist who moves to Calgary (after the oil boom), his daughter a nurse, and my uncle's wife — what to do with her? — his wife, a white woman from Manchester where the English language is now extinct, replaced by Punjabi, Urdu, and Bengali. Enoch Powell, the politest proto-fascist the world ever knew, is fluent in one of these.

Black-and-white photograph: here he is in Lahore, sitting cross-legged by a palm tree, chin tapering to a cone. A hole in one of his red socks. A plate of *shami kebabs* beside his lawn chair. A tall sure-looking woman in a sober whitish sari stands by him. Perhaps his mother, or a distant relative. What do they talk about?

He says, "Did Mr. de Sosa send a message from the Young Men's Christian Association?"

The woman in the sari sways in the breeze. The ghost image in the photograph answers as though the Brownie camera had evolved all the internal biology required to become a motion-picture camera: "No, but your good friend has sent you a telegram from his digging site near Karachi."

"Read it please," my uncle asks excitedly.

The photograph has learned speech. It slowly works up to speech-speed, 24 frames a second, without audio flutter, or waffling, in Sunni stereo. Her lips move, but no sound. Finally, after a few seconds, we have synchronization: a photo ghost. My grandmother on my mother's side reads...some time in 1952:

HAPPY TO SEE KARACHI (STOP) HOT (STOP)
HAVE URGENT FEELING THAT I WILL DEVELOP
STRUCTURALISM IN PAKISTAN (STOP)
MUCH BETTER THAN BRAZIL (STOP) FEWER TREES
AND NICE MANGOES FEWER NASTY NATIVES
(STOP)
HOW ARE YOU (STOP)
WOULD SUGGEST...

The film breaks apart. The projector claws gnaw at Murry's mother. Her image begins to flap on the screen. The sound of their conversation distorts; patrician accents slither to a halt... *Yoong Meeen's Christttiann Asssocciationn*. Click: freeze frame, their image frozen in that afternoon, the leaves in mid-swoop, birds in mid-chirp. It's the stable epoch after Partition — a few minor wars, a small-scale bombing of Karachi, a few soldiers killed in and around Kashmir. Nothing to get excited about.

We slip past the Kennedy exit, Warden Avenue, past Victoria Park Avenue and turn down the Don Valley Parkway. Towering apartments on either side. A snow-filled park. Black dots tobogganing down slopes. Nightfall in Canada's model city. Two historically aware Pakistanis in a used black Mark 10 Jaguar watching the sands of Sind blow in serpentine curves across a highway which dark, short, hard-working European tribals made. It's January, or February, nineteen hundred and eighty something, before my first trip back to South Asia.

"I became friends with Claude Lévi-Strauss when he was doing research in Pakistan on the Indus Valley civilization." I'm told by reliable sources within the family that "Klaaud" gave Murry a vacuum-cleaner demonstration on a site in Mohen-jo Daro.

"But why didn't the fucker go into the politics behind the masks?

What about the politico-paradigmatic complexities of the situation, Uncle?"

He picks up speed, not because I have annoyed him. The Mark 10 slips down the highway at 25 kilometres per hour. The snowploughs have yet to reach this section of the parkway.

"I love motoring in the snow. It is so different from driving in England in the Lake District — though this feels a little like the Lake District with all these hills — no, well no really no it's not like England, so manicured the English countryside is. Why must you call him a 'fucker?'

"And those other big words, don't you know I studied Classical German epistemology — now how can you hope to put lamb's wool before my eyes, bluff me off with big words?"

"I have never been to the Lake District, but I know for a fact that you have, and I think you have lamb's wool on your head, Uncle Murry."

He senses my contempt for his friend. He is preparing to start the airlift story. All is going according to plan. He is not going to have a heart attack; Murry is in narrative-address mode. But just another jab before he settles in.

"I'd like him more if he had gone as far as Jean-Paul Sartre did during the Algerian War. Then maybe all that masks-academic-structural bullcrap profit-making venture could be taken more seriously. At any rate."

I move so I can see the brown uncle directly in profile. The Paki snow slowly covers the Don Valley Parkway. The uncle is motoring. His brain is taking him through the Lake District up to Hadrian's Wall.

"It would not have been very hard to go as far as cross-eyed JP," I mutter. "I mean, any two-bit peace activist in Montréal does so by going to a demonstration, a meeting, a circle jerk-off party up on the mountain in Montréal under the cross of Jesus H Christ."

"What is a circle jerk-off party? Oh! I follow — we used to do that after we'd smoke hash, not opium, near Temple Road in Lahore."

I become a Sartrean for a few seconds. "JP had, however, thinking attached to his activism, don't you think, which is what made him so attractive as a leading figure. He had written a couple of books to prove it — he wrote the introduction to *The Wretched of the Earth*, which made me a fan of his for a while."

Murry carries explosive pills in case his heart stops — winters in Toronto have made him weak. A mind in the image of British India on the Don Valley Parkway. Snake snow telling us that we are not there, his little stories tell me that we are far away from that "somewhere" which we carry with us.

We are both far from 1971 in India, when the lady with a grey streak in her hair fuelled an independence movement. Indira Gandhi's son San Jay had a distant-from-the-original-Greek conception of democracy — he bulldozed the poor from their houses in order to clean up slums, just shoved them off the site, dusted off his hands, job done. Her son liked to fly one-engine planes in hula-hoop patterns over Delhi. She fed a secessionist liberation movement in the then East Pakistan, and her son's plane crashed when he couldn't unwind out of one of his splendiferous spirals. Splat. Parties everywhere in Delhi, Bombay, London, Karachi, Montréal. Indira was so emotionally strong that she went for a tactical meeting on the Assam question the very next day, or the same day after tea.

If Murry had been a little richer he would have been a political leader educated in one of the good universities in England, where he would have been exposed to the right sort of anti-colonialism. Just enough of a leash to contain a reasonable, rational, nationalism; to talk about agricultural reform and to nationalize the banks, sort of, but no further. He would have been a product that the centre could control because they would have shaped his mind in their image; a subtle imposition that might even have worn the garb of a parliamentary democracy — or whatever — for a while. He would have been a nice nationalist had he stayed in British India.

"After the fall of Delhi in 1857, the British would have left anyway. Modernism or no modernism, don't you think we had brains enough to invent some kind of working political models on our own? Besides, who did the Greeks get it from, this idea of democracy — the Africans?" Murry beams out over the Canadian road. "British modernity in comparison to feudalism, given the context, was not the worst option. I mean, look at all those boring endless idiotic religious riots. They were enough to turn anyone off."

His words try to bridge two worlds, one of an overly generative memory, the other based in toy airplanes, model cars, and Meccano sets, which he still collects. My uncle rubs his hands, which resemble mine, along the wooden dashboard that was once walnut and leaves.

"I think I've forgotten her new address — she never used to live downtown," he says, consulting a scrap of paper in his right hand. Curried bifocals.

We hear a different story from the man from Chittagong. It is the nineteen-eighties. He's on the news. General Ershad has sent this one — a "qualified" refugee. He has greenish blue eyes, is small-framed, and speaks very directly; he has enough facial referents to be possibly from Myanmar. Urban intellectual. From that Far East, or perhaps he had a mother or father from Darjeeling? The CBC moron who asks questions found out just a few minutes before the interview, via a memo, the name of the capital of the refugee's country: Bangkok.

Zaffar Chowdhury. Twenty-five years of age. Came to Québec in 1984.

He speaks directly into the hand-held camera.

MR. CHOWDHURY: "I remember the 1971 war of liberation. It was an effort in which I lost three of my family members: my father, my uncle, and someone else. My uncle was a suicide bomber who visited a nest of West Pakistani soldiers. My father died in combat. He went to India for training; he used to say he was not a separatist. He died so others could get liberated. In Québec I worked as a cook in a Greek restaurant and they were cold towards our people. The French Quebeckers are not as racist as people in Europe. In the restaurant I used to listen to their conversations on their own separatism. Italy is really bad. I think people here in Québec have a special feeling for us — they don't like us. I can feel this. I do think I have a future here — in physics or something like that. I know the society we come from is corrupt and there are no easy solutions. I am from the upper middle class and we own land which is the root of all evil. You know, I think that it is appalling that one of the main butchers of Pakistan is now a minister in the feminist government of Benazir Bhutto. Her father really profited by the problems in East Pakistan. You could say the bastard caused them."

Mr. Chowdhury turns to the journalist as if to ask him a question, then continues.

"I don't think we are a split people; we are one, but something has gotten in the way, perhaps our history.

"I see separation everywhere."

Another 747 in the background screeches onto the tarmac. His head turns. He stops, he continues.

"I once saw a murder committed by West Pakistanis. I will never forget it. Some large Pathans, from the North West Frontier Province in Pakistan, beat up one of my countrymen. With a huge knife they cut out his heart. I was small but I still remember everything. And another time I saw some Pakistani soldiers chase a man; he hid in a water tank and they shot bullets into the tank and the water looked like it was boiling downwards."

"It was a hot month."

"What month? Be precise, Uncle Murry."

"I'm being precise. Just a hot month. Why so particular?"

The vultures swept through the documentary photographs of the 1943 famine in Bengal, or was it a less specific narrative than the one in which my uncle plays hero?

Armies of still cameras, satellite feeds biologically attached to open sores: the Brown people chanting a liberation song are cut off in mid-chorus for a commercial break for Japanese cars. The famous famine shows no signs of coming to an end. And soon there will a typhoon for the journalists to report.

Which airlift was it? Could it have been during the 1971 war? Murry has forgotten the dates. Yeah right, Murry. I don't push. He manages to hold it all together. I've produced a few good stories this Christmas break.

We pass the Bloor Street exit. He has missed the exit to the aunt's house. Perhaps he had taken leave from his clerk-in-a-bank job to help out with this mass migration. He says he can show photos with him in his pilot's uniform. Lady Mountbatten, a brown dress; here she is in Delhi feeding *tandoori* chicken to her woofing mechanical dogs. Here he is beside her. The Mark 10 cuts the line in the road; someone honks. There is independence in the air. We slow down; snow accumulates on the windshield.

Bloated bodies, independence. Sounds of megaphones cutting the air: secularism, Hindu-Moslem unity, disunity — whatever the politicians say. Crowds swaying like wheat in fields. Crescent moons burning into one-hundred-percent green cotton. Sir Richard Attenborough signing film contracts. Ben Kingsley losing weight to play Gandhi, the great vegetarian hindrance to human freedom. This is what makes the world go round; someone drawing a line on a map. The grey-streaked woman feeding Kalashnikovs to the hungry hands. "This gun means a neighbourhood pharmacy, this gun means a school, this gun means the end of West-Pakistani domination."

Murry is lifting his dark glasses onto his forehead; the runway lines distort in his shades, dashing white lines curving into the edge of the masculine glasses. He has long suspected his co-pilot of being a homosexual. Small, important details. "It is the way he draws the flight path, the way his long, long fingers touch the scales, and the way he makes his sevens; the way he goes down the ramp to help with people when he ought to be drafting the shortest distance between two nations."

The radio crackles runway clearance in Sandhursty English. Clone-ghosts of Indira Gandhi and Mother Teresa merge into one and float into the airplane to say goodbye.

"Then I stop to refuel in Karachi or wherever we used to stop to refuel in those days. The temperature is thirty-nine degrees, the wind off the Arabian sea is at seventeen knots west, mixed with engine exhaust. The idea of Great Britain; a humming Rolls Royce at five thousand metres. I taxi to a clear runway. I freeze the plane still, as though it were hard evidence in court. The refugees lurch forward, a bit of a jolt for them but who cares, we are off to a safe place."

Fuel gushes into the engines. Propellers lopping up the lost souls of whatever country. He turns to the man with long fingers, nods; reports to the control tower once only, as he leaves the security vector. "Plan B active." Silence for hundreds of miles. Silly wars below the dirty clouds. Too much cabin noise, too much cabin hiss — "These are all signs that the engines could have been better designed; imperialism with its faults — you call this modernism — bah! noisy airplanes!"

The airlift begins somewhere in the southern part of East Pakistan, and ends in highway chit-chat on the Don Valley Parkway. A pink shape in the world map slumps from view. New flags in the starry night.

CHAPTER TWELVE

Québec and the Communal Question

Montréal, 1985

We are moving towards greater extremism which will lead to greater extremism among you. If you beat us, you will turn even the moderates among us against you. The children here already hate you. Shoot us, expel us, turn us into victims in the eyes of the world and victory will be ours.

— *Israeli Mirror*, London; 14.3.85

I have just received another rejection from Kosovo-Montesquieu, a private arts funding agency. My proposal was on the Paris Commune of 1871. This period in French history was about how revolutionary socialists used the Franco-Prussian War of 1870 to oust an exploiting and ruthless government from power in France. Some thinkers feel it was a power vacuum that lead to one of the first workers' governments that emerged in Europe. This socialist vision lasted only seventy-two days and took place when Paris was under siege by the Prussians. It was an extraordinary event by any standard.

The reason for the grant rejection this time (I have had many) is the fact that the Paris Commune of 1871 does not have much to do with Québec of 1990. There is nothing a film on this epoch can provide for the people of Québec. In many ways this rejection is a

way to know about life here, and how historical events – or really
any events – don't much affect the life of this culture. Most dominant cultures behave this way, but some of them are better at playing
and containing minorities.

The québécois regimes, especially the one in power now, are an
allegorical equivalent of many middle-class mimic Western regimes
in Third World countries; lots of Mercedes parked out in front of
renovated houses; little substance, little vision, no courageous debates in the press, lots of technocratic types running the show and
doing what can only be called anti-thinking.

The situation in Québec regarding minorities is sometimes not
totally clear; and yet at times it is xenophobic in a very clear-headed
way. It is a fuzzy set of things that swirl here. As time goes by it
becomes starkly evident that the fuzz and ambiguity is getting more
and more in the way of the expression of the non-whites.

The summer of 1990 at Oka, the Native reserve, proved to be
a proto-fascistically clear example. The reserve is called Kanesatake
and the Natives who live there are Mohawks. They tried in vain to
settle a land claims issue there in 1989, in the "white man's" courts.
The following year there was a summer-long dispute; the Mohawks
were fighting the dominant culture's right to make a golf course on
their ancestral lands near the reservation. As the summer dragged
on, the Sûreté du Québec, the police arm of the québécois province-
nation-state, became more and more hateful of the Mohawk Warriors, who had set up an armed roadblock as an act of protest and
defiance. It became an international issue. Mohawks told me that
solidarity faxes came from thousands of miles away like the balloons
sent out during the Prussian siege of Paris in 1871. Finally, after
facing months of Communard-like resistance, the québécois premier
called in the army.

Many Mohawks, fearing a combined attack by the Canadian
army and the Sûreté du Québec, fled, leaving only the lightly armed

Warriors in a central part of the reserve. As the Natives left the reserve, the local white population, with police protection, stoned them. Windshields were smashed. One pregnant woman was hit with a stone. The Canadian army's siege of Oka had begun.

The Warriors were starved out. Many of these communards, while under detention, had the shit kicked out of them by the Sûreté du Québec. Perhaps the Québec government will exile the Warriors to New Caledonia as the French regime did after 1871.

This is my Québec.

My interview with the person who assessed my film project was curious: within minutes she was telling me that, instead of developing my concept about European history, it would be an interesting idea to research a film on the Indian and Pakistani community here in Québec: "And let's not forget, you could be critical, too – I mean, about Québec society."

I said, "Could I get about $30,000 for one year to research this one?"

"No."

I could apply for anywhere between $10,000 to $15,000 for one year. This figure represented about one-fifth of the bureaucrat's state salary. Now what was burningly present in her brilliant suggestion was not the fact that she was trying to dictate down a screen idea in a cultural politic, but that a certain kind of paralysis of the mind had led her to believe that it was more relevant to have sincere little documentaries on Pakis than slightly riskier questioning works. She had, in fact, stereoprisoned me in the *chapatti* film ghetto.

Her institution funded the film *How to Make Love to a Negro*. The actual translation of the French title is *How to Make Love to a Nigger Without Getting Tired*. Coach House Press in Toronto did not want to offend anyone with the graphic quality of the original title. The book was written by a Radio-Canada journalist who is

Black, so obviously it is not very provocative.

It was clear in my script on the Paris Commune project that I would be using a lot of Third World actors to play French and Prussian historical figures. A Black Bismarck, a yellow Aldophe Theirs with slanty eyes, a Mohawk Louise Michelle. But this rectification of French history did not capture the assessor's imagination at all.

It would be hard to imagine anything other than safe, manageable material being made and aired here. Thick black-dicked stereotypes and white women.

The kind of film she was suggesting I take on may or may not be a relevant project for Québec society, but that she couldn't accept a project on the Commune without feeling threatened excited me … excited me greatly because it always puts me outside looking in: continually renews me as immigrant, places me in what intellectuals call "The Other." It alienates me before the artistic labour has even started. Simply put, she had a parental vision of what nigger filmmakers ought to be doing in *her* society. And yet there was nothing really parental in her suggestion process. It was cloaked. But she did not know that she was working through a larger game plan. A game plan which works like a God of social programs. Where was this thinking coming from? Her society is changing faster than she can comprehend. Her provincialism is amplified by her rejection of valid projects, and this happens frequently with many other disgruntled filmmakers.

They – she in particular – do not know how actually to construct a wide-ranging, rich culture. There is no experiment in Québec, just convention pretending to be more than its European counterpart. It is not. Fucking losers. She mentioned the classical examples of commercial hits in Québec cinema: *Le déclin de l'empire américain* and *Un zoo la nuit*. Two boring films about sex, crime, and free enterprise in Québec. Another example of Québec's cinematic brilliance is the merely illustrative *Jesus de Montréal.*

Québec is, in this way, very much like many Third World countries during their respective post-independence-arrogance-and-revolutionary-excess epochs. I can see the ever changing military puppets in Islamabad making the same decisions, but would they be slick enough to see the advantage of buying off Christians and other minorities? I have my doubts. In the early nineties many churches were burnt down in Pakistan and Egypt.

The contrast is not too surprising, though it seems inexplicably remote and distant. We left Pakistan in 1958 after a tiny coup, only to end up in another colony, Québec; the colony without a metropolitan centre; the periphery of the periphery of the periphery of the periphery.

From post-colonial Pakistan to a province-state based on nothing much really, except a weapons-of-death industry with massive sales to areas of conflict: Israel, Indonesia, South Africa — you name it, Montréal has sold them death and destruction; a highly regional spoken French language and a couple of chicken take-out joints. The French went back and the chicken got fried, with a secret sauce. Québec is a colony of what? What intellection created this? Is it the Goethe Institute on Sherbrooke Street West? Is it New York? Or Colonel Sanders?

To make my position clearer on this issue of the cultural dictation of ideology onto the immigrant body politic, I started to tell the assessor about a wonderful curry recipe I had mastered. She seemed really interested, so I told her exactly what to do:

Recipe for Curried Lamb:
1. Use *ghee* to brown about three large onions in a large pot
2. Turn down the heat to just a simmer
3. Add the following spices:
4. turmeric, about a tablespoon

5. coriander seeds and/or powder, one to two tablespoons, to taste
6. a stick or two of cinnamon, black cumin
7. paprika, enough to make the curry refer to the Hellenic Republic, followed by a touch of chili powder
8. Let the whole thing boil until the meat is soft enough to eat. Boil off all the water.

The bureaucrat was a little surprised to hear about boiling off all the water. She asked if it was traditional to boil everything off. Was it not necessary to leave or add a little water for the sauce? I said adamantly, and with an infallible ethnic authority, "You must dry off all the water — no questions asked."

A kind of siege of the meat in the pot. Let meat burn ever so slightly on the bottom of the pan. The discussion of the importance of the Paris Commune of 1871 had become a distant memory, waves crashing on a beach in Karachi, a summer dust storm seen from a Lahore roof, bird cages filled with tiny birds flying off the roof, dust and moonlight. The immigrants had arrived. Communards on the shores of New Caledonia. After you have made the meat grip the pot, at once turn down the heat, adding a little bit of water and freshly chopped green coriander and finely chopped hot peppers. A siege had taken place: a lamb cooked; the Mohawk Warriors taken prisoner.

She refused my project, accepted the curry recipe, accepted the mild criticism of her culture with its redundant films on the sex lives of a few narrow-minded professors, their wives, and homophobic assholes. I said in French that it was really charming to have met her. Fifty percent of the debate had been in English.

My French was okay, and I am easily understood by people in Paris, Lille, and Algeria. Quebeckers still position their tongues in severe sharpness to ears which are used to other accents. This is québécois demarcation: the army at Oka, the anti-immigrant films broadcast on Radio-Canada prime-time television, and my rejections.

From supposed Muslim intolerance in Pakistan, to some halfwit hick with shit for brains telling me that to think outside of Québec society is not something she can fund, and that I ought to be a good Paki telling nice docu-drama stuff about levels of integration of Asians in Québec. "*Fuck ça tsé.*"

I have started to research a documentary film on the Indian and Pakistani community in Québec. I had no choice — it was either that or welfare. Chapatti Films Limited.

I recently went to see the bureaucrat about my project on the Indian and Pakistani community in Québec. She met me at the elevator and asked me how the weather was. I replied that it was very hot indeed. She said, "But you are used to it, aren't you?" Not really a racist, in fact a nice, unaware kinda gal. She would let her daughter marry a Black man. No problem. Nobody whose face you'd want to open with a razor. The woman was really harmless and possibly a good cook. Salt, to taste.

INTERVIEW WITH HAPPY COUPLE

THIS INTERVIEW WILL TRANSPIRE IN A SUPER YUPPIE PAD IN WHICH THERE IS ONE WELL-GROOMED POODLE WHO LOVES TO EAT CURRY.

OUR CHARACTERS ARE DRESSED IN ZAPPY NEW CLOTHES FROM SOMEWHERE IN ASIA AND IT IS OBVIOUS THAT THEY ARE REALLY HAPPY AND SATISFIED WITH THEIR LIFE IN QUÉBEC.

WE ENTER THEIR HOUSE VIA ONE CIRCULAR PAN

OF THEIR NEIGHBOURHOOD FOLLOWED BY AN ELE-
GANT PRECONCEIVED TRACK SHOT ACROSS TWO
DARK GREEN AUDIS PARKED OUTSIDE.

THE SOUND PERSON'S HAND ENTERS THE FRAME
AND WE HEAR A DOORBELL. AFTER A LONG WAIT, A
WELL-DRESSED WOMAN COMES TO THE DOOR.

WELL-DRESSED WOMAN
Yes, do come in, come in. How wonderful that you could come.
Rather early though, aren't you?

OFF-SCREEN VOICE (CAMERA PERSON)
Sorry, we didn't run into the traffic jam we'd anticipated.

WELL-DRESSED WOMAN
Traffic jam? What, on a Sunday?

LAUGHTER FROM OFF-SCREEN VOICE.

THE CAMERA PEERS INTO THEIR HOUSE IN THE
MOST VOYEURISTIC MANNER POSSIBLE. CLOSE-UPS OF
ALL SORTS OF TRINKETS AND EXOTIC OBJECTS:
WOODEN ELEPHANTS, IVORY CARVINGS. WE PAN
ACROSS A FEW BOOK SHELVES AND SLOW DOWN OVER
A FEW TITLES BY SALMAN RUSHDIE: MIDNIGHT'S CHIL-
DREN, SHAME, THE SATANIC VERSES.

ENTER THE HUSBAND. A LARGE INTELLECTUAL-
LOOKING MAN WHO HAS A BRITISH ACCENT AND IS
GREYING AT THE TEMPLES.

THE HUSBAND
Hello. Yes, well, would you like a drink?

OFF-SCREEN VOICES OF BOTH THE INTERVIEWER AND THE CAMERA AND SOUND PERSON

Thank you very much. That would be great.

THE HUSBAND

Well, what would we like to talk about today?

INTERVIEWER

Why do you have two green Audis? Why two cars of exactly the same colour?

WELL-DRESSED WOMAN

I thought you said this was going to be an anthropological film or some sort of cultural analysis of immigrants and Québec. What do the Audis have to do with anything?

THE HUSBAND

Look here, I'm not sure what you are up to. Yes. Well, actually we like the colour.

WELL-DRESSED WOMAN

Well, to tell you the basics, we have been in Canada since the sixties and, well, Québec has been a very nice home to us. We both rather like it here and we plan to stay till the cows come home.

OFF-SCREEN VOICE

How do you look at the language problem?

THE HUSBAND

It is all political really, isn't it? I mean, everyone is totally bilingual. Our kids have been sent to school in France for a few years to perfect their language skills — the French is so awful here. I remember that when I first came here after a year or so abroad, I was in France actually—

OFF-SCREEN VOICE
Doing research?

THE HUSBAND
Exactly, I was doing a paper connected with wave and particle something or other — I forget. But I am fluent in French and I must admit, much to my displeasure, that I find the language spoken here so poor in quality and accent.

CAMERA PANS ACROSS THE RESPLENDENT FRONT YARD TO THE GREEN CARS. WE HEAR THE TINKLING OF GLASSES AND SEE THE SUBSEQUENT SERVING AND DRINKING OF DRINKS.

OFF-SCREEN VOICE
Have your cultural lives changed since you came here?

WELL-DRESSED WOMAN
Yes, actually. Back home, I could not have been a novelist, nor could I have climbed so high in the teaching profession. There is a serious restriction placed on professional development for women, and I really resented that when I went back home for a visit. It became blatantly obvious to me that Québec, for what it is worth, is not a repressive and brutal society when it comes to women. I lived in the States for some time and I thought it was great there — you know, everybody was an immigrant.

THE HUSBAND
And her novels deal with the relationship between cultural
memory, the old world, if you like, and the new one here in
Québec. I find the work very original and really challenging. And
I don't think that there are any serious writers here. I mean it's
okay, that Tremblay sort of stuff, but it will not hold up
internationally. It is just boring slice-of-life stuff with no real
cultural contortions at all.

WELL-DRESSED WOMAN
I thought he was asking me about my work, dear. Now who
knows what they will cut out or leave in. God forbid that I may be
underrepresented by keeping silent because of my own husband's
propaganda work on *my* behalf!

LAUGHTER FROM THE OFF-SCREEN VOICES.
OFF-SCREEN INTERVIEWER IS NOW REVEALED. THIS
PERSON IS A FAMOUS QUÉBÉCOIS WRITER. THE CAM-
ERA PANS BACK TO THE WELL-DRESSED WOMAN WHO
IS NOW RECLINING ON THE LOVE SEAT. THE HUSBAND
SLIDES HIS HAND DOWN HER ARMS.

WELL-DRESSED WOMAN
Should I continue about my writing or are we going to hear
another long speech about my writing from hubby here?

THE HUSBAND
No, dear, you tell us.

WELL-DRESSED WOMAN
It depends on how — well, you are after the immigrant thing,
aren't you? This is practically how I see it... it's a question of how
one positions the subject, how one positions the discourse. The
wog subject in contemporary Anglo-Québec literature. Does one
position him/her as *nigger supreme* or as *Man Friday*? Or, as
Naipaul does, as nigger supreme, Man Friday, and Uncle Tom.

THE HUSBAND
Yes, that is difficult.

WELL-DRESSED WOMAN
(SOFTLY, LOVINGLY TO THE HUSBAND)
Let me continue.

AMBIENT LAUGHTER.

OFF-SCREEN VOICE
When did you leave Pakistan?

THE HUSBAND
Pakistan? Whatever gave you that idea? We are from Iraq.

CHAPTER THIRTEEN

Deep Relationships

Montréal, 1989

The century 1815-1914 is conventionally (and at times nostalgically) pictured as a century of comparative peace, stability, and progress in Europe. Another way of seeing it, grimmer but perhaps more instructive, is as an incubation period. There have been other such periods. The pre-Napoleonic era (1648-1789), because of the comparatively limited magnitude of the wars, also appeared to be a stable period. But this era too was pregnant with the seed of its own destruction, which blossomed in the French Revolution.

—Anatol Rapoport, Carl Von Clausewitz, *On War* (London: Penguin Books, 1982)

They did it a few times in geographically distinct positions in relation to the television and its programs. His cock and her cunt were being mediated through the cathode. One hand on his nuts, the other on the channel switcher, as Simon Templar's nose vanished into vertical static. Once again he would, ever so tenderly, rub her clitoris while moving his penis in and out of the first millimetres of her vagina. Real love. Tongue in an ear becoming a Gulf-oil-rich liquid, whispering pseudo commands, sex-captain commands in English, eliciting responses in a French that became slightly husky as it crawled down from her mind and reached her mouth. His mediation started as language but came out as a howl. It is a bit unjust to not call this language; heavy paralingustic thoughts during something so ordinary. Sometimes it would change into English midway through her parched mouth. Arse licking. True love. He was accounting for the sex-technical change that nations, ideologies, and individuals have brought about.

In the heat of the moment she, via molecular memory or something, slipped into a well-researched movement, which had a history with no purpose.

He opened his eyes because the rainfall was not part of a dream, it was her sweat falling on his tits. Hot summers. Righteous memories.

Occasionally, as she came he would stick his finger inside her arsehole at just the right moment, when the issue is about to become more mind, less body. This arsehole trigger did something — it pushed her to other areas of thought. They were peaceful harmonious arrivals with a hint of imbalance. She was not totally willing to compromise into the Hellenic world of experiment. This was the best time of their relationship. Incubation for other areas of human experience. Incubation.

There was some discussion of him bum-fucking her, but the whole thing failed and it produced a really misinformed argument in the guise of a debate. In the rueful end, orgasm; they made true love again and as she burst, the following came out as a fax across her abdomen:

— 1947, Indira Gandhi assassinated.
— 1984, Rajiv Gandhi assassinated in London by Richard
    Attenborough.

— 1985, Bertolt Brecht visits Mother Teresa in Malvinas Hospital, where it is reported that she is dying of herpes.
— 1878, Louise Michelle, the Red Virgin, involved in Kanakan uprising in New Caledonia, blows an Algerian fellow revolutionary. Discovers heterosexuality.
— 1986, General Zia airborne for life in a C-130 transport plane.
— 1987, Montréal offices of *Cinema Canada* bombed.
— 1997, Revolution in Panama.
— 1688, Flush toilets installed in Kabul.
— 1990, Saudi King deposed. Thirteenth socialist republic in Muslim world.
— 2030, Palestinian state established.
— 1917, Agra water drainage completed. Again, not a very memorable year.
— 1993, Algeria goes through second revolution.
— 1993, White exodus from South Africa. Canada opens doors. South Africans as political exiles. Immediate citizenship granted. Canadian prime minister sets up welcoming committees at ports of entry.
— 1996, Hong Kong police department marches on Shanghai.
— 1999, Haiti establishes single-party socialist state. Duvalier killed at a ruling-class dinner party in Paris.
— 1884, Berlin conference parcels out Africa among the advanced powers.
— 2025, Central American Liberation Army marches on Austin, Texas. Local residents celebrate.
— 2132, Margaret Thatcher, reelected in 1997, defeated by Labour.
— 2199, First assassination of Canadian head of state.
— 2271, Quarter-centenary celebrations of the Paris Commune in New Caledonia.

CHAPTER FOURTEEN

The Cannibals of Maarra

Montréal, 1985

When the axe came into the forest, the trees said,
'The handle is one of us.'

—Turkish proverb

"ello."

"It's Abouali — I recognize your voice."

"Congratulations. Who is this? I'm afraid I only know one Abouali and he is an Iranian prince who sold his title in '79."

"My friend, I'm not the prince — I'm this Abouali, not the prince."

Slowly a face emerges out of the phone. I'm able to somehow connect Algeria with the accent and the pacing of his words.

"Yes, I don't like Prince."

"What prince don't you like?" he asks.

"I find his music too noisy," I answer. "Who is speaking? Is this a joke or something?"

"This is Abu. Do you remember me?"

"Jog my memory, please?"

"We met at that conference in Algiers in 1987 — that thing about Frantz Fanon. I've been in your Canada since about '89."

"So you've become an immigrant? Yes, of course, I remember I called the Canadian embassy in Algiers for you. What brings you to town — what's the noise in the background? — I hear an airport."

"It's not noise. Just announcements for flights, maybe mine soon. I've been here a couple of weeks. Not at the airport, I mean. In Montréal, staying at relatives. Recovering from a trying year. I did manage to immigrate to Canada years ago and I was teaching until I got fired."

"From refugee to citizen. Congratulations. Why didn't you call me before? What happened? Let's get together."

"I'm at the airport about to catch a flight to Jerusalem."

"That much hope in the peace negotiations?"

"Hope? What's that?"

"Are you still a journalist or were you a filmmaker also?" I ask.

"How easily they forget. I'm just going away for a holiday. I'll be back in two months. So when I come through again I'll call and we'll get together then. I apologize about not having gotten in touch with you before."

"You're forgiven," I say.

"Well, I've had a difficult time in Canada. I was not fairly treated by a cultural studies department I was teaching in."

Abouali went to complain to the head of the cultural studies department whose office was located in a snowy Canadian city. When the head of the department spoke with the Arab sitting across from his desk, his hands moved in tiny, repetitive arcs. Sometimes, depending on the emphasis he was trying to place on a word, or even on the gesture itself, he succeeded in making elliptical shapes with his hands which would ultimately usher Abouali out of the department, onto the street, and onto the welfare rolls.

"I'm a little troubled that the cultural studies department has not taken my job application seriously," Abouali tells the head of the department.

The head of the department responds: "I understand that Mr. Hacking, the person responsible for hiring in that area, doesn't think you are qualified to teach in this department."

Abouali responds, "I think I am qualified. I have the experience — look, it's all in my CV. And if one thinks about the others in this department and their qualifications, then yes, comparatively speaking, I'm absolutely qualified."

The head of the department is slightly scared that Abouali will accuse the university of racism. Racism is all the rage at North American universities. Many students are challenging faculty, hiring practices, and curriculum.

"So, my friend, the bastard was right, I fanned the flames of racial equity just to get the job," he tells me over the phone.

"Actually, Abouali, if I remember correctly, you're not qualified in cultural studies, in the strictest sense of the word, are you? I do remember you to be an impressive intellectual — but Canadian universities don't want that," I offer.

His degrees, some of them earned in the West, don't impress anyone. He has the usual degrees in the related humanities, but — and this is his only defense — there are other people with jobs in this department who don't have a PhD either.

"Now why do these lucky few all have secure jobs?" he asks.

I explain, "Back then, when all these white fucks got jobs, only an MA or BA was required. It's a historical thing. Listen to me, Abu — control that rage."

His laughter mixes with the echo of the flight announcements.

I say, "Why not get the required PhD? It'll make things easier."

"Ideally, I ought to return to school to get the doctorate, but would it really make a difference? I mean, there a few members of this department who don't have anything but MAs, and it goes without saying that there is a race thing in these places."

"How did the interview go?" I ask.

"The head made me feel like a grovelling political refugee claimant in front of an uncultured immigration officer begging entry," Abouali says.

On the head's table is Abouali's file filled with articles. He looks at it. Abouali thinks to himself: Please, Mr. Head of the Department, consider the facts. Count up the points. Look at my CV and compare it with the semen receptacles of both sexes who work in this department. If I am not qualified, what about the others? Are they qualified? All they do is run home from conferences and adjust their CVs.

Abouali tells me, "The only reason they have jobs is because they are willing to discuss the semiotics of culture rather than imperialism or because they are married to someone with tenure — that helps."

"Abouali, you don't think that's an exaggeration?"

"No. Not really."

"Are you going to miss your flight?"

The air conditioning hums in the university office. The head of the department will not admit the slightest bit of nepotism transpiring under his nose. "This department has included many radical Third World subjects." He leans back in his chair and braces for the race card to be played.

"Oh sure, after arguing with the head, the bastard gave me the job. I mean I should say that after I threatened to stage a demo outside his fucking office, he caved in."

Abouali taught only once, in a section of cultural studies, and then he was fired by the university, which is 6,947 miles away from his hometown, Maarra.

Professor Hacking is in charge of hiring for the section that Abouali will be considered for. Abouali is seen by some as a very radical commentator on cultural politics, a threat to people's security. Hacking is seen as a hypocrite who pushes gay and lesbian issues that are safe. However, students who are knowledgeable in socialist politics know that he is a typical cultural studies type. And Abouali has unhesitatingly propagated this view of Professor Hacking at the few conferences he has been fortunate enough to have been invited to. The conference organizers always get Abouali to present papers on the Third World.

"Oh yeah, my ex-boss Professor Hacking is in physically great shape. Because of his high income, he can afford expensive anti-aging vitamins and growth hormones which make him look very attractive. Lots of leather clothes which he only sometimes wears to school. I've seen his wardrobe in his house. For the younger generation of intellectuals he is a beacon of civility and erudition. They say he has a splendiferous sperm fountain which has delivered many lessons and has been captured on Polaroid film. Those that participated got A's."

Abouali thinks Hacking is a sleaze who uses bland minorities and their safe affirmative-action ordeals and sexual politics to further his own career in a country where the slightest squeak against the system makes one look like Rosa Luxemburg or Lenin.

"They have degrees in desk-top fucking," he tells me. "What do they publish? Sweet fuck-all. They sleep in the Canadian snow."

But this charge, like all the others he has made, is false, and to some extent he is at least as much a hypocrite as Professor Hacking. Some of the faculty met their spouses while teaching at university. However, many others within the university had smoothed the way to hire their lovers and friends. A natural enough process that ought not to be tampered with by affirmative action.

"Be fair, Abu, you want to show films against the Israelis," I say.

Abouali was a passionate watcher of the scene in other countries, especially the United Kingdom. He frequently made the mistake of comparing Black British commitment to justice and intellectual life with Canadian intellectuals. He was not able to judge Canadians fairly. He would say, "The CBC radio and TV are government lap-dogs. Lots of programs about how to make your dog jump over four-foot fences."

The head of the department says, "But, Mr. Riza, we have minorities in this department." Ah yes, the head is referring to Mr. and Mrs. Lesbian, the gay and lesbian professors. What he is saying, albeit indirectly is, Mr. Abouali Riza, you know *that* is political.

"But that's not fucking political."

Abouali believes in the profound importance of sexual politics, especially when connected with "a critique of the representation" of social issues such as AIDS, and of course he's been dying to do some research on gay and lesbian culture back in his riot-filled Palestine: "Homosexual Practice in Palestine, from Deir Yassin to the Current Israeli Occupation."

He pauses, then says, "And then the department head's eyelids move slowly down over his eyeballs, like a lizard's on a hot day."

"Really, like a lizard's. Show me how?" I ask.

"Next time we see each other."

In the head's office, Abouali floats away for a few moments. "I mean," he muses, but drops what he is about to say. The head is silencing him. He thinks: Look at all those missiles and submarines that Canada is making and selling; that's all sexual politics. Missiles. Abouali thinks of testing a missile right there and then. The head of the department has read his mind. The head is frightened. Abouali can sense this fear after years of dealing with Israeli soldiers who are fearful when confronted.

Abouali says, "Students used to talk about international politics and have demos. But now it's about condoms."

Perhaps he was just constructing malicious counter-productive approaches with which to justify his own failure at not getting in the department permanently. Did he really have a valid complaint? Was it really racism that was keeping him out of the department? International economic and cultural rape and Canadian complicity? Forget teaching that sort of stuff here.

"You see, Abouali, here we require qualifications," the department head drones.

Abouali is a heterosexual configuration. A hero breeder vaguely from the Third World elite who has been reduced to a welfare recipient. Haifa to Algiers to Alberta, to — once again — Mirabel Airport.

He is somewhat like Professor Hacking, someone who uses the Third World to create a career.

Professor Hacking said once that he couldn't show a short film Abouali had made because it had effigies of Ariel Sharon and Menachem Begin being put to flames. As images of these leaders burn off, images of Ronald Reagan are revealed behind them, like a curtain of political doubt being lifted. Professor Hacking feared that a Jewish student in his class might call him an anti-Semite and have the cultural studies department closed down just like in the Occupied Territories.

Professor Hacking has recently published a book on "radical" art in and about the Third World. Sort of like Germaine Greer's recent romp through the Third World.

"The bastards would rather study the history of disco than the other stuff," Abouali says.

The irony of the situation is that Professor Hacking, even though he did not like Abouali much because of his often rough approach, ended up using Abouali to demonstrate a pluralism that didn't exist in his department.

The head's eyes move across his large desk. He is silent, badly dressed, and powerful. The head of the department asks his slave to photocopy Mr. Riza's file. The secretary comes back into the room and softly places a pinkish folder on the dean's table. Her nails click as it leaves her fat hand. The humming air conditioning fills the silence again.

"So I said to the European tribal: I think the department has a racist hiring policy and if you don't give me a fair chance I will go ahead with the demonstration. That would make this institution look real liberal, wouldn't it? Then the fucking arsehole started to notice me. Ah yes, many of my friends are journalists. They would just love to expose the spectacle: *Arab demonstrates over race relations*."

Abouali is sure his journalist friends wouldn't cover his story unless there was violence – a condition Abouali was not prepared for. He didn't want to be reminded of home that badly. Excluded minorities always use extreme means to get even, even if they are not qualified.

The demo idea has scared the head, who now calmly says, "Well, in that case, if you feel so strongly about the matter, please resubmit your application. We'll review it. You'll get a fair hearing."

Abouali was wishing rather vindictively that the dean had been a student at his West Bank school. Abouali was wishing that the dean would call him sand-nigger, or whatever the right-of-return Americans used to say near his house. Abouali was wishing that Oum Kaltoum, the Egyptian singer, would sing his favourite songs from Omar

Khayyám's *Rubáiyát* as he kicked his face into a bloody mess. He would hear the head of the department gurgling, "Quota, yes, quota, quota, it's not such a bad idea."

This was the head's country even if he did come from West Germany some years ago. Abouali had just come here a few years ago from an Arab town, Maarra, where in 1098 blond crusading knights cannibalized a large part of its population. Babies roasting on spits. Abouali, in the nineteen-eighties, was in the presence of a descendent of these huge knights and he did not have the rites of passage.

Some of Abouali's best friends would suggest that this issue was based on his international views, not the colour of his skin. But he would whine: "My work has been shown internationally, I have published, and I have had some prestigious grants from Canada and UNESCO. And they still will not give me a job."

"Yeah, I got the fucking job. But they made me include the work of many moronic Canadian intellectuals. Mimic Americans," Abouali says on the phone.

"Are you going to miss your flight?" I ask.

"Getting bored listening to my narrative of oppression?" he asks.

"No, not at all. Continue. I want to hear everything. I'd like to interview you for my next film — on minorities who live in Canada. Was the course popular?"

"Very. Highly rated by the students. Students not officially enrolled in his class would often show up to hear the discussions. The jealous dead-fucks who fired me ought to be sent to geezer land — Florida — where they would hopefully die of skin cancer."

"Heroic," I say.

Some years after his teaching career was snuffed out, Abouali found himself walking in the Chinatown of a small Canadian city. He was back on welfare at $400 or so per month. Government budget cuts. The rent had been paid, the gas, hydro, and telephone bills as well. He was hungry, looking at all the lunch specials in the prosperous Chinese windows. "Lunch Special $4.50." He had two dollars in his pocket, two dollars and sixty cents in the bank. Abouali wanted to give the faculty third-degree burns on visible parts of their bodies with hydrochloric acid. He wanted to see them do their politically correct lectures with melting faces.

"I had become too poor to move. Then I decided to borrow some money and head home again."

To escape his predicament he would dream of his Middle Eastern homeland. He would often make the bearded Sufis appear in his memories: the Sufis in their private garden in Maarra near his parents' home. He could see them through the green fence. They would look at patches of sunlight in the shade of the fruit trees and sway. Sometimes they would gather in a circle, play music and dance. It was all so peaceful watching them seek out the effulgence of the inner soul.

"Maybe I ought to do a PhD in Sufi dance floors?" he suggests.

He would poke fun at white gays and lesbians; they were just out for themselves and not for a larger international mandate. At conferences, he would express solidarity with "progressive gays and lesbians," but he would tell his dearest friends how stupid he thought they all were: "People without anything larger in their minds than the next grant application and how to do something creative on the AIDS issue. Or how to fund another boring cultural studies conference."

His barbs at Professor Hacking made even his closest overweight funding allies in Ottawa call him a homophobe. But, of course, he was nothing of the sort.

"I can't understand being kicked out of the department. They were such zeros that I could not begin to feel inferior. My direct boss, Professor Hacking, was a pale imitation of the kinds of scholar/activists I had known.

I mistrust these fucks more than the elites from my own country. Imagine that. I've actually said that. Ignorant these fucking pink-skinned arseholes are.

"I want to go back and live under a nice massacre-hungry dictatorship. That'll make me happy."

"Don't be silly."

Once Professor Hacking had profited from Abouali's visible minority presence within the department, he refused to re-hire him.

Professor Hacking is in the habit of bringing important left-wing Third World intellectuals into the classroom. He gives a course on post-colonial "politics." When Third World intellectuals visit, he invites them to give lectures. He puts his arms around their shoulders, buys them drinks, has dinner parties, and makes his ugly-tasting white-man's curries for them.

Hacking will always have a job. Abouali has been rendered a permanently unemployable marginal. His friends used to call him a professional victim. He would blurt back, "You're just a bunch of cock-sucking Toms with all your corporate jobs, wives, carpets, and televisions."

Now Abouali lives in fear of the welfare officers. Professor Hacking will have holidays in the wintertime. Very sunny ones. He has a garden where different birds come to feed. He loves to have minorities as friends. They have such nice recipes.

"I just heard something about an El Al flight going to Jerusalem," I say.

"Yeah, you're right. I've bored you, haven't I?"

"No. I've been taking notes. I'll interview you when you get back."

CHAPTER FIFTEEN

Report of an Officer Who Was Educated in the West

I bent the head over the sunlit chair and the pressure of the other olive-skinned hand broke its throat. We clutched the throat with our fingers and twisted it: screams were emitted from the person's mouth.

The narrator of the events became caught up in a use of descriptives.

I took out the single-edged razor and slashed blindly across the back, peeling the skin like a sweaty shirt. Seconds later I peeled the skin again in smaller sections. Sunlight from the window made a clean triangle about the lower torso. The composition was neoclassical.

Then we made deeper incisions. Other olive-coloured hands helped me to part the increasingly detailed flesh. Draino was poured into the mouth. A series of "X" slashes were made, using the anal sphincter as the centre. We stopped for a few seconds, then started again. The other person came in with his anxious face and white coat, took the pulse, and said there was life. He was the doctor.

A rusty hacksaw was used to detach the hands. We sawed off the gums. The bleeding got out of hand. We tried hard to arrest it with the Draino — it was all we had. We cut deeply into everywhere until things looked like asterisks all over. We put the limp, not-at-all-dead body on the toilet so the fecal matter could fall endlessly.

CHAPTER SIXTEEN

The Starry Night I Met Begum Akhtar

Lahore, 1984

Moi, Hassan fils de Mohamad le peseur, moi, Jean-Léon de Médicis, circoncis de la main d'un barbier et baptisé de la main d'un pape, on me nomme aujourd'hui l'Africain, mais d'Afrique ne suis, ni d'Europe, ni d'Arabie. On m'appelle aussi le Grenadin, le Fassi, le Zayyati, mais je ne viens d'aucun pays, d'aucune cité, d'aucune tribu. Je suis fils de la route, ma patrie est caravane, et ma vie la plus inattendue des traversées.

—Amin Maalouf, *Léon l'Africain* (Paris: Jean-Claude Lattès, 1986)

This view must have been, I thought, Cyril Radcliffe's vision of the Punjabi landscape on 8 July 1947. Radcliffe was the geographer of Partition; he followed instructions to divide this part of the continent into many parts: East and West Pakistan, India, and Kashmir. Before Radcliffe flew back to England, his plane was thoroughly combed for a bomb.

Landing clearance. I touch a city which I left twenty-three years ago. There was nothing romantic about it; no Proustian tactics, no magical biscuits dipped in cups of tea.

A Punjabi customs official who inspects my suitcase looks behind shirts, pants, underwear. I can see one miniature bottle of Bell's Whisky in each of his eyeballs. I am safe. No alcohol. Twirling his long moustache, a thud to the passport, he clears me.

I engage in the hectic process of trying to get a cab. The airport parking lot swarms with cabbies who try to snatch your suitcase from your hands and settle you into the back seat of a Japanese-made car; Pakistan does not have a national car manufacturer, unlike India.

I get ripped off, but at only, I find out later, three times the normal rate, not such a rip-off if one considers what political scientists and historians are writing about.

We move along Jail Road. I recline in the back seat, watching street lights, palm trees, roadside fruit and nut sellers with hissing lamps, then Fatima Jinnah Road. The cabby turns, gears down, gears up, slips along past the concrete-banked canal. With a series of wrestling movements at the steering wheel, we proceed to a neighbourhood of large houses with huge lawns, servants, and palm trees. I recognize nothing.

A few days after I arrive, there is a huge dinner party at my distant relative's house; the gathering is for someone returning from the UN. Silk saris and silk *shalwar kamezes* blend with heavily perfumed men and women. There is curried chicken which the Moslem guests eat with their hands and the Christians eat with a fork, pushing morsels of rice and *khura gosht ka masala* mixed with *ratha*, a mixture of thinly sliced cucumber and yogurt, onto an opposing spoon.

A Christian servant who pretends he can't understand a word of Urdu brings in a huge tray of *biryani*, a dish made with lamb or some other meat layered with *basmati* rice and almonds. Of course he understands Urdu; he's a liar.

The rice is followed by a bright red dish of curried lamb ribs. On one side of the table is yellow fish curry, decorated with large

hoops of onions and bits of plucked coriander. On the opposite end
of the table is a plate of *karhi*, balls of *basan ka atta* in a neon yellow
sauce laced with cloves of garlic. The smell of fresh coriander makes
me dizzy. Beside this yellow dish is a mound of deep-fried triangular
pakoras — fried pockets of flour with bits of vegetables and meat.

The party slowly moves out from the drawing room, leaving the
Schubert sonata by itself. The guests orbit around the food table to
load up their plates; some settle into chairs or the couch, others just
stand around, plate in hand, talking: *gup-shupping*. In between the
chicken curry and *pulau* is a thirty-centimetre-high stack of flat bread
called *basan ki roti*, cooked with bits of dried onion. An older woman
servant brings out the salad.

The men at this party are all powerful members of the estab-
lishment. Some, however, are followed by the dreaded Central
Intelligence Department. Everyone feels secular tonight. Moslems
come traditionally dressed, though mostly all the men wear suits and
ties. A friend of my uncle's turns to me and says, "Many Blacks in
Canada? You know, I work for the UN and I go to New York often,
in fact I even live there at times. I must say I'm allergic to the Blacks."

"So you have difficulty with Black people?"

"Yes I do."

I turn towards the food but he sticks to me, plate in one hand,
fork in the other. "Looks good, all this food. You know, I divide the
whole human race into two — the civilized ones, like us Pakistanis,
perhaps a few Indians even, who understand the use of green
coriander, and those who don't — those Eastern European tribes.
What do you think — is it nice to be back here?"

My aunt is sitting in front of me in the palatial front room which
has a twelve-foot Christmas tree subtly decorated with only one
colour of balls — light blue. Taste.

I have been here only a few days and already she seems to know
me well. She is about to have a little fun with me. "Our Julian is a

strange case. He comes back all this distance to talk to the opposition for a hobby. To talk to a few left-leaning people, to talk to the opposition who have gained their fame by going to jail. Julian, didn't I tell you about all the delicious food all those prominent left people have sent to themselves in their jail cells — with the approval of government?" I am about to offer a reply, but her slender hand goes up to hush me. She moves her professional hands in a slow beautiful musical arch. She has on an expensive perfume from her shopping spree in Paris.

Her husband always wears a suit, even to bed. He looks at me, smiles, looks directly back at his wife, replies in Urdu. "*Jee ha mere jan*. Yes, you're right, dear, he comes back to talk to the opposition people just for quick chats, 'for interviews,' he says, and then he will swoop off back to Canada without, without — and this is most surprising of all — he does not even think of taking back a wife. Yes, you're right — *ajeebe* this one is."

He gathers up some rice with his spoon, a little bit of yogurt, a small piece of mango pickle, and it all goes into his mouth. Some years later, after Zia's plane is blown up, I will recall this conversation with this man and his morsels of mango pickle mixed with rice and curried chicken and Zia's floating body. Spoonful after spoonful descending his throat. The bomb on board Zia's last flight, my mother tells me, was concealed in a crate of mangos given by the head of a province.

The daughters have invited college girlfriends. We are surrounded by the greatest concentration of beauty and brains I have seen in years. There are some horny young men here; dicks growing out of their eyes.

I'm sweating — the curry has been made especially hot tonight. My aunt gives me one of her looks, eyeballs to one side of the head. She wears a silk grey and blue sari with a pearl necklace, large oval hoop earrings.

The distant aunt continues her flirtation. "You know, this is what surprises us all the most — you've come all this way and no interest in a wife? Explain all this to us, will you — a lot of other hyphenated-Canadian or hyphenated-American boys have come back to have the roots experience, which is all and well up to a point, and we love having you here, don't misunderstand me, but you can also look for just the right woman. So many here, so many women want to live in Canada — most prefer America, of course, but Canada is acceptable — Montréal or something like that."

I get the impression this bit of theatre has been planned. She has an audience of bilingual young women who are listening to her every word. Her fork disconnects from her spoon. She arranges both the fork and the spoon neatly near the outer circumference of a plate with red borders, gold lines. The plate is perfectly balanced on her knees.

She is a highly respected professional, the head of a section in the government — a woman — a minority right up at the top. "Now why don't you send flowers to that nice girl you met at your other relative's house? I know that nice family — isn't that right, Yasmin?"

"Yes," responds a college girlfriend. Yasmin's voice has the enigmatic authority of Begum Akhtar, the Edith Piaf of the subcontinent. She is making me weak at the knees. Green-blue *shalwar kameze*, oval silver bangles, three of them, a hint of kohl around her eyes which are shaped somewhere between Northern Pakistan and the Chinese border. Urgent breasts. A Marxist. Something sets her apart from the other college women; she has sandals on, without socks, during a secular winter evening.

The distant aunt is taking me for a ride. "Look," I say, "this is just a holiday." I'll never get Yasmin to love me if I am made to look like an idiot. I am wearing a beige dinner jacket with blue jeans. Very hip. People notice the jeans. There are several very well decorated guests around me. One of the drop-dead-beautiful single Pakistani women giggles.

"I have just come to see how this place has changed over the years. I'm too scared to start a wife selection process just now. I just got off the flight from Delhi five days ago," I say with confidence.

Yasmin, leader of the college women, puts down her glass of boiled and distilled water, says in Urdu, "Julian *jee*, we're feminists also."

Another femme fatale, Jamila, joins the chorus: "Yes, you should look for a wife. Can we help?" Giggle giggle. "Where is it that you live? Canada. Oh yes! Pierre Elliott Trudeau. A very intelligent civilian leader."

This one might be the perfect choice. But it's Yasmin I want. The distant aunt is right. I should find a wife, teach at the local arts college, write political pamphlets to gain credibility in my spare time, and settle down.

Yasmin speaks many languages, has lived in London, Washington, has met Benazir Bhutto twice, and is, my aunt whispers, "doing her doctoral thesis on 'Women, Continuity and Change in the Medieval Islamic City.' You'd be aiming high if she's the one." I move towards the table to get more rice, and some relief from the social pressure.

I ask Yasmin, knowing fully well that she is Moslem, "Would you like to come to a midnight Christmas service with us?" My only nearly successful question of the evening. Yasmin reorganizes her long wave of jet-black hair over her shoulder. Her eyes are greeny-greyish. I feel the surging of a wave collapsing on my neck, such is her beauty.

She picks up her glass of boiled and distilled water. "Oh Julian, please let's hear you say something in Urdu." Ah! she said my name in that raspy international English-Urdu. The malaria, the delirium, the twenty-four hours' air-time has been worth it all, even the night when I will see Begum Akhtar.

My well-rehearsed Urdu floats out, the beginning of a poem by Ahmed Faraz — about political prisoners, the Zia dictatorship, and how allegorical candles fade in the wind of the coming of the American-backed army. A fat bystander says, "*Kamal*, he speaks Urdu. You know, Faraz and I studied history in Forman Christian College. He's a good friend of mine, I'll tell him about you. Maybe you could interview him?"

Yasmin is impressed. She is caught unaware. She sits down not because she is overcome with my missionary Urdu but because, I think, it is touching for her to see someone come back to Lahore after so many years. She had to leave here sometime in her past, too. The transnationals have touched.

The servants, called "domestic help" in India, bring out tea and hot sweet *gulab-jamins*. A winter night outside, a Christian-Moslem-non-military dinner party inside. I ask Yasmin if she likes banana splits, and if Zulfikar Ali Bhutto really politicized the servants and workers. I say, "There is one servant who works here who claims to not speak any Native language except English. Do you think it is a put-on? Or do you think a tight slap across his face would liberate his tongue?"

"Yes, maybe, but your aunt tells me you are a left-winger. What's this about slapping-shapping the oppressed minority? Let him do what he wants."

My aunt's undying requests for me to seek out a wife are beginning to work on me. I begin to see every woman I meet with a view to a proposal, especially Yasmin: You wanna marry me and live in the hip Plateau Mont Royal area of Montréal, make feminist-semiotic curries and play post-colonial exiles?

I've just got to get her phone number. But, arsehole, this is

Pakistan. You can't just ask her out on a date. I may never see her again, unless the college daughters set up a meeting.

I make it a hobby to go with the driver to pick up my aunt's daughters after school every day. "Just for the drive." The daughters are on my side. This is an elite college. Paths to the various buildings are surrounded by palm trees with swishy large emerald-green leaves. Occasionally, a poorly dressed janitor with grass-cutting tools walks by. He looks me right in the eyes. Maybe he is defending the students in the college. The uplifting effects of Zulfikar Ali Bhutto, I assume.

Reddish paths under a tunnel of palm trees lead to the various squat buildings laden with more flowing *dupattas*. Women in uniforms. Navy blue sweaters over light blue *shalwar kamezes*. After school; jeans and the latest air-filled running shoes from America. "Let's have a peanut butter sandwich," whines one of the daughters. Certainly not a fixed traditional society. Everywhere, the illusion of progress and not.

It is too easy to say that traditions are static, traditions are constantly not being traditional. There is no fixed Islamic past, so I can weasel out how to fix a date without feeling guilty.

Prostitutes, for example, use the veil, tradition, to hide themselves from the Godly faces of the doormen at the various five-star hotels in the major cities.

It only takes a few weeks of being in Lahore to discover that everyone has a modernism-versus-traditionalism tale to tell. The best story I heard was of a young Pakistani performance artist who, after quite a few years of studying in an American art school in Chicago, returned to Pakistan. He did the most extraordinary thing. He decided he'd put on a street performance just like the rappers in America. After all, Pakistan has a historical tradition of street performance – public flogging, military parades. The act was to somehow connect Islam with progressive Black American rap music. Sections of Black American society have to some extent embraced Islam: the early and developing Malcolm X, and Louis Farrakhan, to mention just two leaders.

This young returning Pakistani performance artist had taken a recording of a local prayer reader and dubbed it with samplings from Grand Master Flash and Lata Mangashker. The sound pulsated; synthetic electronic drums with Pakistani equivalents of the abrupt stopping and restarting that DJs do in the West. An audience formed around his sound system. He had been away from Pakistan for a decade or so. He had badly misjudged his audience. His sound system was turned into a heap of colourful Japanese wire, a twisted stylus, punched-in speakers, and a punctured left lung. His visiting American video artist friends were dumbfounded. The following day, they left for Bangkok, where it is rumoured there is more religious freedom. The Pakistani state faces test match after test match.

Other less Western-influenced opposition activists I met all hated Gandhi, admired Faiz Ahmed Faiz, and loved shitting on Richard Attenborough's malignantly flawed eulogy. I remember one intellectual telling the story of how some Calcuttan "untouchables" emptied a large bag of cobras into a packed cinema that was showing *Gandhi*.

At first, the language of political discussions seemed confusing, but after a while I reassured myself that they too were confused and divided on many issues. I remembered Yasmin saying during that dinner party, "The left here is like a chicken with its head cut off — one minute running to Moscow, the next stopping, turning around, then heading off for some Peking duck." And when we had moved away to a corner of the dinner party she would, with a full smile, say, "Fucking opportunists — the whole lot of them."

Some of the older activists were capable of letting you have Hegel and the latest theory on Kabul in one ear and why they did not really want to talk with me in the other. Mazar Ali Khan, editor of a leading magazine, said, "Well, Mr. Samuel, I am glad that you took the time to visit us here in Pakistan, but I am afraid that I don't have the time just now to do an interview." This remark was followed by a cagey pause in which his eyes tracked across the sunny desk over some papers, and then, noble advice.

"May I suggest — " he hesitated " — that you talk to the Moslem League."

Only a few political types wanted to give an interview. The regime had terrified everyone: the unions, the peasants, the workers. In Urdu, I must have sounded like an American missionary; in English, there might have been enough of a linguistic twist of empire that I might be a CIA agent. An agent? Who, me? That would have been great husband material for daughters. Fresh flowers, and a job in DC.

Within the first few days I fall sick. Not an exotic sickness, but the worst combination of flu, stomach flu, super-runs, delirium, and dreams which shake apart my national identity and bowels. The country takes you, then it rejects you, turning your shit to water. A kind of unofficial long-term visa. All the pills in the West cannot save me. One particular night, I count thirty trips to the washroom. I dream about various world systems, books and articles I read in preparation for this prodigal saga. Words as large as a cinema screen float across my vision: "The Secret of Primitive Accumulation," "Genesis of the Industrial Capitalist." It is all to get much worse.

Hours and hours of sitting in a plane. Jet-lag for weeks afterwards. My anal sphincter is in direct contact with all the activist types who have in one way or another played a role in encouraging me to visit my "homeland."

In one of my dreams I saw my Urdu teacher from university. She was the only Canadian of Dutch or German origin I knew who was fluent in the language, even though her spoken Urdu was bookish and wooden.

I asked her about the sources of certain words; she, in her show-off way, started writing them, first in Arabic, second in Farsi, third in Sanskrit, and last in Hindi. If we had not stopped her, I am sure she would have given us the equivalents in Dutch, German, and Spanish as well. She didn't have a talent for wearing her education lightly. She wore the heaviest jewelry the subcontinent had ever produced. When she wrote on the board, the hundreds of bangles and earrings became instruments in an orchestra tuning up. Her fingernails caught on the blackboard. She jingled in the halls like an elephant in Rajasthan.

At five in the morning, after powerful megaphones blast out the day's first prayers, in my malaria-like condition, I start to hear Begum Akhtar's ghostly voice oozing from the walls. She is known throughout India, Pakistan, and many other places where we live.

Not everybody is affected by her music. My Indian friend, the historian of slave labour, introduced me to her. Once one has developed an attachment to her voice, one never loses it, or if one does, it is only for a while. My mouth is parched.

Begum Akhtar is as important to India and Pakistan as Ahmed Ben Bella was to the Algerian revolution. She sings the poems of nineteenth-century Mirza Ghalib or the twentieth-century Faiz Ahmed Faiz — the most important poet in Southeast Asia, one is constantly told here. I cannot remember exactly whose words she is singing. My knowledge of Indian or Pakistani poets is very slight. I know more about English literature, a more or less unhappy admission.

Her singing tangles into my dream. I am flashing through bits of Satyajit Ray's film, *Jalsaghar – The Music Room*.

We are landing in Kuwait to change planes. The migrant labourers returning from the cruel racist Gulf States burst into joy, even tears, at the sight of lights over Delhi or Karachi or wherever we are stopping to refuel.

Begum Akhtar flickers in front of my eyes. The film is scratched and worn in parts, unprojectable: there are so many scratch lines she seems to be singing in a jail cell. However, her voice is sharp, exact, as though it is being played back on a video disc. She sounds like the middle-aged Begum Akhtar, but she inhabits the flesh of a nearly extinguished body.

The shadows in the film are black and rich grey. I can see objects through her. I hear the sound of rain outside. There is a power in her singing. The poets are never wrong. Faiz, not impressed with Partition, asked, "Is this the dawn we have been waiting for?"

Ray's film is about an old man who uses his family fortune to put on concert after concert in the spacious music room of his mansion. The room has portraits of key British political figures of the epoch. It is twilight. But tonight his money has all but run out. No music. His friends have left him. He is consumed in a desperate drunkenness. He is crying and mounting his horse. His house is beside the sea; his white robe narrates the Bengali wind. The film is about to end; so too, an epoch. The white Arabian horse bursts out across the sandy surface. Man and beast, tiny in the sealandscape, move from one end of the screen to the other, hooves not touching the ground. The horse falls. A hole in the sand. It is fatal for the rider. The horse's leg is broken at the knee. British India is about to define itself. The largest democracy in the world.

Begum Akhtar stops singing after a stanza — right in mid-song. A harmonium attempts to fill the gap by politely mimicking her voice. Her eyes close. She steps out of the black-and-white film world, appearing as a living woman.

She sang in the period just after the Raj. She may have been born in 1917 or earlier, before the Lucknow Pact. I see the young Begum Akhtar, fully decorated with jewels, singing in front of a portrait of George V.

When, sometimes, I can't understand an Urdu line she sings, the sound of the morning prayers seeps into my fever and I remember bits of the Koran my Moslem friends exposed me to:

"And the believers, men and women, are protecting friends
of one another; they enjoin the right and forbid the wrong,
and they establish worship and pay the poor-due, and they
obey Allah and his messenger."

Another favourite of my Iranian Shiite friends was:

"Fight them; Allah will torture them by your hands and
bring them to disgrace, and assist you against them and
heal the hearts of a believing people."

The message of the Prophet (Peace Be Upon Him) expires into the static drone of a megaphone buzzing in early morning. I listen attentively: I can hear the sensitive microphone pick up the Mullah touching his fingers to his tongue, turning pages.

Begum *jee's* voice returns, layering the Prophet's message. She is turning slowly as if sitting on a slow-moving luminous Frisbee thrown out from the wall.

The Farsi-influenced verses are like a cool rain on my hot-and-then-cold-then-hotter-again body. She is by my bedside. I wonder if my girlfriend back in Montréal has started her experiments in lesbian sex. I am trapped in a 747 that cannot land in the West, that cannot land in Pakistan.

With an incongruous movement, Begum Akhtar turns her back to her younger black-and-white double in the film. I feel sure that if she looks at her image she'll vanish — *poof*, just like that — so I keep trying to talk to her to prevent her from becoming an empty sari. She turns and blankly looks at me. Does she see or recognize her younger self, I wonder.

She comes near me, putting her bluish celluloid hand on my quilted thigh. The *rag* intensifies into a vortex of sound: the European-introduced harmonium, the older *tablas* and *sarangi*, a *tampura* vibrate with codas and smaller instrumental references to her rising and falling voice. Codas within codas pull her back into her flickering, scratchy black-and-white world.

She sings poems of broken friendships, shredded hearts, permanently parted ways. I see in her melodramatic renditions of verse EM Forster rejected by India and Dr. Aziz.

My malaria-or-something-like-it has no time to make the English writer a real entity in my returning-to-Pakistan psychosis except in one scene. He says goodbye to me at a Lahore train station; an epoch slowly puffs down the tracks: Amritsar to Lahore, and for another people, Lahore to Amritsar.

Begum *jee* comes out of the film again. Satyajit Ray's *Jalsaghar* freezes, just as my uncle used to freeze the brakes before take-off on the various transport planes he flew.

Ray's film flutters. A freckled white horse wheezing in pain as the Bengali crabs and a green high tide fill his panicking nostrils and lurching eyes.

Begum Akhtar is slowly turning towards the screen, but I manage to pull her into our conversation. I keep her talking. I don't want to suffer the effects of Pakistani antibiotics alone.

"Why do you sing Sufi music?"

She cannot say *zamine* but says *jamine*, the Urdu word for *ground.* She replies in Urdu with what I confuse for a Lucknowesque accent. She cannot make the Arabo-Farsi-influenced *z'ah* sound in Urdu.

"I don't sing Sufi music, Julian — that is your name, isn't it? You aren't Moslem, are you? You see, I don't sing music, the music sings me, the poets make me."

An expression that looks like it may become a laugh forms on her face. The next time she chuckles she'll vanish. Her teeth are red from the endless chewing of betel nuts in *pan* leaves.

"I sing love poems. It's not Sufi-shoofie music, you know." Her leg is warm and close to my hand. Now my body is suddenly cold, cold as the winters in Montréal, thousands of degrees below zero.

I ask, "Do you know the function of Fluconazole, Begum *jee?* Fluconazole, Begum *jee*, this is an anti-fungal drug with no side effects that my friend with AIDS is using.

"Begum *jee*," I say, "you see my friend is suffering from toxoplasmosis and is taking AZT and N-acetylcysteine, a hypo-aller-genic." Begum *jee* goes blank. She is still in British India, I am in the AIDS era.

Night. Rain falls in the military state. The temperature too is falling. Sure to be frost in the morning. The man from the UN with the bullshit theory about coriander and civility sections into the room like Muybridge's *Locomotion* photographs. Fades. My aunt, in a silk green nightgown, comes in to give me pills. She leaves.

"But, Begum *jee*, I thought you sang about directly communicating with God?"

She moves closer to me, pulls part of the chequered quilt over her knees.

She has on a polyester sari, not silk, not cotton; she smells like an airport lounge. The sari rustles in my hand. Formaldehyde breath. Her pupils are dark with thin crimson blood lines zig-zagging like railroad tracks on a map. She disappears from view as my sickness fades.

She is not the young Begum Akhtar that I remember from Ray's film. There are streaks of grey in her hair. Black dye has been used to give the impression that she is greying only at her temples. Fat chance.

"I can say that there are some singers who—" Her direction changes. "Julian, you're not Moslem, are you? I didn't think you were, Julian. *Sahib*, there are those who sing directly to communicate with God because they don't want to talk to representatives of God on earth. And where is God? Don't you trust the representatives?" Her head cranes round to look directly at me. "I sing about love, friendship." Her hand soothingly touches my chest. Her fingers are looking for my nipple. But this can't be true. She is a respected singer. Don't make her do this in your dream, I say to myself. Her hand moves against my body. She mixes up songs with which I am sort of familiar:

> I don't remember
> any Gods
> or any ghosts,
> my hands are joined in prayer.

> Was the news so bad
> that the rivers
> started to flow backwards?

> You be the flower,
> I'll be the gardener,
> I'll be the demented lover,
> you'll be the master,
> then I'll be master

then you'll become the flower,
I'll become the
unfortunate lover also.

Ray's film spins backwards. Sounds of conversations are just woops and waaaps. Cigarette smoke flows back into cigarettes which become unlit. Brown hands put them back into packs. The characters walk back through doors and knock on them. But no one smokes cigarettes in this film. The characters smoke *hookahs*, not Goldflakes, not the Goldflakes that Sa'adat Hassan Manto used to puff away on.

She sings a line: "How is one to hide the tears from one's eyes?" Her accompaniment comes to a halt. The musicians are obedient soldiers.

"All my songs are a farce; people who like my singing are donkeys, do you hear me? Donkeys." Her hands turn subcontinentally outwards from her breasts. "I don't know why they like my music. Sufism is about a straight line to God without the bearded ones. God matter to you?"

Her gritty chuckle grows louder, ends with her coughing and spitting red betel bits on the floor. As she moves back across the room to where her image flickers, her steps are studied, as though she were a member of the Paul Taylor Dance Company.

"Please don't leave me," I beg her.

On the wall, a thin black wind of coal starts writing verses from the Koran from the left to the right. It smells as though someone has just lit up a cigarette. I vomit. Homecoming.

"Please don't go, Mrs. Begum Akhtar. Mrs. Begum Akhtar, are you leaving because I am a Christian?" The pea-green puke runs down my front. "I know about your first name, your first name before you became Begum Akhtar — it was Akhtari Bai Faizabadi, wasn't it? Tell me, Begum *jee*? Ha! your name was Akhtari Bai

Faizabadi, wasn't it? And as soon as people started calling you 'Begum' your singing got worse – isn't it true? – and you started drinking – true, isn't it? You're nothing but a *mujra* singer – admit it, for Christ's sake. I'll sing Beatles songs for you. Please don't leave." I cannot control the dream – I dream I am splattering back brown watery wisdom to my exile gurus. I can't even insult her into giving a response.

All like a bad acid trip, I tell myself. Why am I here? General Zia is here. Pakistan is a military state. I am not used to a military state. Canada is a pleasant liberal democracy. In Lahore, people in prison, torture – the whole repressive apparatus I've read about. I am a Canadian. I am from Montréal. No, wait a minute. I am a British subject from Warlingham, Surrey. There are too many television sets in this house. I am not a Pakistani, maybe yes maybe no. So what? I've had Jewish girlfriends. I went to Saint Patrick's School in Karachi, where I was given a caning. There was a German kid in my class who never got this treatment. Who is this singer coming into my life?

I have run out of the antibiotics I brought from the West. I'm dependent on this fucking Third World country. I don't need Begum Akhtar, nor her red teeth. I have travellers' cheques. I scream after her: Listen, Mrs. Bobbies Achar, I have American Express Travellers' Cheques. I show her fading body all my American Express TCs. Fuck you, Mrs. Akhtar. "Molluscum contagiosum," I yell after her. The slave-labour historian pushed Begum Akhtar on me in the first month of my stay and now she's here in my malaria? The country tries to re-own me, but I can't stay. I must go back to where I am clearly a nonentity. There is no unemployment insurance in this country. The state of public medicine is a Thatcherite dream. Just down the street is the church I was baptized in. My grandfather never used to spit near it but he spat everywhere else. Lahore is filled with his asthmatic globs.

It's morning now. A woman servant comes into my room. Tea with ginger is supposed to work as an expectorant. There are red bits in my vomit. My aunt's Siamese cat crosses the floor. I sneeze. I want to reach down the cat's mouth and pull out its lungs. A door is opened. Sunlight in a trapezoidal shape crunches down on the grey tiled floor.

The servant leaves. The house is empty. Everyone's at work. This always happens when I visit my friends abroad – they are at work, I am in their house smoking cigarettes. It is eleven o'clock in the morning. I smell garlic frying in the far-off kitchen. Someone is revving up a 100 cc motorbike. The garlic smell mixes with motorbike exhaust.

I try to fall asleep. The servant has very nice eyes, her husband is working in the Gulf. The daughters are at school. Will she come in again?

The background drone of music pulls me down into an earthy feeling of dust, rustling bones, mud, blood mixing with wine, betrayed love, poison gas in villages, cloven hooves running across a dusty street in the rainy season. Begum Akhtar's teeth in EM Forster's throat, Dr. Aziz on the white horse of modernity lurching upwards.

Her words pull me skyward to my kite-filled childhood in this city. I get up yet another time and shit my guts out.

Some days later I am better. An oppressive stone lifts itself from my chest.

The sky is clear. A crescent moon over Nulakah Church. The cool night air revives me. I feel like Wallace Stevens in Havana, lots of travellers' cheques and all the time in the world.

I do get to meet Yasmin again. We go for a long drive along the canal, but we pass through the old city first. Her father is progressive, friendly, wears Nana Mouskouri glasses, and dresses in a serious

Moslem fashion. He gives her the car for our evening date.

As soon as we get off the driveway the cigarettes come out. She uses words like "fucking military bastards" to shock me, to prove that women in Pakistan can say what women in Montréal can say without any damage to their reputations, souls, and lives in the afterlife. Soon enough, though, her decorative curses fade. Her hand flicks on the right indicator, then the left indicator. Logical turns are made, or so they seem to me.

The Renault winds concentrically out of the old city, and the narrative of the malicious oppression of women begins as our evening together unfurls against the brightly lit Badshahi Mosque and the silent ancient canal water flowing to Mohen-jo Daro.

She tells me the story of a certain year during the dynasty of the Generals; a Mullah in a market slapped a women he did not know, merely because she was not wearing a *dupatta*. Many women organized a protest in the same market; they did not wear their *dupattas* over their heads.

Pakistan in the eighties is far from static. Despite all the sexual distraction Yasmin is offering, it is great to listen to her. Women in Islamic Pakistan have elaborate interpretive devices they manipulate. According to a group of activists, Yasmin says, "It is patriarchal feudalism and capitalism within a Koranic context that makes being a woman in Pakistan a crime."

The way the Women's Movement fights against the so-called Islamic Injunctions and Hudood Ordinances of 1979 is to quote the Koran back to the regime, offering more progressive and credible interpretations of the Holy Book to refute the reactionary ones. The rules are always stacked against women. If a woman is raped she has to produce four pious Moslems who actually saw the act of penetration. "Now what do you think of 'pious'?" Yasmin asks as we park in front of a roadside restaurant. "Julian, I suggest that you get a take-out order. I don't want to eat inside — not enough women in this place. I'd feel odd, they'll all look at me."

I go into the small restaurant to get kebabs. The menu says "Order by numbers." My eyes pan down the numbers until they reach "Political discussions and drinking strictly forbidden." At the bottom I read: "Rendezvous of the Elite." I mention all this to Yasmin.

"I can understand why all this is exciting for you," she says, lighting another cigarette.

"Is Benazir Bhutto going to do much?" I ask, munching down on a kebab.

She laughs. "Here, Julian, are her words: 'I would not like to be the person to come in the way of the enforcement of the *Shariat.*'"

Within feminist Lahore there are debates as to whether or not women ought to work within an Islamic context, whether one ought to go left in the Western Marxist sense of the word, or invent an applicable women's solidarity across classes. The in-fighting is the best I have ever seen. It seems so much more real than the in-fighting in Toronto and Montréal, where the repercussions are obviously not the same.

It is dramatic to watch the Western-educated ones get torn to shreds by the ones who were educated both by Western universities and the experience of the various military regimes that have plagued Pakistan since 1947. These women have a commitment to one day come back to Pakistan to change it into a nicer, freer, classless place. Their sense of counter-Islamic reinterpretation and manipulation is thrilling; it has so much hope attached to it.

We back out of the restaurant's mini-parking lot. My informative evening with Yasmin is coming to an end. Past the canal road, I roll down the window. She pulls out a hash joint. "Julian, you're in the land of plenty — have a puff. All the taxi drivers are totally stoned all the time, you know."

It has been a great evening. I feel very connected with her. I now have a comprehensive history of the women's movement inside me. She drops me off at my relatives'. There is some goodbye tension as I think about touching her hand, holding her waist, nibbling her Lahorie lips. But I can't take the risk. I shake her hand and hold on to it for slightly longer than is polite, by Western standards. She does not let go, either. I should make my move, but, no, I must protect my integrity as a man genuinely interested in women's struggle. Any miscalculation now could ruin the future possibility of a fuck.

Javid, who I've been asked to look up by some Montréal friends, comes by to visit me. We drink tea, Scotch is offered but refused — good boys don't believe in drinking and driving. We make a quick plan and announce that we are going to visit Heera Mundi, a red-light district in Lahore. Better to be direct about it. Dancing girls in silk. My distant aunt protests, "Don't you dare."

"But, Aunt *jee*, I must see every side of this city. I am just going as a Canadian sociologist — don't worry." I won't poke my sex-starved pole in anywhere. Anyway, Auntijee, the tragic condition of the prostitutes is enough to wilt anyone's dick.

His motorbike hums to life. We drive past the fruit and nut sellers with their gas lamps hissing away on this cool crisp night. The temperature is like that of a cool September night in Montréal. Past more street vendors who sell *guavas* and fresh fruit salad. Others fry chick peas in large pots. *Chapattis* flap on large black pans. Almost-teenagers wash pots under the hurricane lamps.

I tap Javid's shoulder. "I'd like some fruit salad."

"Weren't you just ill?" He replies without turning his head, keeping his eyes on the caravan of traffic: packed buses, hooting scooter taxis, smaller minibuses criss-crossing each other. He gives the throttle a crack, downshifts.

The motorbike comes to a smooth halt. He zaps the throttle

again just before he takes out the keys. When the fruit-salad maker is putting the spice mixture on my bowl, he says, "*Halka, halka*" — lightly, lightly. As custom has it, he refuses to let me pay.

We remount the water-cooled Honda 500 cc, threading through the ancient caravan. Somehow we have worked our way to an open space where there is less traffic. In front of us is a free lane of highway, a mile or so. Javid Cyprian, the Christian, accelerates to some truly unreasonable speed. The seat is slipping from under me but I manage to hang on.

At Heera Mundi we park the bike by the roadside and begin our short walk through the winding paths. The hookers are fully clad, making come-in gestures with their hands. Their pimps stand uninvitingly nearby. Distorted Urdu disco blares out of cassette players. The fruit salad is trying to find a quick way out.

Sa'adat Hassan Manto used to hang around Heera Mundi. Hookers, incense, music through fractured speakers. Maybe he even fucked some of the older hookers, but that's impossible. Manto's short stories are about resentment, passions that become foolish, manipulative religious fraud, murder, looting in the pre-Partition days, and one story about fucking the dead. In fact, a literal translation of "Thanda Gosth" could be "Cold Meat," about a beautiful woman who is raped when she is dead. He was sued by the Christian community in Lahore because he published a nasty story about them. He published many ironic stories about Moslems as well. He translated Oscar Wilde's "Vera" and Hugo's "The Last Days of a Condemned Man" into Urdu. He was influenced by Gorki, Chekhov, Pushkin, and Maupassant. Manto drank himself to death here in 1955.

My relative's house was not far from Temple Road, where I was born in a humble kitchen. In the two months I was in India and Pakistan my accent in English changed; I found myself straining not to lose the mixture of Canadian British and the precious though slight Urdu inflection. But I was losing; Pakistan was winning. I was starting and ending sentences with *yaar* and *jinnab*. The fruit salads were not presenting problems.

I returned to my original colour. The hints of bride-search got boring but not the idea of a few hot one-nighters. My relatives thought I was an accountant or a big filmmaker in Québec with a safe job at some complacent place like the National Film Board of Canada. I could afford to fly to Pakistan, so it was not wrong to think I was financially successful. I suppose life for well-off Pakistanis is black and white; there is an automatic assumption that those who followed the line of gold to the West have made it. As of 1 September 1995 I hadn't.

My comfortable relatives insisted rather strongly that I was in Lahore to discover my past. They had been conditioned by the TV program *Roots*. No Joycean epiphanies for me. It would be unfair to expect them to understand my struggle for a visionary post-coloniality imbricated with an avant-garde anti-Eurocentric projection in the overall rejection of traditional theories of perspectival representation.

How were they to know about my life? My friends there had ordered and exactingly framed lives, lots of parties, a little legal fraud here and there for a new car or a fridge. They were nice to their servants, who were well-paid and loved, and treated like they were "part of the family."

My relatives' servants have more job security than I do. I don't even have a job or a regular source of income, except for the provincial government's welfare cheque or arts grants. Their servants don't live in fear of being evicted from their simple houses in the back of the real house. I am always worried about what my landlord will do next.

My relatives sent their kids to arts schools. The only cultural queasiness they ever felt was that they were Christian in a Moslem state. Even though Zia had personally bid them all the best at Christmas, their daughters and sons were leaving Pakistan, just like my parents' generation.

The Zia regime had appointed some of them to high posts in the military, and these Christians stayed.

Some years later, Zia's body, along with those of a few American advisors, became air, smoke, and water by the simple act of fermenting mangos — that's my mother's explanation — "It was the crate of mangos that someone gave him in Quetta." General Zia was cross-eyed — a true descendant of the Prophet.

That day when I first got back to Lahore, when the taxi drove up to their house in that well-to-do neighbourhood...suddenly, as I was getting out of the taxi, something happened which still divinely confuses me. I excitedly thrust open the car door. There was a crack. A man riding a bicycle had slammed directly into the door's sharp corner. His cheaply printed-in-Lahore books strapped to the bike with a knotted old belt, his thick-framed glasses, went splat. He lay writhing in pain on the road. Luckily, this road was not busy, otherwise he would have been hit by several cars and lorries. Lahore streets are usually busy.

I rushed over to him.

"You have killed me, you have killed me."

I picked up his undamaged glasses, got him up to his feet, and walked him to the side of my relatives' house.

A woman servant came out to greet me. I told her what happened. She took him to the servants' quarters for a glass of ordinary tap water. He recovered like a stunned bird. I peeled off a few notes from my limited wad of rupees, paid the smiling cabby, and walked into the house. I had been in the motherland for exactly forty minutes.

CHAPTER SEVENTEEN

Hong Kong and the Boat People

PART ONE: Hong Kong, 1989

To the Editors:

I disagree with the letter headlined "Refugees can make useful contributions." The letter stated that in order to make the refugees behave better, we can train them so that they will not be idle, but I think their behaviour is not due to their idleness. The riots that have taken place are conflicts between people coming from different parts of Vietnam.

Furthermore, providing them with training will pose more financial and security problems for the government. However, I think the most important point to remember is that the Vietnamese come to Hong Kong because they want to go to Western countries, or to take some money back to Vietnam as a volunteer of the repatriation scheme, so I don't think they will work hard in Hong Kong even if they have been trained. As a matter of fact, interviews from the TV stations with the refugees who have worked for local factories show that they are not interested in working at all.

Furthermore, they complain that the wages are low and the lunch-boxes are not tasty, but they forget that they are just refugees.

It is a mistake for the writer to compare the Vietnamese with the Chinese refugees who came to Hong Kong in the

late forties and early fifties. For those Chinese refugees were
really political refugees who came here to earn their living.
They seldom caused any trouble and they were responsible
for the development of Hong Kong.

But the Vietnamese never do anything for Hong Kong.

Sincerely, Chung Chin-Wai, Mid-Levels

— Letter printed in *South China Morning Post,* 21 October,
1989

Penny, my lawyer friend, picks me up at the airport in Hong Kong.
She wears a dark blue raw silk blazer, shiny grey skirt to her knees,
and a sheen of lip gloss. She is beautiful, in her late twenties or early
thirties. Red sandals made out of wire-thin leather tied into swirly
knots. "Pleasant trip?"

"Really bad, and we had to stop in Bombay and I almost
accidentally drank the water." We filter our way through the crowd
at the airport and settle into a red air-conned taxi.

"I've been fine, though this year was difficult." I decide to hit
her with all the petty problems in my life within the first two minutes
of our encounter. "Well, an ex-girlfriend of mine is pregnant; she
and her boyfriend have broken up, she hasn't any job in sight, is
still on welfare, and I am not able to play surrogate father because
I need to find myself in London. Montréal is small and, you know,
one is still an outsider in little Montréal — no matter how long one
has been there."

I am astonished by Hong Kong's architecture, but I continue
my monologue: "And I have just finished a love-hate relationship
with someone who drank a lot, and my best friend has tested HIV
positive — his T4 cell count is lower than forty and he keeps talking

suicide, with a sense of humour. Apart from that, everything is fine."

The taxi driver, who speaks little English, guides the car past the Bank of China building, the tallest building in Southeast Asia. There is a constant hissing of the taxi's air conditioning. I see no smog. This is not Calcutta, nor is it Delhi. This is Milton Friedman's dream with bamboo scaffolding. Lots of badly compensated deaths on the job site.

The red taxi curves along Robinson Road, begins its slow climb up to the Middle Levels. "Penny, how's the job? What is intellectual property – is it as easy as proving that African nationalism was a series of Brechtian plays orchestrated from the Colonial Office in London?"

"Who is the one with AIDS?" she asks.

"I don't think you remember. It may not make a difference anyway." Her blazer rubs against her skirt, making a sound that means she is employed. "Yeah, he might have been around in those *McGill Daily* days when you were a member of the Conservative Party."

She interrupts, "But I was only a member for a few weeks, Julian."

"Yeah," I reply, "it looked like you were committed to Progressive Conservative forces within Canada – I mean, how else could we all have been invited to that luncheon for Peter Pocklington?" There she was, in the reception hall of a downtown hotel dressed in an outdated seventies near-hippy dress, unaware of class and race as concepts, let alone as instruments of oppression. A glass of wine tinkering in her hand.

Our taxi pushes up past the impressive corporate buildings. Her deep blue eyes point out all the architectonic constellations of beauty. "Here is the one an Aussie designed, and the press critics said that it even looked Australian because of the koala-bear-like structures up along its sides."

In relation to Hong Kong, the cities of the West look and feel as though they are in a state of decline. Montréal has more garbage on the streets than this place. Last year's trip to New York City also proved that; the city's government looks after its homeless like the Israelis look after the Palestinians — maybe not even as well.

I say, "London is closer to Calcutta than it is to Hong Kong."

"This is Caine Road, dear."

All my letters to her were delivered here. A name, her name among all the others. A number. Rude people. "Chinese shit-heads with cellular phones — how did these people do it?" I can't come to terms with the difference between India and this place. I try to use the old Marxist-history/mode-of-production arguments; those don't scare Penny any more.

"Calcutta will never catch up to this place. This place was never ravaged as much by the British Empire, I suppose — and there must be a huge injection of capital from somewhere. How could they have done all this?" She has no clear answers, just her income. I look at her lips moving and she is suddenly back in Montréal playing Franz Schubert's Three Piano Pieces, D. 946 No. 1 in E-Flat Minor. Her hands still look strong.

She seems good at concealing her tilt to the right, but there is nothing really right about her except her mode of money production — she loves art, books, visible minorities, animal rights, holidays in the Southern hemisphere, armed liberation movements, save-the-elephant-tusks clubs, kids — all the things that left-wing intellectuals like me like. And she loves me as a friend. One fall she even exchanged a painting I had done for a plane ticket to Hong Kong.

We arrive at her small apartment in the sky. Twenty-seven floors up. The kitchen is small. There is a round glass-topped table in the dining area. Her furniture is Chinese, bambooish with lots of plump cushions pinned in the middle. In the corner beside the CD player is an arrangement of wooden flowers in pastel colours. Across the room is a wall covered with a huge mirror.

I pull out the cheap duty-free from my small bag. She is very impressed with how lightly I travel. "Oh, you shouldn't have done that." I start signing travellers' cheques to pay for the pre-paid plane ticket in Hong Kong dollars. "Oh, don't worry about that now."

I ask, "You have a calculator?" We fill our glasses with ice and Scotch and head towards the stairs. "Awfully cramped, these steps."

"Yes, Julian, be careful. Don't sue me."

We surface on the rooftop patio – very spiritually uplifting. A panoramic view of Hong Kong harbour and Hong Kong. A city that has produced no serious filmmakers, one novelist who is a pissing bore, and no poets that I can think of right at the moment. By the end of the trip I am to be proven wrong on some of my initial observations. But I am not proven wrong in an impressive way, just perfunctorily; there are moneymakers here. She is one of them and consequently has scored the top floor of this apartment in the Mid-Levels in a mainly Chinese building. Some of her neighbours don't like her and express it by writing graffiti in Chinese near the elevator door: "The people in Apartment 34 are pigs, or nerds," a friend translates.

From this height and distance, the harbour looks silent. White trails of slow boats and jet boats shooting into Macau's various Portuguese holes of entry, fertilizing it. Soon, I shall be out there in the harbour itself when my stay in Hong Kong comes to an end. She will have used her connections in the most important law firm in the world to get us a visit to the USS Enterprise, killer of Libyans. The trip to this aircraft carrier made me a campus radical for a day, filled with quiet anger. The ship has many polite queens who work in the souvenir shop. They meticulously fold souvenir T-shirts and are nicer than the marines on board.

We sit around the picnic table on the roof. The sun is setting. I have not seen her in a few years. So I must not sound too unfamiliar, otherwise we won't hit it off and I'll feel like a guest and not part of the family. "Why is your boyfriend moving out?"

"It's all taking different directions; he is into his human rights thing and I am taking this very markedly different direction, as you can see. You know how these things have a terminal cancer in them — think of it this way."

I say I understand. "When a relationship is in a blissful state, think of this period as incubation for the stresses and strains, mini-wars of jealousy, quarrels over intellectual and emotional territorial possessions — for that new state of war."

Her legs are as tanned as they ever get. Her feet are white like Canadian snow. There is a shine on her nails. She exudes a wonderful friendliness.

She used to work in a Canadian city as a human rights lawyer, but couldn't resist going for an interview for this current job rather outside the field of human rights work. The company based in Washington is innovative in the way they interview potential employees. She told me that after she had been checked out on the bare bones of the workings of a law firm, the remaining interview was conducted the following day by someone else, in a slow walk in front of the Vietnam Memorial in DC, cherry blossom season.

The boss, veiled as casual friend, asks her what she had thought about the war in Vietnam.

"I was young," he says. "I mean I was younger. I remember resenting the American involvement." The general tone is set. The lawyer with all the international experience guides the conversation but leaves enough space around things. He has on a medium-priced Rolex. And instead of having the company driver drop them at this place, they use the DC Metro which has no stops in the Black parts of town. He continues, "Yeah, some of my friends were actively involved in protesting against this war."

Penny is still not thrown off course, but she is taken aback. This is supposed to be an interview for a job in Hong Kong? But there is nothing to be surprised about. The discussion is a way for him to understand the workings of her mind, how it actually negotiates, questions, and balances power. It is a way to examine how her mind weaves through what is acceptable to say and what requires a certain occulting, a reformulation. One's mind can only go so far with the moral arguments connected with refugee and immigration legal battles. And, she says, "this was definitely not an interview about my tits."

The conversation is friendly, as though they were long-lost friends. He guides her deeper into the memorial; the list of names grows taller and taller. He is very tall, a Florida tan. Penny loafers with pretty new pennies in the slits. "Oh yes, these are Canadian centennial pennies." Occasionally they see a parent of one of the names touching the wall and crying.

"I am sure," Penny says in a hushed tone, "that this war did not improve life for anyone – the Christmas bombing – awful – and what was wrong with self-determination for the Vietnamese? These Americans can't see very far, and besides–" she uses the short form for North Vietnamese Army in case he has any doubts about her having studied the period " – the NVA was a better educated army." The international lawyer is impressed. The sobbing parents caress the black marble and move on.

There is a disturbing mischief to the collection of death. The names are cut in triangular striations into the stone that taxpayers have paid for. "Were your older brothers or sisters engaged in any kind of opposition like I was?" Penny glances at the long lists of names; her hand reaches out to touch the products of the great fraud but pulls back into her navy blue cotton power suit. Past resentments lead to yuppie heaven. He sees the respect she has for human life. "My brother is younger than I am, so he was not as aware of the war as I was, and still he does not question American involvement as much as I do and did." Her first responses are on course.

Her beautiful frankness got her the job. She left for Hong Kong at the tail end of the eighties.

"Finished your drink?" I go down to the fluorescent kitchen to bring up more scotch. Night has fallen.

Texans come to see and ask her to set up fast-food joints all over the south of Asia and she does it; from fixing the locations of the electric plugs to appointing the managers. The Japanese let her bosses in Hong Kong know that they wouldn't like the concept of having a woman at the helm leaving a trail of cherry blossoms. This progressive intellectual property company says: Look you Japanese fellows, fat Texans, go fuck yourselves. This is our woman: don't like her, then piss off. However, this Christmas she told me that the Japanese are winning; she is being kept off their cases. The East rises. Will blue-eyed Penny sink to Europe in 1997?

It is a sunny day. Clouds are reflected in the names dug into the black marble. Crying parents.

Vietnam found it very difficult to get imperial loans from the International Monetary Fund and the World Bank. Reconstruction loans were impossible. Decades of napalmed forests; leaves scared and reluctant to grow. Leaves ground in black marble grindstones until they are a green pus. The American names can be scooped out from the deep creases and laid out on the grass to dry.

In my many trips to DC to do research and visit friends, I have seen mothers and fathers touching the monument and maybe remembering the Tet Offensive, Operation Rolling Thunder: the heady Nixon days of peace. The carpet bombing in Hai Phong, William Casey's beloved Phoenix Program which eliminated many innocent Vietnamese. Casey was tried in *absentia* in a Vietnam war crimes tribunal and found guilty. Agents were sent, to no avail, to drag him back to Vietnam à la Eichmann.

Looking at the memorial makes me think of the People's Army knocking gum-chewing Yankees out of helicopter gunships. Small American fighter planes being shot down by thin, elegant eighteen-year-olds in the NVA; operating anti-aircraft guns during the siren warnings, planting rice and dismissing and/or loving Camus during the lulls. In my trips to DC I would find it so uplifting to see these names in this state of grace. Perhaps it is unfair to say these fuckers got what was coming to them. My friends are not with me on this. They say it was a manipulation by the American ruling class — gas-station attendants one generation, White House illiterates the next. Yeah, so what?

As a teenager, I had just moved to the States with my family. We were living in Pittsburgh then. The immigration officers asked my brother and me to register for the draft. I was not going to fight in this war or any war on the side of the Americans. I left the States to live in Toronto. As one rounds out of this little piece of outdoor marble theatre, one faces the Washington Monument, symbol of indecency rising high in the sky.

Penny walked that day into the deepening list of names. I ask, "Did he ask you about the Christmas Bombing — more bombs dropped there on Vietnam than in all of WW II? Did he question you about what you thought of Kissinger getting the Nobel Peace Prize? About how the Vietnamese negotiator, Le Duc Thu, from the Paris Peace Agreements, did not accept the Nobel Peace Prize?"

The Vietnam Memorial looks black and orange as the sun tilts into the innocent afternoon. There is a lovely smell of cherry blossoms. The interview for her Hong Kong job was rather long. It was all worth it; from the hard, mannish-looking woman who tested her letter-writing skills to that dreamy and easy-to-navigate interview in front of the elegant morgue: fifty thousand Americans, two million Vietnamese. The figures may be inaccurate.

"Your father being Trade Commissioner to the Palestinians might have given you confidence to handle that kingpin in front of the black slab of shit. With all those names looming down on you, your upper-class manners were crucial."

"True. Enormously true," she says.

It is my second week in Hong Kong. Penny just got a raise. A mere $20,000 US or so. She has stopped in on the way home at Land Mark, a Hong Kong store for the well-off. She has blown $800 US on a brightly coloured shirt, a blazer top, and a loose swishy skirt. I offer to marry her. "It isn't for the money, Penny."

I will return to my dull life as grant seeker in the second largest bilingual place in the world. "Penny," I say, "we have fucking Bill 101. And you, Penny, what do you have? You have the excitement of 1997? This new skirt? A job? All these intelligent Asians to de-Europeanize you. This wriggling young body. This ability to destroy the negative stereotypes women have suffered in patriarchal history. This UNHCR boyfriend to poke your morals."

She mimics my roll by operatically stretching out her arms and saying, "Penny, you got everything. Don't ever come back to Canada. At least under Hong Kongese rule, and under soon-to-follow subsequent Chinese domination, you'll still be able to make money."

Another evening. Our drinks thin out. It's just Penny and me. Night settles into Hong Kong's twiggy apartment construction. The sound of construction never stops. Jackhammers forcing metre-thick foundation bolts into the island.

Apartment windows emit light sometimes yellow and sometimes fluorescent blue. I say, "It is like a Mondrian painting, perhaps 'Broadway Boogie Woogie nineteen-forty-something.'" We hear the cracking of a game the Chinese play: *Mah-jong*. Snap snap. Surplus value. Snap. 747s made of shiny bamboo skin; fuselage hulls tapered to a needlepoint, splitting air. However, no toilet paper in the washrooms at eight thousand metres. Bamboo toilet seats, bamboo mirrors. Jet-needles of water to clean your dirt chute. Fat American tourists get used to it; it is Eastern jet technology pumping rose-scented water into the rectums of the West. Just compensation for everything, including the opium.

I leave with her in the direction of downtown. We stand smiling at each other in the aluminum elevator. She uses her fast-fading French with me as floors are lit up: 26, 25, 24, 23, 22. The doorman is, she tells me, a racist. Penny's blue eyes get the cold shoulder more often than my Pakistani features.

We hit the ground floor. The door slides to the right. There he is with his frozen shoulder. "Hello," I say rather loudly in the direction of the racist. I will not be ignored. He greets me with a wide smile. Penny cringes.

A warm winter night. Caine Road. Just below her apartment are Third Worldy fruit and vegetable stalls. Flipping fish. Handcuffed frogs. Jittery quails in baskets that look like large flattened oranges. A pen knife slits them open. A hand puts them in a plastic bag. Outdoor restaurants with a few polite hungry dogs with square faces. They never get too near the tables.

"What's that chanting, Penny?" Around the corner we see brown-robed monks – sounds like a rehearsal for a film – *Indiana Jones in Hong Kong, Part 5.* A sliver of a view between the buildings reveals the Hong Kong and Shanghai Bank. We descend one of these twisting rising and falling roads onto Hollywood Road. The narrow sidewalks are terraced above some of the roads. Cars whisk by. Antique shop after antique shop. Paintings on rice paper. Culturally rich, consequently boring, very expensive, consequently culturally rich. A small herd of miniature jade elephants crawls in and out of the arsehole of a sixteenth-century wooden lion. Our pleasant walk takes us to Sri Lanka. Lions roaring endlessly into Milton Friedman's necromantic night.

"Julian, they do an okay buffet here." Some perfumey Chinese beer arrives. John, the refugee-camp boyfriend, is due, joining us after a week in Hanoi. Penny is excited; she whispers, "Julian, I think he is fucking someone else."

Moments later John arrives.

"So how do you like it here?" I ask.

"I love it here."

"John, you followed Penny here, didn't you?"

"Yes, as a matter of fact I did."

"What would you like to drink?"

"Same as you, buddy — fuckin' Molson's, eh?"

"How did you get the job?"

"She told me about an opening." His hand reaches for her. "Hi, sweetie."

"Oh, so you used her again."

"Again and again," he says.

"And now, little hick is no longer a little Canadian of simple working-class origins. Tell me again how you jumped out of your class? McGill your ticket to freedom?"

"Yeah, that and all that Penny did for me. You know, she took me to New York — first time I saw a subway with so many lines. I suppose I am more international because of her. I owe it all to her."

I ask, "John, you had ice-cream before?"

"It's all right, John, you don't have to thank me — he's just playing with you."

I say, "She tells me that you were frightened when she first took you to New York."

John is a nice Canadian. Hockey. Beers. No sodomy.

A Christian relativity to anilingus.

"Yeah, I owe her everything – including a friendship with you. My very white Pakistani friend."

Penny, in mock-maternal mode, says, "Have something to eat, love?"

I keep up the polite chatter. "So, what is it that you do? I am so interested by what Penny tells me."

"I'm working at the Vietnamese refugee camps – refugee determination." There is humility in his voice. Canadian humility.

He returns to the table with his plate loaded.

"Eat much, John?"

"I listen to the boat people and then decide if I am going to defend them. Would you like to visit the camps? The Hong Kong police determine their status first. Then we try to form a UNHCR perspective."

He continues, "To alter the original decision in an effort usually to bring justice to the situation, which means opposing the Hong Kong fuckers."

"Humanitarian," I say.

"Does this mean that you are reading a lot of history about this conflict?"

"Yeah, loads – especially the history books with lots of pictures."

Penny makes $260,000 US in one year and is investing in a local stock exchange. She gets the company junk when international guests come to visit. We all went swimming in the South China Sea because of her. We made friends with the boat's captain. I am told that all international guests do. Nice Chinese guy with no shoes. He is friendly. John makes about $45,000 US working for the UN as a refugee lawyer, and the only boat ride he gets is in the morning, on the way to Lantau Island, the refugee camp.

John puts down his beer. "Today we had to listen to the case of a major in the South Vietnamese army, and he was claiming that he would face certain execution if he were repatriated."

"And you have decided to help him?"

"Yes, he is here claiming refugee status."

"But don't you think that he's a kind of war criminal? I mean, he did have connections with the French and then afterwards with the Americans."

All of a sudden I think of fucking his girlfriend. Maybe like this. No, maybe like that, and with her nails in my tits. She moves in her chair. A concerned girlfriend. This is her major boyfriend number 3.

I continue: "Do you know what that major might have done? He could have been part of a nasty chain of events. How do you know he was not in charge of interrogation? How do you know this South Vietnamese soldier was not deeply connected with the actual torture of 'communist sympathizers.' How do you know he didn't pull out fingernails?"

"Look, I'm just a UN lawyer," he says slowly.

"No. Asshole. You are part of a process of saving an Eichmann type."

Penny is happy to see us exchanging ideas in this way. The process internationalizes her boyfriend and makes him more presentable to her colleagues at the firm. She orders more beer. The waitress in Jackson Pollockesque South Indian sari with invisible feet trolleys over and sets the beer on the table.

Penny has blue eyes. Thin lips. Blond hair. *Vogue* ideology beauty, but in radical contestatory relationship to it, because she is eight kilos "overweight." She was a McGill feminist. She was almost a McGill lesbian. I think she once had carnal thoughts about me. If she had lived during World War II she might have done something brave, and would not have been thrown back into a kitchen afterwards. God only knows what she would have done after World War II. She may have become the successful daughter of a greengrocer, like Margaret Thatcher.

"The major might end up joining the KKK if the Americans let him in, or better still, and this is more like it, keep low and make a lot of bucks with a restaurant chain."

"You minorities so easily slip into racism."

"Sorry," I say.

"The UNHCR keeps its hands clean. They try not to get involved in the repatriation shit. That would make them look totally bad. The UN wants voluntary return, i.e., those that lose their appeals ought to go back to where they came from.

"The UN is facing a hostile Hong Kong government. The UN did not have any input into designing Hong Kong policy. The UN is a fucking joke. The UN is filled with well-dressed men – well-groomed, well-mannered men with degrees. This refugee problem was caused by the UN ten years ago. In June of 1988, the Hong Kong government was accepting everyone. The 16th of June was the cut-off date. Fuck all the others who were fleeing Vietnam. These poor fucks had to go through to a refugee determination procedure – you know, a screening. The UN sleazes were acting as if there were not going to be a refugee problem – American pressure."

John continues, "But I am not here to moralize. That is for freelance intellectuals like you who travel around the world making films. I am just here to save lives."

CHAPTER EIGHTEEN

Indonesian Restaurant

Montréal, 1985

Our summer is young. End of May, perhaps even June. The humid hot days of thirty degrees for weeks on end are to come. I have yet to go to a conference in the then West Germany to present "Rushdie in the Age of Reason," a paper on Salman Rushdie's rescripting of the life of the Prophet. I am to be crucified by British Black intellectuals at this conference: "But how can you imply that he is a racist? Look at his anti-imperialist positions on Channel Four."

"Was the great Gandhi not a little anti-Black in his South African phase? Was he not an 'anti-imperialist' at the same time also?" I answered. I remind the Black British intellectuals that Rushdie makes fun of grassroots Black activists, but they ignore me and prove beyond a shadow of a doubt that I'm the most simplistic person alive.

"The industrial revolution in the West could not have happened without cotton from India," I say.

"Serfs hitchhiking rides in historical Volvos?" Michael interrupts.

I continue, "Displacing the growing of food...generations have paid in various sicknesses and other conditions brought about by malnutrition."

"For what?" Ian asks.

"Well, for a nice Occident, silly," Michael says gleefully.

The waitress brings more food. She appears like a cross between Mary Magdalene and Indira Gandhi, in boulevard Saint Laurent black, red lips parted, black stockings, black shoes, tiny bows, tightly drawn, regal, Harvard in September. The darkness at the back of the restaurant swallows her again. Seconds later, the kitchen gushes her out into the sunlight as though she were adrift on a skateboard: "*Autre chose?*"

"I am thinking of giving our dyke friend a positive role in my book so our other dyke friends will not get pissed. I will call this section 'How to make love to a stereotype without being called a feminist: Eyeless in Gaza, at the mill with AIDS.'"

"Yeah, okay, that's a great idea," Michael says nostalgically. "I remember when it was okay to taste sperm. Now, dicks are like poison darts."

Utterly out of the immediate context, but truly within the larger realm of things, I mention a cultural studies professor whom we all knew; he has just come back from India and Pakistan, where he was doing what's called "work" on "political" literature: women's health plays, environmental films on Bhopal, industrial pollution, films on Indira's emergency, and the Naxalites movement – a revolutionary movement in India. He was going to expose the horror of it all to students back here in Montréal. It would make for a cosy, concerned class. The Canadian connection was going to be kept at a very safe distance. The capital generated by the papers he would publish on marginal Pakistani cinema would be great and it would help the universe expand. Departmental slaps on the back. Intertextuality. Piracies of perspective. Subsequent papers at hot-shot conferences in the Southern American states, blow-jobs of admiration. Respect in the form of international solidarity. Perhaps some respect from most

second-generation Third World students here, excepting of course
the ones who might see through it. Lots of those around. He has
enough money in the bank to have winter holidays. Enough money
to buy vintage LPs of Cliff Richards singing "We're going on a
summer holiday."

Michael looks upward to take the kink out of his neck. Smoking,
Michael is always smoking. We become silent again. The arguments
have puttered out. He crushes the ciggy in the full ashtray, toys with
the pack like he used to years ago. His lips compose words; he is
about to say something, or to say nothing, or to eat something more
even though lunch is over and the plates have all been taken away.
Ian will be returning to Ottawa some time tomorrow.

Michael's hands join as though in prayer. His white fingers
spread; left-hand fingernails encroach into the fingernails of his right
hand. He ends the lunch with, "What argument? What relations?
If you are claiming that our marginal existence is accepted here,
straight Pakis and dying fags...because liberalism is linked to the
great imperial ravage. No problem accepting whatever the fuck you
want to call it — a theory — whatever the fuck. However, I am not
sure if Ian is accustomed to these trajectories, though I'm sure that
he does have an understanding of unforgettable evenings in the
parks."

My friends were testing HIV positive. Deadly good time we were
all having. Inexorable Anglo-Saxon recession. No university jobs.
Authoritarian feminists who were no longer exciting to listen to. We
knew their fucking scripts by heart.

In Marx's time cotton fuelled the Industrial Revolution. There
is another material fuelling the West these days. Boring intellectuals
with big ears and dicks hungry for dark erotic holes — cultural
studies Marco Polos. Canada's thinkers, concerned intellectuals
who take Indian "political" culture and convert it into CV points.

Visionless, inane, careerist postmodern prattle.

My friends pick up the tab for the Indonesian lunch. Najama Akhtar is playing on the sound system as we leave.

5 September 1993, 12:15

Years have gone by. Michael is bedridden in a hospital on a hill somewhere where the #144 bus passes Pierre Elliott Trudeau's house on avenue des Pines. Transparent tubes of this and that with this and that amount of potassium, etc., regulated by an occasionally functional computer flow into Michael's skeletal body. He is reluctant to eat. His parents have come to visit him. I sit beside him and beside a box of ridiculously optimistic chocolates. His mom has gone for a stroll down the fifteenth-floor hall to leave us alone for a few minutes. Old friends. A stunning bilingual-biracial Haitian nurse with blue eyes comes to fiddle with the beeping computer which regulates the flow of solutions into Michael.

I try to strike up a conversation with her. She smiles and, when she has finished resetting all the beeping buttons, leaves. I hope she'll return. Perhaps I can get her phone number. Oxygen mask mists up near Michael's face. Dried-up egg sandwich behind plastic in front of him. Shit-and-piss smell.

"Are you happy your mother's here?"

He looks directly into my eye with his one functioning eye. He has lost vision in the right eye because he is dying. I admire his sense of humour. Cotton patch over his eye. Kleenex over his mouth. With just one eye and oxygen vapour misting out into the room he makes me crack up just by looking at me. He groans in pain and mutters slowly, "Sort of happy to see her." A phlegmatic milky cream clogs his mouth, his breathing, his eating. He stops trying to talk. One Kleenex after another: a hand slowly lifts up to his mouth, and then down again to the side of the bed, then again, then again.

"Please open the window." A cool September wind seeps in and he asks me to cover him with a blanket. I cover him, nestling the hospital blanket under his Somalian hips. I cover my friend, white and skinny and now it's only a matter of weeks. The thin blanket ruffles as his leg slowly moves. He is a little cross with me for missing our last scheduled visit.

"I'm sorry," I say.

Lungs sloshing full with a slow pus which will not leave, will not leave my friend. The TV mounted on a metal arm crackles in the background. Our new less-than-average-IQ prime minister, Kim Campbell, is busy campaigning; according to reporters she does her own shopping and knows the price of a litre of milk in several provinces. A self-righteous CBC reporter is doing a holier-than-thou critique of her for buying helicopter gunships while kids in Montréal go to school hungry.

16 September, 11:35

The elevator looms up to the fifteenth floor. He's asleep. The oxygen mask hisses innocently around his mouth. His mother slowly walks in behind the curtained-off room which he is sharing with one other patient. Michael inches out of the druggy sleep. His body is nearly all paralysed on the right side. A tube juts from his stomach. Hospital food, like it or not. I touch his long fingers. I stay for three minutes and leave. He may come home to die; the doctor has given him the pills to do so. He can't die using the pills at the hospital because of legal complications. Ian, whom he was living with again, tells me he'll be home soon. I think about our dinners, drinks, walks at night in Parc Jeanne Mance, his anger, his poverty. He says, "I don't like to be left alone." His mother is almost living at the hospital.

28 September

Michael has moved back home – into Ian's apartment on Saint Hubert near Sainte Catherine. Bedridden. A hospital bed with wheels dominates the living room. The neighbourhood is just south of where we used to play. A few safe-sex hookers wander around, and there are used condoms in the parking lot across the street from Ian's large light-filled pad. Leaves of droopy trees flutter in the wind. Michael's father has arrived.

30 September

Right side total paralysis. Blind in both eyes. Morphine makes him giggle from time to time. Sleep frequently overtakes him. I stay for a few minutes and politely say bye to his parents. Green door. Silent brass key on the inside of the double safety lock.

2 October

I dream that I've come to visit Michael in his borrowed hospital bed with large wheels. But the bed is empty. No one is home. Ian's bed is not in Michael's room. They had separate bedrooms this time round. A slight breeze visits the apartment. It thrills through some sheets left bunched-up in a corner. I leave. Green door – oil paint. Key in the inside. I take it out and try to lock the door behind me. The key gently breaks, one half in the door, the other in my hand. I throw my half inside. I wake the Coptic Egyptian woman I'm sleeping with. She expresses an interest in my dream. Polite. Middle of the night. The same thing is happening in her life, friends with cancer, AIDS, incurable headaches. "*La mort est partout,*" she says sleepily. I prattle on about our winter trip to Cairo, where I will be doing research for my next documentary on the rise of religious fundamentalism and architectural space. "Do you know about the caliph Omar? How did Ibn Toulin die?" I ask.

"*Laisse-moi dormir.*" She fades, pulling the sheets tightly around her. Classical Egyptian preparation for life in the world after death.

CHAPTER NINETEEN

Hong Kong and the Boat People

PART TWO: Hong Kong, 1989

On the boat to Lantau Island, John, the UNHCR lawyer, shows me the places where the HK Immigration Department burns the Vietnamese boat people's boats. Even from this distance I can see scorched, gutted, cindered holes in their hulls. Courageous HK police boats slip back to central command.

The boat glides up to the small island's harbour. The road to the camp is steep, surrounded by trees with long narrow leaves. The sailors unload potatoes, rice, and various very green vegetables.

An eight-metre-high fence outside the compound. Two fences in some parts of the camp, the innermost topped with a forest of razor wire. There are children in multicoloured clothing running about freely. Everyone has flip-flops on. *Slip slap*. John gives me a tour of the city-state. Young Vietnamese approach us smiling.

Young women and girls giggle. "Is it my beard?" I ask. Maybe they will give my life meaning by taking me hostage. Maybe they will give my life meaning by taking the UNHCR fucker hostage. We walk to the sleeping areas. Box-like corrugated buildings about ten metres high and about thirty-five metres long. The bunk-bed structure runs three high and stinks. Cages.

"Nice place to review your sense of history, eh?"

"Was it an invasion from the north? What the fuck are these people doing here living like this, tell me, *Montréal socialiste*?"

I say, "I don't care what the fuck you show me. This is the fault of the Americans. The country was screwed after liberation. What'd you expect — cherry blossoms?"

"Whose liberation? Fuck the theoreticals. This is the fruits of socialism. What political artists are fighting for. This is the NVA. This is Ho. This is Vietnam. This is General Giap. Cut the revolutionary romance," John says.

I see a box of American detergent. Fights break out frequently. Tempers heated to fever pitch, ground to a full hate by black marble. The electric power was cut off recently because some men in the camps tried to use it for light and to heat water. Accidentally, someone was turned blue by electrocution.

"Julian, why do you think the world is full of socialist angels? I thought you'd lived in England. Welcome to what those hours of street demonstrations amounted to...all those hours of admiring Angela Davis and her leadership."

"You're wrong. There was nothing wrong with watching all those protests on TV." I am thirty-eight. The UN lawyer is twenty-nine. Back then we both would have been too young really to do much. Besides, we were more or less in Canada. Land of peace.

Some women are working in the sun-filled camp, scraping up scraps of filth and burning small fires. I hear birds. There is an acrid smell of antiseptic mixed with rotting rubbish. Birdsong scales rise and fall. I pass my hand over my passport pocket, the scale changes: another bird has taken the lead.

I say, "I want to have supper in a really expensive restaurant tonight."

INTERVIEW WITH REFUGEE IN CAMP CHIMAWAN, LANTAU ISLAND, OCTOBER, 1989

UN LAWYER (to refugee, via translator)
"Tell him I am here to help him and that I will listen to his story in full."

The refugee, a man in his mid- to late-twenties, nods. His eyes are directed onto a single area of the table. As he answers, his eyes territorialize the edge of a pen. He is small. The legal game is large.

UN LAWYER
"Does he want to make any changes to his statement?"

The question shuttles from English into Vietnamese. After a few seconds it becomes a response on the man's red face.
"No, not really" trips back to us in English.

UN LAWYER
"Tell him I want to ask him some things about his statements."

Various factual questions and answers are made through the tireless translator. He is from Vietnam, and does not pad the answers. He is wearing expensive glasses.

UN LAWYER
"When he was fishing did the Vietnamese government let him have a licence?"

The English becomes other sounds in the translator's mouth. The camp man's face shows something. The other noises become English.

REFUGEE CLAIMANT

"No."

UN LAWYER

"Did he have a *Hau Khau* – a household registration book?"

REFUGEE CLAIMANT

"No, they did not let me have one because my father used to dust the desk of a French officer. I was punished for what my father did. I was being punished for this."

The lawyer thinks this is good, and can be used.

UN LAWYER

"Did his father have anything militarily to do with the French?"

REFUGEE CLAIMANT

"No."

UN LAWYER

"Were you allowed to go to school?"

REFUGEE CLAIMANT

"No. I was not allowed to go to school."

UN LAWYER

"But you said before that your sister was allowed to go to school?"

REFUGEE CLAIMANT

"Yes. But she was only allowed to go after all the others had finished their classes."

UN LAWYER

"Did your sister study the same subjects that other students were taught?"

REFUGEE CLAIMANT

"No. They taught her different subjects."

UN LAWYER

"Getting back to your job...did your fishing boat have a motor?"

REFUGEE CLAIMANT

"Yes."

UN LAWYER

"Did you need to have a licence for the motor?"

REFUGEE CLAIMANT

"No. I had the motor without obeying the law."

UN LAWYER

"I wonder what he is getting at. Did you try to organize a group of people to make the voyage to Hong Kong?"

REFUGEE CLAIMANT

"Yes."

Coffee break. A thin woman in her twenties approaches us and, through the translator, is told that her case is going well and that she might get status. Her face forms hope. She is young, like the women in that *Time Magazine* photograph. Nude, running. An air strike by some heroes. Maybe My Lai. There is a socialist lump in my throat. My eyes track the wire walls. Spring in DC.

She asks, "When?"

John pushes the idea of hope without precision. No dates: the objective of professional philanthropy.

"Why no date? Tell her the date. Tell her," I say.

"Nothing is fixed yet."

The journey from Vietnam to Hong Kong by boat takes two to four months. Many perish en route. There are many cases of piracy. Women have been pulled on board, raped, and thrown overboard.

Another UN volunteer fieldworker with heavy-duty Doc Martens and black shorts shows me photos of a refugee camp birthday party. She is glowing with nice feelings for the refugees, and for the enormous good she is doing. She likes one refugee in one particular photo. I assume the obvious. Australian sex heat.

At the camp we have a lunch of sticky rice and a few bits of meat. It is hard to imagine a constant diet of this kind of food, days into weeks into months into years, and then perhaps forced repatriation.

That night after the refugee camp visit we eat in an expensive restaurant. Hundreds of HK dollars.

We return home to the Mid-Levels area of Hong Kong. There is a refreshing shower of rain. Penny's legs are wet. The automatic banks are covered in sheets of water, Asians standing outside to get the bucks. Minimum withdrawal: $100 HK.

Another evening. Tones of the musical scale. This is the doorbell. We are having a party before I leave Hong Kong. We are having a party at Penny's place. My friend's apartment on the twenty-seventh floor, $2,500 US a month. I just got off welfare. I wonder in very simple terms why we are still friends. We are still friends because we love one another. I got a mini-research grant to pay for this trip. We're having a soirée. I am her friend. Shared views on many things; our modes of production are different.

The party is in my honour. These people all have jobs. I am a drifter — grants, and when I am lucky, part-time teaching. The guests are professional philanthropists — the UN lawyers and fieldworkers — about ten of them — and about an equal number of people from Penny's company. A professional asks, "How are you enjoying your stay here in Hong Kong?"

"Our trip to the night market was great. Opera on one side, fortune-telling birds and cats on the other. These birds have a greater predictive quality than Mrs. Gandhi's astrologers."

A philanthropist with Penny's firm asks, "Birds?" These professionals don't know about the birds because they never check out this part of Hong Kong; like the Wasp literature teachers at the university. No real attachment to Hong Kong — just the job of implanting English culture.

"Yeah, birds. During the night oldish men bring out their small wooden cages that look like these apartment buildings. The particular evening we went, there was a slight wind so I am not sure if the birds were on or not. Night wind has an effect on their skills." Dust ethereally picking up bits of garbage. Birds with red beaks, learned minds. "The man holds out a fan of cards. The birds are trained to pick out your future. They dart back into the cage, meditate upon the span of cards, and dart out again."

I can count at least a dozen small, tight twitchy birds directing the lives of the old men. The UN philanthropist likes my story.

On the other side of the birds are the Chinese operas which take place in tents merged close together. The performances are loud enough to hear if one stands directly in front of them, while soft enough not to interfere with other operas to either side. Very respectful.

On a nearby street we see large live civet cats in cages. In front of the cages are large boiling pots of water. We care too much for the nervous cats to place our orders. Also, this is the season for snake soup.

Tonal music — that doorbell again. I tinkle down the rooftop steps to receive a friend from my Montréal days. I have already had a few drinks with him. He is a UN son. Privileged from the cradle to the UN. His father left the foreign service when the army started firing on textile workers. High deeds. Instant international cred. Moral high-standing because of class. Poor people never get this chance.

In Montréal he used to keep busy fooling women with his androgyny act, sticking his cock in whenever it got hard. We used to call him PIA-discobunny. He is now a rising star within the UN. In his Dad's footsteps. He was, I was told, responsible for saving hundreds of lives in Ethiopia. He had wells dug, hospital tents set up, wheat flown in. He had a very large rose garden in the Addis.

In Hong Kong he was to negotiate a settlement between rioters in the camps and the cops who had helicopters flown over barbed fences. There were a few gunboats. He was to deliver his compromises from the dock. He was to go no further than the landing dock because they might take him hostage. He had changed. Disco-UN-Iqbal standing at the dock's edge stopping a riot in the camps. Handmade shirt puffing in the South Asian wind. Saving souls in Ethiopia. Saving souls in Hong Kong. He had come such a long way since our university days.

He is friendly and continues our conversation as though we never really stopped having that drink at his apartment. "Listen, I've been thinking about why you're having difficulty getting funding for your radical films: it's because you are too radical."

"And you are so slick, I suppose?"

"Don't get upset, Julian. I am just trying to help you with

suggestions on how you can face-lift your political approach, that's all. I mean, you're a non-white and non-whites are *in* these days. That's Toronto. It is all a question of tactics and strategy, *jinnab*."

"Yeah, yeah, you remind me of this Jamaican man in Toronto. He is getting all the race-culture artsy curatorial jobs and he thinks it is because of his 'refined tactics and strategy, *jinnab*.' Oh yeah, he's a nice dresser." But it has nothing to do with his tactics which only seem refined because radicals like me made the anti-racist noises in the beginning. He gets the gigs and grants because we were the first ones to kick down the doors. Then the nice powerful bosses put the moderates in the house.

He swirls the expensive scotch in his glass, stops, and looks me in the eye.

I remember that there is a massive picture book of Lahore on his coffee table. Cost: $250 Canadian. He is here in front of me now. Talking with me. The book is at his apartment in the clouds all alone. Perhaps he has left a light on. Perhaps his answering machine is now picking up a call from his friend in Khartoum.

His apartment was on the millionth floor of two giant towers that flee upward to heaven, maybe purgatory, maybe the HQ of the UN in New York. Tower B. I momentarily wish that I could have been a UN fieldworker instead of an artist grovelling for grants. This fantasy passes, as does the temporary urge to be a lawyer.

Another ring at the door. A Swedish blond bombshell who was in HK to sell Swedish food. Dried fish. "Isn't it Gravlox or something?" a British androgyne asks. This one is the most boring woman the world has ever put arms and legs on. Perhaps the ex-pat community would be the only people to try this boring food. Market specificity. I suppose a life on steak-and-kidney pie could open up one's trap for dried fish.

Beautiful Disco-UN-Iqbal realist (realist because repatriation did not scare him like it did all the other UN moralists) quasi-quivers in his handmade shirt. He is acknowledging the breeze. The beautiful Pakistani looks at her. She sees the potential: a cultured, refined UN fieldworker in his late twenties. He has read and understood James Joyce. Knows the last paragraph of "The Dead" by heart. Enjoyed *My Dinner With André*.

The trendy British mag *The Face* is going to do a feature interview with him on how UNHCR fieldworkers ought to dress when working with Third World refugees in the camps. Perhaps a photo session by the River Ravi, another in Khartoum. He looks at me and delivers, in flowing Urdu, "Dried fish?" The words fall from his oval-shaped brown-red lips as though he were a court jester in the time of Shah Jahan.

A metre-long plume of educated smoke is exhumed from his mouth. A gust of night wind moves through his loosely rolled cuffs, puffing his forearms with wind, making him look like Popeye. Asian silk, Asian labour, needle to silk, the sewing needle picking the outer layer of the silkworm's naive flesh. The tailor, a few hours' flight from HK, gets Pakistani rupees for hours of work.

Our conversation collapses into Urdu: "But I do find her attractive," he says. Closed-circuit discourse: super-feminist angels in English. Pure cunt-licking-bum-blasting-schoolboy-altarboy-feminist vulgarity in Urdu.

I remember that he saved lives in the Sudan. I respect him. I can share his sense of humour. We both burst into laughter. She falls out of his attention for a moment. Dried fish to a Pakistani brought up on *kride gost*, curried ochre, *basin ke roti*, and cucumbers in yogurt — not much impact. I start telling him about my two-night excursion to Canton, People's Republic of China.

I draw him back into Urdu. "Don't be such a sister-fucker — go down on her afterwards — surprise her about Moslem men — nothing better than a surprise. She is making all the right suggestions.

Perhaps a little salsa after the party. Think of all the post-colonial retaliation."

"Julian, you sound like Kipling or that sweet liberal anti-imperialist, EM Forster. Besides, what does she have to do with the British Empire?"

"The situation is reminding me of the four hours I spent in Macau before boarding the bus that took me to Guangzhou."

He changes the subject. "So the next project is to do with what?"

"What's my career to you?"

"I am only asking for the fun of it, do you mind if we come back to this topic?" I oblige. Iqbal moves his Punjabi fingers through his modern haircut. I remember him from his Montréal days. At a Hallowe'en party he was decked out in a turban, lipstick.

His Popeye silk shirt ruffles flatulently in the wind, deflates, then rebloats, taking on a life of its own. His arms return to their normal size, hands now in proportion to the body. His cheeks fill with smoke.

The dried-fish woman has turned her beautiful head into the wind, her blond hair hesitantly quivering at the roots. Her lips are stereotype red. Her forehead is small, very pale, not the slightest potential at all for getting a sun tan. We have salsa on the ghetto blaster. Celia Cruz, the exiled Cuban singer, sings about how hard it is to face a world in which Fidel exists; the song opens with "*Cuba es muy triste.*" Celia Cruz would like to pull Castro's beard and put him in a Miami prison, for life.

The fish woman drifts in and out of various conversations — some even more inane than the one with Iqbal and Julian; others on the brink of showing massive earth-shattering social commitment to intellectual property law or the boat people. Her hips move slightly as she turns to talk to this or that person. The salsa is affecting her. Disco-Iqbal notices this. He notices Julian looking at her long white slender legs.

Julian looks out over the harbour, imagines how inadequate his historical perception of this harbour must be in relation to that of many other outsiders who have passed judgement, been descriptive, or even visitors who have described it with the intensity of Thoreau describing a riverbank. He thinks about the Chinese critic Lu Xun and how his understanding of Hong Kong is so much more informed. Ah! so fucking what? Each to his or her own, as they say these days to avoid persecution. He continues to ponder how easy it is for some writers to churn out books on a daily basis.

Julian inhales deeply on a cigarette, looks at the Black Senegalese-American woman's even pink toes, wondering how her day might have panned out at the Vietnamese refugee camps. She works with Iqbal.

Julian turns to Penny. He blurts out the smoke in three discontinuous shafts, silently slurps at a caving-in can of beer which has sprung a leak. A politely sucked-in burp goes by, marginally acknowledged.

Disco-Iqbal enters Julian's arena of thought, his shoulders moving; a file of silken ripples shuttles across his shirt as though he were an august Pakistani bust on a rotating pedestal. His words break as Julian puts down his leaking can of beer:

"Why the Paris Commune of 1871, yaar? Who in fuck's name is going to fund such a pretentious film? You think those progressive zeros at Channel whatever in London are going to give some Canadian Paki money to reflect on European history? Besides, I think there is already a film on the Commune made by Ken McMullen. Paris history is more his business than the business of some Paki."

He twiddles his cigarette in a way that a *pukka* pre-Partition *Sahib* might have done. "Why should they not fund films on unemployment lines or films on a short history of all the beautiful launderettes in Winnipeg. You know — the usual liberal themes." He falters and turns to the Black Senegalese-American woman, then turns back to Julian, and continues:

"Why shouldn't TV fund films on Black poets conventionally thought to be heterosexual who turn out to be queens on the Hershey highways of gay history? Or films about how difficult life is for single mothers in their fight with bad, terrible things like the state welfare system?"

He looks Julian straight in the face and adds, "The Paris Commune – ha! Dream on. It is people like you who make sensible people like me vote for the right. And I hate voting for the right."

Scotch makes Iqbal more lucid than he is at the refugee camps. The wind inflates him. His squirrel cheeks deflate. Julian remarks that he seems like an accordion on such a night. Iqbal does not understand the remark.

All those years of being a freelance intellectual have dulled Julian's brain. Disco-Iqbal is on one of those rare conversational highs. The audience is polite. There is an audience. The refugee camps are hours away by boat. Julian tries to wear his years of education and subsequent marginality lightly. "Hong Kong has not produced any serious filmmakers, questioning writers, or journalists. Everyone here is too willing to give or get a golden hand-job."

Iqbal says, "Listen, why take out your lack of success as an artist on these poor bastard Hong Kongese? Besides, what the fuck do you know about what's going on here in Chinese, huh? Tell me about this? What's all this ethnocentric snobbery? Montréal *coot key chutney?*"

Julian's embarrassment dissipates. Penny comes to the rescue, beaming at Iqbal. "Iqbal," she says in an accent more English than usual, then mediates a courtly pause. "Is your Urdu so good these days that you can read Chinese with it?"

Iqbal laughs. The charge of ethnocentricity, like many other charges and countercharges, is valueless. A white cloud of smoke lingers in his elegantly open mouth, then swishes down into his throat. His cigarette is pinched at the very ends of his fingertips. A UN son: elegantly held smokes.

Julian laughs. Penny looks at Julian. All friends. It is a big joke right from the paper-pushing dumb questions for the boat people to the very nice clothing stores on Queen's Road to the legal process of putting little basement violators of copyrights into Hong Kong's dungeons and on to the picking-up and subsequent fucking of Filipino girls in Wan Chai. Life is good. Everyone is under forty.

The Senegalese woman is also involved in the process of refugee determination. She has very long hands and fingers, and is intelligent in a non-theatrical way which makes her very rare at this party. Disco-Iqbal is jealous of this, her finesse and calm.

Julian feels she is on the wrong side of Black history. He is sure that her thoughts orbit the arena of an old Athenian culture of questions, but not deeply. After all, she is essentially from America. "So what is this all about?" the Black woman, Rachel, says. "I don't think there is much going on in Hong Kong, either. Iqbal, since when did you become an expert in Chinese society? Is it because you have been spending all that time in Wan Chai?"

The crowd is getting giddy. Julian looks out at the fluorescent harbour. This city resembles Algiers, a city of solid streaky roads accurately built into hillsides. Local labour, foreign brains.

Rachel takes an interest: "What do you mean Langston Hughes was gay? He is one of our men — our pride and joy. Our children grow up on him — he was not gay, he was straight."

"Well, this Black British filmmaker, Isaac Julien, has just made a film in which he shows beyond a shadow of a doubt that Mr. Hughes was a homosexual." Julian magically holds the word *homosexual* in front of her. The night wind hovers around it and then he flings the word out to sea.

The Senegalese-American woman says, "Even if he was gay, why tell the world? All this undermines the integrity of the Black community."

Julian again calculates his response. "I suppose you'd side with the NAACP's vision of Black America's purity from homosexuality."

Her fingers interlock, her drink descends to the table. The conversation tapers in sex-ridden smiles.

Julian has played his cards right. She is going to become best friends with him. In the days that follow they catch a ferry called Man Fat out to Lantau Island. The punctual, hill-crawling yellow bus takes them to see the construction of the largest Buddha in the world. The Buddha, high up on a pleasant tree-filled hill, is surrounded by bamboo scaffolding. The Buddha's fat face is covered with bamboo toothpicks. He is still being constructed. A late afternoon lights him.

A continual sparking of welding torches stitches the pious sheet-metal bits together. There is peace and quiet here in the evening shadows, and priests clad in brown sacks. The buzz of Hong Kong is far away. Silence. They stroll together, smell jasmine together by the phoney aromatic incense-burning temples, hold hands and discuss what kind of man her husband-to-be is like. They catch the ferry back to Hong Kong and pick up some take-out food. Back at her apartment they listen to House music. She makes up her mind to be slightly unfaithful to her boyfriend back home in America.

It is three o'clock in the morning. The roof party still has life. Penny nibbles at some stray vegetables. She is talking with some UN arsehole.

Penny is on occasion naughty. "I have this strange legal prob-lem-client," she says, smoothing her black dress against her legs. "We have this Chinese firm that has a trademark called BLACK MAN, and in order to avoid the charge of racism we are registering the trademark with an African country. With a Black African country, that is. That way if any of the politically correct church groups get upset as they did with Mrs. Negro's Toothpaste, we can always say, look — I think it was some attention-grabbing British or American Black politician who was threatening to sue the manufacturer — then we can always say, look, it is a Black African trademark." Penny is flirting. Rachel acknowledges the complexity of what Penny is saying and doing with her life. They interracially bond on this point for forty-five seconds.

Iqbal is not going to leave off the Franco-Prussian war and the siege of Paris. "Julian *jee*, are you telling us that this whole issue has been shifted to the margins of anti-colonial history because the film funders in Québec did not give you a production grant?"

Julian bookishly utters, "Would you not have wanted to see a film on the first socialist government in Europe? It lasted seventy-two days."

In a Peter Sellers Pakistani accent, Iqbal waddles out what Julian has said before, complete with hard interdental "T"s and guttural aspirations: "It is occulted history. In history departments throughout the world it is not ess-studied."

Julian offers another banality. "And what a tragic thing — I mean, to think that the monuments of European history are being discussed in Hong Kong seven years before socialism itself arrives here."

Iqbal returns with a freshly filled glass of Penny's best scotch. His old-fashioned pen catches the glow of a naked lightbulb on a swaying string of bulbs.

A large largely unpicked-at fish rests on the table with its ribs showing. Iqbal loosens a morsel of flesh from the fish. He dislodges a shard of lemon, removes the parsley, and moves his open mouth over the full fork.

"So where in HK are you thinking of opening a restaurant?" Iqbal interrupts the dried-fish woman. She turns a naked white shoulder in the direction of the wet fish. Her face cuts the wind. Unselfconscious, but nonetheless theatrical. Diageses of hotel management.

"I am not sure that we have as yet done that kind of market survey, but we think that it might be in Lang Kwai Fung."

"I see a lot of UNHCR defenders of human rights making your resto a hang-out. You know, after a hard day's work on the plantation," Julian adds. And for good measure, so Penny will not outdo him, "But I don't think you would have to spice it up just so it won't seem too European. A sort of merger of flavours. Everything here's a merger."

Iqbal hounds Julian: "Do you think that if there had been a Vietnamese boat people crisis in 1871, the Communards might have given asylum to all these people fleeing a communist government? Without asking dumbfuck questions and making all those deliberations?"

Julian looks at the dried-fish woman. "What do you think — would the Communards have gone for it or not?"

She senses a male trap to belittle her. But there is no trap to belittle her. It's just her imagination. "I think we might have made a Communard special with mayonnaise. You could think of it as a contribution of the Swedish people to these very important socialists," she says.

My last night in Hong Kong. I am having a dream. The life in Canton, PRC, goes round and round. Special Economic Zone. Those French people I met are locked into my dream. They are spinning, round and round the same corners, making the same observations about the same old ridiculous churches, temples, that lost Moslem mosque in the Chinese cultural haze. "*Existe-t-elle? Cette mosquée... quand même durant cette période de la grande liberté?*" Referring to the same guidebooks, getting ripped off by the same street sharks, eating the same little Chinese surprises. Being shocked by June 4th liberalism.

Their French fathers fought in the great Indo-China war, were crushed on May 7th of that very special year two years after my birth in Lahore. Their children are here now to sell things. Just a few years between their defeat somewhere nearby by General Giap: General Christian de la Croix de Castries riding his white horse in what to some must have been the most uplifting of Vietnamese nights. Bare feet. Bicycles to carry the guns up the muddy slopes. A siege around the French mind.

A few years down the road these French soldiers were politically, though not militarily, swallowed up by the Algerians who, like the Iranians, experienced their six or seven months of post-revolutionary euphoria. Now their French children were here to sell electronics, cars, or something. These French youths speak beautiful Chinese.

Some of the wretched refugees change status. Others are sent back to Hanoi, which may have faced no period of post-revolutionary excess. The refugees are kicked in the face, thumbs tied behind their backs with nylon wire, screaming shit about democracy this democracy that. Hero hunger strikers. Smashing little heads into some nicely carved black marble. Seven-foot-high Hong Kong authority anti-riot figures kick them on board jets and strap them in their seats. The little jade elephants crawl up roaring assholes. *Time Magazine.* LBJ. Fuckers. Thatcher gets election points. The UNHCR humanitarians get paid, eat in nice restaurants, get suits cut in raw silk. Their friends become international feminists by writing papers on the connection between water purification plants and the liberation of Java's women.

The bamboo jets bring them home to Canada for Christmas. God saves them also. Souls are saved, creased between heaven, hell, and purgatory. A leaf from a brown branch slowly creeps out to hear the B-52's. Somehow it's Christmas. There is bombing. The Vietnamese government in Hanoi wants to befriend the Americans. Well, not exactly.

1978-79. Refugees could come to Hong Kong: unconditional acceptance.

June 16, 1988. Citizens of Hong Kong pressure its government to stop the flow of refugees.

June 16, 1988. Comprehensive plan of action. Signatories: Thailand, Philippines, UK, USA, and Australia et al.

Obvious exception: Japan. What else is new?

Agreement that asylum countries implement screening procedure, and terms are set out under the Geneva convention of 1951 and the protocol of 1967.

Some countries even shoot at them on the high seas.

The sea pushes them up. The sea pushes them down.

The dead grey TV screen reflects her approaching body. Penny has come into my bedroom to give me that goodbye kiss. The curtains are light blue. The walls are light blue. My bed is a brand-new fold-out couch. She has to have lunch with someone big today; lawyer-dark-blue suit, intelligent perfume, not aggressive, not manly, not womanly. Her arms are around me. She is happy that I came to see her. The Canadian boyfriend in his shorts in the background mutters his heartfelt goodbye. I am alone in their apartment.

I take my last walk on Hollywood Street when the two of them are at work. Power lunches and refugees. I talk with two Aussies who are looking into buying bracelets or a fourth-century bookshelf for $45 US. The Star Ferry takes me to Kowloon side. The boat's bow pushes deeply into the green water. Here and there massive Far East jet foils move by at the speed of light; Mao's comets. 1997. Here and there old crescent-shaped junks filled with vegetables and shrimps chug, splutter, and writhe in the green harbour water.

I resentfully pay the $100 HK airport tax. Abu Dhabi to London, where I stop for a night with my union activist friend.

And I meet with my Pakistani architect friend – the one I went to the Warlingham woods with. He takes us to a party somewhere in Central London. Lots of people dressed in black. Boring food; carrots sliced lengthwise. There is a trendy square cut into the ceiling. We witness an architectonic accident. A large stereo speaker falls eight feet onto an American student's head. Blood. "Oh wow, man, like it really hurt. Like I think I am really hurt." An ambulance. No real damage.

The following day, Piccadilly Line to Terminal Two. Friendships these days mean a long streak of blackness, then a diaphanous dawn; a brief descent in a great European capital followed by more compressed days and nights to a friend at an airport; weeks of jet lag. The British Airways flight is delayed two hours. I pass the time by buying multicoloured socks which fall apart in two weeks. We follow the St. Lawrence River to Montréal.

GLOSSARY

ajeebe	strange
array	surprise
bhenchood	sister fucker
cha	tea
choudie	fuck, to fuck
chouth-key-chutney	cunt chutney
choutias	cunts
djellabas	long flowing robe
dunnia Arabia	the Arab world
dupatta	scarf worn around the chest and head
fata-a-futt	quickly, on the double
Fatwa	Islamic verdict
gandoos	fuckers, hoodlums
gazals	form of poetry
ghee	clarified butter
Ikhwan	the Moslem brotherhood in Egypt
jamun	purple fruit tree
jee	dear
jinnab	sir (polite form)
kamal	good, excellent
Khuda-hafiz	goodbye, God follows you
Khusras	hermaphrodites
ma-ka-laura	the cock of your mother
mather chood	mother fucker
mujra	a *very* refined form of entertainment
nalies	open sewers
paan	betel-nut and spices in a pan leaf
Qawwali	a form of Sufi music
sahib	a well-off gentleman
Salam	a Moslem greeting of peace

Shariat . . . . Islamic law

shalwar kameze . . a long shirt and baggy pant which fits closely around the ankles

soosth . . . . slow and lazy

souk . . . . bazaar

tongas . . . . horse and buggy carriage

turra . . . . turban

ulama . . . . clergy

yaar . . . . dear

zabah . . . . to slaughter

Acknowledgements

This work would not have been possible without the help
of: Abouali Farmanfarmaian; Ackbar Abbas; Alix and
Christine Parlour; Allan de Souza; Allan Samuel; Barb
Young; Bruce Ferguson; Bita Hamid and Sonia Gremala;
Catherine Mayers; Charles Acland; Cheryl Simon; General
Giap, who has made my birthday meaningful: on 7 May in
the mid-fifties the people of Vietnam brought the French
regime tumbling down at Dien Bien Phu; Harana Para;
Huda Lutfi; Ian Mclachlan was helpful with the spelling of
Asian names; Jocelyne Doray; Linda Leith, an uninterfering
editor at *Matrix*; M. Nourbese Philip; Matthew, Daniel, and
Richard Clive and Penny Sanger for liberal support;
Michael Neumann; Mona Fahmy; Naushad Siddique, who
was patient with some of my Urdu-English translations;
Scott Proudfoot, whose name has to be added to the
inexorable list of concerned proof-readers; Mohammed
Azhar, who for five minutes linked the United Kingdom
with Lahore, Pakistan, in the woods outside a little English
town. My parents; Abigail McCullough; Natasha
Mukherjee; Fred Reed; Nadia Salah; Paula Sypnowich;
Rabin Lai; Richard Flint, the instant expert; and John Flint;
Rob Conrath; Salimah Valiani; the British Museum, and
the Bibliothèque Nationale in Paris; Saleem Kidwai; Sarah
Amato, whose commentaries were useful; Shaila
Parthasarathi; Suzie Goldenberg; Colin Tomlins; the man
from Burundi whom I met at Hourai Boumedienne
Airport; the Algerians who organized the conference on
Frantz Fanon. The confused and talented Greek man who

sometimes leaves me for dead. David Wilson; Vera Frenkel; Christine Gosselin; Waqar Ahmed; Ron Poulton. The man from Chittagong who chilled me with his story about the West Pakistani army; the two French women in Guangzhou; the woman in Warlingham; the woman who drank too much; the woman from Wakefield who did radical theatre during the miners' strike. Harbinda and Jesh Hanspal; Rob Holton; Raj at Have a Very Good Time Travelling; the man on the bus ride on the way to Lundi Kotal; the Algerian colonel who gave orders to fire on the teenagers; Stuart Ross, the generous and patient Mercury Press editor; Beverley Daurio, for her deeply thoughtful re-sequencing of chapters and challenging editorial suggestions.

Without the critical letters of Sean Kane, this work would not have progressed at all.

The chapters "Plague Years in England" and "Lipstick on Your Collar" were published in slightly different form in *Matrix* (Montréal) and *Bazzar* (London). "Plague Years in England," under the title "Holly Trees, the Plague and the Press" also appeared in US/THEM (Amsterdam). Draft excerpts from "The Starry Night I Met Begum Akhtar" appeared in *Montréal Serai*, as well as a version of "Grandfather at Noon: Lahore, 1957."

This work was supported by small grants from The Canada Council, Conseil des arts et des lettres du Québec, and Secretary of State (Multiculturalism) (Status of Women).

—Julian Samuel, Montréal, 1988-95

Bibliography

Ali, Tariq. *Street Fighting Years: An Autobiography of the Sixties*. London: Collins, 1987

Lowry, Bullitt and Gunter, Elizabeth Ellington. Editors. *The Red Virgin: Memoirs of Louise Michel*. The University of Alabama Press, 1981

Brecht, Bertolt. *The Days of the Commune*. London: Eyre Methuen, 1978

Fanon, Frantz. *The Wretched of the Earth*. New York: Grove Press, 1968

— *A Dying Colonialism*. New York: Grove Press, Inc., 1965.

— *Towards the African Revolution*. New York: Grove Press, Inc., 1967

— *Black Skin, White Masks*. New York: Grove Press Inc., 1967

Ferguson, Kathy. *The Feminist Case Against Bureaucracy*, Philadelphia: Temple University Press, 1984

Gardez, Hassan., Rashid, Jamil. Editors. *Pakistan: The Roots of Dictatorship, the Political Economy of a Paratetorian State*. London: Zed Books Ltd., 1983

The Guardian — NYC., various articles 1987-90

Horne, Alistair. *A Savage War of Peace: Algeria 1954-62*. London: Penguin Books Ltd., 1977

— *The Fall of Paris: The Siege and the Commune of 1870-71*. London: Penguin Books, 1964

Khan, Asgahar. *Islam, Politics and the State: The Pakistan Experience*. London: Zed Books Ltd., 1985

Lenin, V.I. *The Paris Commune*. New York: International Publishers, 1931

Lissagaray, Prosper-Olivier. *Histoire de la Commune de 1871.* Paris: François Maspero, 1970

Maalouf, Amin. *Léon L'Africain.* Paris: Jean Claude Lattes, 1986

Mason, S. Edward. *The Paris Commune: An Episode in the History of the Socialist Movement.* New York: Howard Fertig, 1967

Roberts, J. M. *The English Historical Review.* Edited by J. M. Wallace-Hadrill and J. M. Roberts, Supplement 6, *The Paris Commune from the Right.* London: Longman, 1973

Sabatier, Robert. *Aids and the Third World.* London: The Panos Institute, 1989

Schulkind, Eugene. *The Paris Commune of 1871: The View from the Left.* New York: Grove Press, 1974

Shari'ati, Ali. *On the Sociology of Islam: Lectures by Ali Shari'ati.* Translated from the Persian by Hamid Algar. Berkeley: Mizan Press, 1979

— *Marxism and other Western Fallacies: An Islamic Critique.* Translated by R. Cambell. Berkeley: Persian Series, 1980

Wallerstein, Immanuel. *The Modern World System, Vol. 1.* Academic Press: New York, 1974-80